Two Doors Down

JOSEPH BAILEY

Two Doors Down

Cover design by ebooklaunch.com
Edited by BK
First Edition: November 24, 2025
Published by Open Palm Press
A story born on The Alchemist's Path
ISBN (Paperback): 979-8-9987213-0-4
ISBN (Hardcover): 979-8-9987213-1-1
ISBN (eBook): 979-8-9987213-2-8
For more information, visit:
www.josephbaileyauthor.com
Printed in the United States of America

To My Kids

You didn't just witness the creation of this story -
you were part of the strength that made it possible.
Every late night, every quiet moment I spent writing…
I was thinking of you. Thank you for your patience, your laughter, and your unconditional love.
You've each given me more purpose than I could ever put into words.
May you always tell your story.
May you always know your worth.
And may you always feel, without question, that you are deeply, and endlessly loved.

- Dad

Chapter One

The cool concrete bites at my bare feet. Beyond the tall trees, the river stretches out—choppy, endless, always moving forward even when the surface breaks into whitecaps.

Most mornings, I wake up too early. Sometimes it's a sound, other times a vivid dream. Stress does weird things to a woman's body. Last night, it was the one that always comes back—the memory of when it all started. I remember it like it was yesterday.

Nora's first day of daycare. We both worked back then, barely making ends meet. That first day broke me—my first child, my first separation from her. We picked her up together, and I remember running from the car straight into the classroom. She held up a drawing—bright colors, messy scribbles of our family. I turned to Nathan, expecting a smile… but it never came. From that day forward, we drifted—one missed smile at a time—until I woke up in a life I didn't recognize. When this dream happens, I lie in bed a little too long, staring at the ceiling, wondering how I got here. Not just this house or this life, but to this place where I no longer feel seen, cherished, or loved. I used to believe we could weather anything—that if I gave enough of myself, I could hold it all together. But now… I'm starting to think I was wrong.

When those thoughts hit, I usually text Maya. But I already know what she'll say. Marriage is work. It's just a season. No marriage is easy. I've heard it all before—maybe it's a broken record on repeat, or a prayer murmured in the back pew—but I wear it like armor. It's the thing I use to shield myself from this life. But the truth is, I don't know if we're in a rough patch… or if we're just pretending not to notice our world is crumbling. Because behind our front door, where no one sees, something broke a long time ago. That something… is me.

"Ella!"

Nathan's voice slices through the air, sharp and strained, snapping me back to now. I know what's waiting before I make it to the door. Nathan is overwhelmed again. The kids are too loud. His frustration spilling over—like always—onto me and them. Moving is never easy, but it feels more complicated now. It's not just the exhaustion of motherhood and marriage—that's weight enough. It's the emotional heaviness. The strain of keeping everyone happy while I quietly unravel. Every box I open feels like another part of me getting packed away. It feels like more than just a change of address this time—it feels like a test I'm barely passing. Boxes are scattered everywhere, toys are piled in every corner, and I'm physically and mentally exhausted, barely able to keep my eyes open at the end of the day. My body aches, my mind races, and my eyelids feel lined with sandpaper, but I keep pushing. Because the kids need me. Because Nathan expects it.

And because if I stop, even for a moment, everything might fall apart, for the kids, for him, and for us.

Maybe the movies have it wrong. Maybe love doesn't sweep you off your feet. Maybe it's something you settle for because life is messy, people are complicated, and happy endings aren't gift-wrapped. Since we've been married, there have been worse moments than I care to admit, but I do what I'm supposed to do. A wife puts her husband's happiness first. That's what I've always been told. And for too long, that's exactly what I've done. Our move is just a lateral one—we're still living in Eastwell, a sprawling city with too many people and not enough soul. It's supposedly the largest city in the state, full of noise, endless bridges, and people who never look you in the eye. But none of it has ever felt like home. We've moved into a private gated community called Whispering Oaks. I've never lived in a gated community like this before. Even though the house is nice, it doesn't feel like ours yet, and Nathan's short temper only makes it worse. He works as a systems contractor for an aerospace firm, bouncing between day and night shifts, sometimes gone for days at a time. It's unpredictable, which makes everything harder. But even when he's home, it still feels like I'm doing it all alone.

Three weeks.

That's all the time we had after the owners decided to sell the rental and gave us barely any notice. No warning, no room to plan, just a deadline and a scramble to find somewhere new. We packed up our lives in a blur, labeling boxes between naps and tantrums. I scrubbed every baseboard on my hands and knees, sweat dripping down my neck—meanwhile, Nathan sat scrolling through his phone, barely lifting a finger. That's Nathan, always caught up in something, always assuming I've got it covered.

It's not just the physical toll, it's the sharp sting of his indifference, the way he acts as if my efforts are invisible, as if I am invisible. But it's not like I have a choice. I keep pushing, the way I always have.

I don't mind cleaning, though. There's something cathartic about knowing the kids will come home to a clean space. There's something in the shine of a clean floor that feels like control in a life spiraling out of it. But it's thankless—and that's what stings. A month ago, I spent an entire evening cleaning the kitchen counters, reorganizing the pantry, and mopping the floors until they sparkled. Nathan came in, dropped his jacket on the chair, and stepped over the freshly mopped floor without a word.

Not a thank you, not even a glance. It's not the lack of gratitude so much as the quiet assumption—like everything I do happens on its own. Like I'm the background noise of this life. No one ever really taught me how to do this—how to be everything for everyone. I guess I just figured it out on my own.

Sometimes, I wonder if I'm trying to give my kids the childhood I never had. And sometimes, late at night, when I'm alone with my thoughts, I wonder if it's even possible.

Moving to this neighborhood wasn't my idea. The gates, the constant feeling of being watched, I never wanted to be contained. But there's something strange about it, something oddly comforting in the safety of it all. It's a nice neighborhood, even if every house resembles a carbon copy of the next.

Ours is a two-story duplex tucked at the top of a quiet hill. From the driveway, I see the river shimmering in the distance, just beyond the top of the tall trees, its surface choppy with white caps as far as the eye can see. There are a few perks. The grocery store's nearby, Nathan's work is only fifteen minutes away. The community center down the street offers all the usual amenities; playroom, a pool, pickleball courts, volleyball courts, and even a movie room. The kids will love it. It's not home, not yet, but at least it's something.

I hear Nathan's voice again, louder, as he scolds the kids for their noise. His words hit like a gut punch, sharp, and mean; settling in my stomach like a weight. My breath catches, and for a moment, the air feels thick, suffocating, as if his frustration fills the entire world, leaving no space for anything else. I know it's not their fault, just their excitement getting the best of them. But he doesn't see it that way. He never has.

He yells. I don't know why I still expect him to do better. He knows it bothers me when he does it, but he doesn't seem to care.

I turn back and catch a neighbor's curtain shift, a sliver of eyes peeking through. Whispering Oaks didn't miss much. I sigh as I step through the front door and find Nathan in the living room, his face a picture of frustration. "Yes?" I ask, my voice already softer than it should be. I can see it all over Nathan's face, the frustration, the barely contained irritation. "What's wrong?" I add, bracing myself.

"Can you take care of these kids? They're bouncing off the walls," he snaps, motioning toward the living room like the chaos is my fault. "You know the courts don't look kindly on unfit mothers, Ella."

I glance at Nora and Emmett. They're frozen, wide-eyed, too scared to move. It's not their fault, and I hate that they're starting to feel like it is.

"Go on upstairs and play in your room," I say, kneeling beside them. "I'll be up in just a minute to help unpack your books."

"Yes, ma'am," they reply, voices small but obedient.

The stairs creak under their weight as they climb. I wait until their door clicks shut before I turn back to Nathan, forcing calm into my voice even though everything inside me is tangled and raw.

"Why do you always threaten me when you're in a bad mood?" I ask. "They're kids. They're excited."

"It's not like I'm in a bad mood all the time," he snaps. "It's just this move; and all the responsibilities we have now—two kids, work, everything. It's a lot."

It's not the words—it's the way he says them, like I'm the problem he can't solve. I swallow hard. For a fleeting second, I remember the Nathan who used to pull me close on nights I felt overwhelmed, tracing lazy circles on my back until I fell asleep. "We've got this, El," he'd whisper, his breath soft against my hair. "You and me against the world."

I'm not sure when "that" Nathan started to fade.

"I'm trying too," I whisper now, hoping he'll hear the hurt beneath my calm. But he's already moving on, lifting a box, shifting the weight without a second glance.

"I've got to move these boxes upstairs," he says, grabbing one labeled Master Bedroom. "And there's still a whole garage full I'll have to handle later. I don't have time to babysit while you wander around."

"I wasn't wandering. I was just getting some air."

"Well, I'm working. While you take strolls and let the kids run wild."

"They weren't running wild," I say flatly. "And it's not babysitting if they're your kids." He stops, eyes narrowing at my tone. He's not used to hearing this version of me, the one who doesn't flinch. I brace for his rebuttal, but he only shakes his head and vanishes upstairs. I watch him go; box balanced in his arms, and feel something inside me shift. A crack, thin and threatening, forming in the foundation of everything I've been desperately trying to keep together.

It wasn't always like this, at least, I tell myself that. I

remember the way he used to kiss the top of my head after dinner, even if the dishes were still dirty. That version of him feels like a dream I might have made up. But even in the beginning, our connection was built on convenience more than passion. He proposed at the kitchen table, a toddler on my lap and dishes in the sink. "It just makes sense," he'd said, practical, not romantic. I'd told myself this was enough; that practicality could fill the space love left empty. I just smiled and said yes. But part of me knew what I was agreeing to. No candles, no grand gesture, just something that felt safe. I dropped hints about the kind of ring I wanted, something simple but thoughtful. He missed them all. When the box came, I smiled anyway. I told myself it didn't matter. That love wasn't about diamonds or dinners. That if he stayed, it was enough. I clung to practicality like a lifeline, convinced romance was a luxury we could live without. Now, years later, I'm not so sure.

I need to breathe.

I grab my purse from the kitchen counter, suddenly needing air. My fingers tremble as I dig for my keys and step out the front door. The air outside is cool, the kind that stings your skin and refuses to let go. I blink against the brightness, grounding myself in the details of the street, neatly trimmed lawns, perfect sidewalks, the distant hum of someone mowing. My SUV is parked along the curb. I open the trunk and pull out a folded comforter I forgot to bring in earlier. As I straighten, I catch movement from the corner of my eye, someone down the street.

A stranger, maybe late thirties or early forties, kneels beside a small boy with a red helmet. The child is wobbling on a bike, feet barely touching the pavement. The stranger is patient, steadying the handlebars and offering quiet encouragement. The boy nods his head and off they go. The stranger steadies the back of the bike, jogging beside him. His steps slow as the boy finds balance. He lets go and slows his jog to a walk, watching intently. The boy swerves, nearly topples, then steadies again.

I pause behind my car, frozen. There's something about the stranger's attentiveness that holds me in place. Something about the warmth in his voice when he says, "You've got it, buddy. Just keep looking ahead."

It's not romantic. Not really. But it's unfamiliar. The softness. The presence. The way he's tuned in.

Nathan stays standing, always. Separate. Removed. I used to think it was a difference in style. Now I think it's just a difference.

"Whoa…" I step forward instinctively, the comforter slipping from my arms as I reach to catch him.

The child swerves just in time, tipping sideways as I instinctively grab for him, and we both tumble into the grass.

The stranger rushes over, crouching beside me, his hand wrapping gently around my forearm as he helps me sit up. "You, okay?" he asks, his gaze flicking over me, then landing on the boy. "Did he scare you?"

"A little," I admit with a breathy laugh. "He came out of nowhere."

"That's what he does when he's overwhelmed," he says. "Races forward before he's ready."

The boy nods solemnly, like he's just faced a dragon. I smile despite myself.

"I'm glad you were there." He flashes a crooked smile. "Good people are hard to find… trust me, I know."

He straightens. He's wearing a faded long-sleeve T-shirt, sunglasses over his eyes shielding them from the sun, and there's a sheen of sweat at his temples. He looks over at me, not flirtatious, just attentive. Present.

He smiles, just a small one, but it lights up his face, as he removes the sunglasses. Then his gaze meets mine—and I see it. Recognition. He actually sees me. I force myself to look away first, my heart beating faster and faster. The comforter is heavy as I lift it from the ground into my arms again. I say nothing and turn toward the house.

As my bare feet press into the damp grass of the front lawn, something stirs beneath my ribs. Not attraction, exactly. More like a breeze brushing across a closed window.

When was the last time someone looked at me like that?

I glance back once before I shut the door behind me. The stranger is crouched again beside the boy, pointing toward the end of the street like they're mapping out the rest of the ride.

Inside, the silence welcomes me like an old friend. But this time, it doesn't suffocate me. It breathes. And for the first time in a long time, it feels like possibility.

Chapter Two

The next morning, the house feels smaller—the walls closing in inch by inch. Unpacked boxes loom like silent accusations, as if nothing has changed. The air smells of cardboard and stale coffee. Nathan left early for work, leaving me to wrestle the kids and the clutter alone.

Barely a day here, and the house already feels suffocating. I need to get out. I need to breathe. "Let's go check out the nature trail," I say—half to them, half to myself.

The suggestion ignites their excitement, and their energy suddenly funnels into giggles and shoe retrieval. I need to feel the sun on my face, the hush of trees above me, the quiet that only lives off pavement. The thought of winding through a shaded trail with nowhere to be feels like oxygen.

As we step off the porch, I spot him two doors down—loading something into the back of his car. He catches my eye and offers a quick smile, a neighborly wave. I return it, my hand lifting in an automatic gesture. But something about the way his eyes hold mine for that split second lingers longer than it should. I should've introduced myself yesterday when we crossed paths, but I froze. That's not like me. I can talk to anyone—except him. Maybe it was the way he looked at me… like I was staring into a soul I already knew.

I shake the thought away.

We wander toward the edge of the neighborhood, where a narrow trail slips into the trees. The sidewalk ends, replaced by gravel that crunches beneath our shoes, then softens into packed dirt. The oak trees' branches stretch above us, twisted and tall, as if they've been here for generations—weathered and steadfast. The canopy surrounds us, and everything falls silent. It's cooler here. Quieter. Like the world has turned down its volume just enough for me to hear myself think.

What I thought would be a short walk stretches nearly a mile, but the kids don't mind. The trail finally opens into a quiet clearing, and just beyond that, the river comes into view—broad and winding, sunlight dancing on the surface like scattered glass. The faint rustle of unseen birds scores the morning. There's no playground—just flat rocks, soft grass, and the ever-moving sound of the water. "Look, water!" I say, pointing as the river comes into view.

Emmett bolts ahead without a second thought, racing to the shoreline. He crouches to toss something in. Nora scrambles over the rocks, her laughter echoing off the trees. They scream into the open air, and somehow, it's everything I need. I sit on a nearby tree stump and let the sun warm my arms.

"Watch, Momma!" Nora yells, throwing a stick into the water.

"I'm always watching, baby!" I call back. Moments like this make it harder to admit how tired I really am—but it feels good to hear them laugh, to remember that I still can.

Eventually, the water calls to me—it always does, offering

a momentary escape. I stand and drift closer to the riverbank. The sun catches the surface of the water, flashing tiny beams of light in every direction. It's mesmerizing—choppy, broken, yet somehow endlessly steady.

The shoreline is scattered with pale rocks, smooth and flat like someone placed them there with intention.

"Let's try skipping some stones," I say.

Emmett and Nora scan the bank, crouching low to find the perfect rocks. Their laughter echoes as stone after stone plunks into the water—none of them skipping, but none of them caring.

To my left, an elderly man sits in a weathered lawn chair, a fishing pole resting across his lap. He chuckles softly as he glances toward the kids. "I hope they don't fall in," he says, his voice worn but kind. "I'm too old to jump in after them."

Emmett spots him and, of course, barrels straight over.

"Emmett!" I call, chasing after him, breathless and apologetic.

"Sorry," I pant.

The old man smiles and waves it off. "No problem. He's fine. Does he fish?"

I hesitate. "He's been a couple of times—with his dad, mostly his grandpa."

I don't know why that catches in my throat—maybe it's the reminder of what's missing.

"Did you catch anything today?" I ask, changing the subject.

"Not much," he says, tapping the handle of his pole. "But that's fine by me."

"Oh?" He shrugs. "I don't come for the fish. I come for the view. If I catch something, that's just a bonus."

His gaze drifts toward the river. "Do you like the water?" he asks, his voice unhurried. The question lands softly, but still heavy.

"I do," I say before I even think about it. "My uncle used to take us out when we were kids—kayaks, canoes, whatever he had. I've always felt drawn to the water."

"So did your whole family go?"

"No," I say quietly. "My parents were too busy working. My sister and I… we spent a lot of time raising ourselves, especially in the summer."

He nods again, slower this time. "That's tough."

"It was," I admit. "That's why I'm so intentional with my kids. I want them to feel supported, not just seen, but truly known. Like I'm really there—not just physically, but emotionally too."

He studies the water again. "You know what I love about rivers?"

I shake my head.

"They don't stop. Not for rocks, roots, or man-made walls. They shift. Carve new paths. Always moving forward." His voice softens. "They're stronger than they look. What you see on the surface isn't the whole story. Sometimes, the deepest parts are hidden underneath."

I follow his gaze. The river glints in the light, current flowing even when I can't see it.

"That's… beautiful," I say.

He nods. "Just like life."

Before the moment stretches too long, Emmett squirms on the rocks and calls out. "Momma, I have to pee!"

Of course. And just like that, life reminds me it doesn't pause for reflection.

A faint laugh escapes as I gather our things. "It was nice talking to you."

"You too," he says, smiling like he means it. "See you around."

I herd the kids back toward the trail head, one last glance over my shoulder at the water—shimmering, broken, and unbothered.

I stare at it longer than I should, jealousy rising in my chest. The river flows forward without hesitation. And me? I've been circling the same questions for years. Maybe I'm not like the river at all.

Maybe I'm just another stone—stationary, worn, and waiting. Or maybe, even a stone shifts…when the current's strong enough.

Chapter Three

I wish we were all unpacked and settled in, but that couldn't be further from the truth. The rush of moving has faded, but it hasn't been replaced by calm—just a silence that clings to everything. Thick, all-encompassing silence that hums like a wire stretched too thin.

Nathan and I barely speak anymore. When we do, it's clipped, transactional—about the kids, the bills, the house. Never about us. Not really.

The stranger, though? I haven't seen him since that first afternoon in the street over a week ago. He made an impression—and then vanished. And yet, I catch myself scanning that same street every chance I get. I glance out the window while folding laundry, linger in the driveway after grocery runs, hoping to get a glimpse of him. It's maddening. I tell myself it's silly, that he's a stranger. A kind stranger, sure, but nothing more.

Some routines have stayed the same, like driving Nora to school, a thirty-minute trek each way. Those drives feel endless. I drop her off, take care of Emmett at home, then head back to pick her up—only to repeat it the next day. It's exhausting, but I tell myself it matters. I have to give her stability during this transition to a new home. Keeping her in the same school is one small way I can shield her from the chaos. And luckily, Emmett will start preschool soon.

I've started indulging in a little ritual during these drives—stopping for coffee. It's my one luxury, a small rebellion against the monotony. I sip it slowly, savoring every drop like it's the only thing tethering me to myself. Nathan, of course, calls it a waste of money. He says it like it's a fact, not an opinion, and I've stopped bothering to argue. Some mornings, I feel like that coffee is the only thing keeping me sane.

And today, I decide to stop at the small gym I noticed a few blocks from the new house. I haven't said it out loud, but I think part of me wants to feel something again—anything, really. I've been meaning to get back into a workout routine, even just to remember what strength feels like.

Nathan hasn't noticed me in months, and I've gotten used to feeling invisible. But this morning feels different. Not because of him. Because of something else. Something I can't name yet.

I'm in a T-shirt and black yoga pants, so I figure I'll just stop in and have a look around—maybe even join. The lot is only half full when I pull in. I park, gather Emmett from his car seat, and push open the glass doors to a wave of dance music and the rhythmic clang of weights. Emmett clings to me, his head on my shoulder, wide-eyed and curious.

As I round a corner, my heart stutters.

There he is—the stranger—standing by the free weights, talking to someone I recognize from the neighborhood, Colby. Athletic clothes. Posture sharp. Demeanor easy.

Our eyes meet for half a second, and something shifts. I adjust Emmett on my hip and try to appear unfazed.

"Coffee and the gym this early?" he calls out, smiling. "You're setting the bar pretty high."

It startles me. I wasn't expecting him to speak. My heart races as I glance toward him, unsure if I should answer.

"Me?" I ask, my voice unsure.

"Yeah, you," he says, his tone light and playful. "Looks like you've already had a full morning."

I manage a small laugh, bouncing Emmett lightly. "Dropped my daughter off at school. It's about thirty minutes away. Figured I'd stop here on the way back."

"Oh," he says, nodding. "So, you're keeping her there for now?"

"Yeah," I reply, shifting Emmett to ease the weight on my hip. "We figured it was best. And I get to grab a coffee as a bonus."

"Well, if anyone deserves a coffee, it's you," he says, his voice genuine and sincere.

The compliment stops me short. I glance up, and for the first time, our eyes really meet. His gaze is steady, unguarded, as if he is genuinely seeing me. My breath hitches, and I feel a flush creeping up my neck.

"Thank you," I say softly, unsure what else to add.

"Do you always pick up coffee," he asks, his voice teasing but curious, "or do you prefer the ritual of making it at home—the sound of beans grinding, the hiss of the coffee maker, the way it fills the kitchen with that comforting aroma?"

"I almost always pick it up on my route to school," I admit, feeling a little self-conscious under his gaze. "Honestly, I'm not even sure which box the coffee maker's in. It's probably buried under a mountain of kitchen gadgets I won't touch for weeks."

I let out a small, nervous laugh. "By the time I find it, I'll have already adapted to living without it, or I'll buy a new one out of sheer desperation."

He smiles, just enough to make my stomach flutter.

"Well, if you ever need a cup in a pinch, let me know," he says. "I usually make a full pot at home. Most of it goes to waste. Hard to finish a pot on my own."

"I just might take you up on that someday," I say, my voice light but laced with something I can't name—curiosity, maybe. Or longing.

"You've got your hands full," he adds. "But from what I've seen... you're doing an amazing job."

I blink, startled by the kindness in his tone. "What makes you say that?"

"I've seen you outside with your kids," he says. "You're present. You don't check out. That kind of patience. That kind of love. It's rare."

His words hit me like a gentle wave, soothing and unearned. I blush, caught off guard by how much it means to be seen.

"That's... kind of you to say," I manage.

"My name's Callahan. Jack Callahan," he says, offering a hand.

I blink, a little thrown by the smooth delivery. Jack Bond. I bite back a smile.

I set Emmett down, praying my hand isn't sweaty as I shake his.

I hesitate, suddenly aware of how intimate a name can feel.

"Eliana Morgan. But everyone calls me Ella."

His hand is warm, steady. When I let go, I feel the absence of it almost immediately.

Just like that, the mystery is gone. His name is Jack.

"Nice to meet you, Ella," he says.

The way he says my name—like it's familiar and new all at once—makes something shift inside me. It's been so long since anyone said my name without frustration. Nathan says it like a chore. Jack says it like a discovery.

"Morning, Ella," Colby chimes in. The moment shatters. I force a smile. We met a couple of days ago at the mailbox—he was chatty, neighborly, the type who remembers names.

"Hey, Colby," I say, still too aware of the man standing beside him.

The conversation drifts, and I know it's my cue. I gather Emmett and make my way to the door.

"Nice to meet you, Jack... and to see you Colby," I say, hoping my voice is steadier than I feel. My eyes linger on Jack just a moment too long. "See y'all later."

Even walking back through the parking lot, I can still feel his gaze. It trails me like sunlight—warm, uninvited, too close.

Back home, I unlock the door and step inside. Emmett trails behind me. I close the door softly, press my back to it, and slide down until I'm sitting on the floor. What am I doing?

I can't believe I just met him. Jack. The neighbor.

No longer a mystery with quiet eyes and a careful smile. Now he has a name—and a voice I'm still hearing in my head.

Emmett tugs at my arm.

"Momma? Are you okay?"

His eyes search mine, too wide and knowing for a child.

I smooth his hair. "I'm fine, baby," I whisper.

But it's a lie.

I reach for my phone. I need my girls—Maya, Claire, and

Tara. My lifelines. The ones who won't let me get away with glossing anything over.

I already told them about the neighbor. Now… I know his name.

I pull up our group chat and type fast, my fingers trembling.

Me: *I just talked to the neighbor again.*

Responses fly in instantly.

Maya: *WHAT?! When? Where? DETAILS NOW.*

Claire: *OMG spill it.*

Tara: *Shirtless? Please say yes.*

I bite my lip, already smiling.

Me: *No shirtless moment; sorry to disappoint. I stopped at the gym after I dropped-off Nora at school. He was there.*

Maya: *Ran into him? Or were you accidentally standing in front of the squat rack, waiting for fate?*

Claire: *Fate or strategy? Be honest.*

Me: *Not planned. I swear. But... we talked for a few minutes.*

Maya: *A FEW MINUTES?! That's basically a date in mom-world.*

Tara: *What did he say? What did YOU say?*

Claire: *How long did it take you to stop blushing? Asking for a friend.*

I shake my head, grinning.

Me: *He asked about the kids. Complimented me. Said I'm doing a good job.*

Maya: *Shut. Up. That's flirting.*

Claire: *Or foreplay.*

Tara: *I think he likes you.*

I groan and type back.

Me: *Stop. It wasn't like that.*

Maya: *Was there eye contact? Lingering pauses? Did he lean in? I freeze, fingers hovering.*

I can still feel the warmth of his eyes on me. Like he saw

more than I meant to show.
Me: *Maybe.*
Claire: *Maybe? Oh, honey. You're in trouble.*
Maya: *Serious trouble.*
Tara: *OMG, I'm so excited for you!*
I exhale, thumbs still.
Me: *I know.*

And the worst part? I mean it.

I lock my phone and set it down, my heart thuds against my ribs, as if it already knows something I don't.

Chapter Four

Life pretended to move forward—carried by loads of laundry, school drop-offs, and the fragile lie that my marriage still worked. Somewhere in that blur, I started counting down to this trip. Two weeks in Coral Pass, at my dad's house by the water, felt less like a vacation and more like a lifeline.

The drive north isn't long—just a few hours—but with two kids, three bags of snacks, and an SUV packed to the roof, it feels like a full-blown expedition. We wind through backroads lined with pine and marsh grass, the sky opening wider the farther we get from home. Nora sings off-key to the radio. Emmett asks for snacks every ten minutes. Nathan drives in silence, hands gripping the wheel, eyes on the road, like we're all just passengers in his world. He only speaks to curse at traffic.

Coral Pass is a sleepy little town tucked beside the Gulf, where the docks creak like old bones and the sunsets make you forget how lonely family trips can feel. As we pull into my dad's driveway, I feel that familiar mix of emotions—comfort and tension, joy and grief, all tangled together.

Even with the short drive, these trips always feel like beautiful chaos, equal parts magic and mayhem. This year will be no different. I pack everything for all of us—right down to Nathan's toothbrush—while he complains he can't find his socks. Like that's my fault too.

I don't know why I bother folding everything so carefully, double-checking outfits and shoes. He'll probably still yell at me for forgetting a specific shirt or pair of pants he suddenly wants to wear at his parents' house. How am I supposed to know what he wants? I'm not a mind reader.

When we finally arrive at my dad's house, Nathan is the first one out and through the door. He grabs his single bag—mine and the kids' still in the trunk—and disappears to scroll his phone before I've even unpacked the kids' things. Bouncing between two households—my dad's and his parents'—makes the trips even more chaotic. After I unpack, cook dinner, and get the kids to bed I tell Nathan I'm going out and he just shrugs. Doesn't ask when I'll be back. Doesn't even look up. Just says, 'Don't be late,' like I'm his teenage daughter sneaking out past curfew.

☾☾☾

I texted Maya, Claire, and Tara a week ago to lock down our annual girls' night. No loud clubs, no awkward party invites—just the four of us at a cozy local wine bar with soft lighting, real conversation, and a few glasses of red to blur the hard edges.

Nathan agrees to stay with the kids at his parents' place in Pine Hollow—a quiet little town about thirty minutes from where I grew up. A rare win.

There won't be hangovers or strangers trying to make forced conversation. No makeup, no pretending. Just women who've seen me—before the stretch marks, the exhaustion, the parts of me I lost trying to hold everything together.

I need this tonight—just a few hours to remember the version of me that still knows how to breathe.

The wine bar is tucked on the corner of a brick building, with flickering lanterns above the door and fogged-up windows that make the inside feel like a secret. As I walk in, the warm hum of conversation wraps around me like a blanket. Candles flicker at every table, soft jazz plays beneath the hum, and the aroma of cinnamon, wine, and something baking in the back lingers in the air.

I spot them right away—Maya in her oversized sweater, Claire already laughing at something Tara said. Their glasses are half full, cheeks flushed, eyes sharp. I slide into the booth and exhale.

"You look exhausted," Maya says, handing me a glass. "Nathan let you pack everything again, huh?"

"You know it." I take a long sip. "I swear he'd forget his underwear if I didn't do it for him."

"Honestly, same," Claire mutters. "We should start a petition. Minimum husband standards: pack your own damn bag."

"Agreed," Tara says. "Step two: don't act like you are doing us a favor by watching your own kids."

We laugh, and this time it's easier.

"Okay," Maya says, leaning forward, her tone changing. "How are you? Really."

I sigh, swirling the wine in my glass. "Tired. Stuck. Like I'm always running on empty, but if I slow down, everything crashes." They nod in sync. This isn't new territory—but it still hurts to say it out loud.

"And Nathan?" Maya presses.

I shrug. "Same. He works. He's cold. I feel invisible most

days. Like... I could vanish and no one would notice until laundry didn't get done."

"Jesus," Claire whispers. "That's not how it's supposed to feel."

"I know." I blink hard, swallowing the ache. "I just... I don't even know who I am anymore."

"Well," Claire says, lifting her glass, "that's why we're here. To remind you."

"And to drink until you believe us," Tara adds, clinking her glass against mine.

But Maya's not done. "Speaking of reminders... tell us about the neighbor."

I freeze. "What about him?"

"Don't play coy," Claire grins. "You left out so much last time."

"I didn't leave out anything. We just talked. Briefly."

Tara arches a brow. "Was this the sweaty gym incident?"

"Technically yes," I say, trying to sound casual. "I had no idea he would be there and just ran into him."

"You rerouted your whole morning to 'accidentally' run into him, didn't you?" Maya teases.

"Shut up." I laugh, shaking my head. "It wasn't planned."

"So, what happened?" Claire leans in, eyes wide. "Did he flirt? Did he ask you out?"

"No! He... just said I looked like I had a full morning. Asked about the kids. Complimented me. Said I was doing a good job."

All three women freeze, eyes narrowing.

"That's flirting," Tara says.

"Big-time flirting," Maya agrees. "Was there eye contact?"

I hesitate. "Yes."

"Lingering pauses?"

I nod reluctantly.

"Did he touch your arm? Brush against your hand?" Claire pushes.

"No. But he said he's seen me with my kids outside," I say—though even to me, it sounds like a deflection. One that neatly distracts me from the thought of Jack touching me.

"THAT'S FOREPLAY," Maya nearly shouts.

I laugh so hard I have to set my glass down.

"He's just... nice," I say. "And yeah, it felt good. He made me feel seen. And not like... 'Wow, you're such a great mom' seen. Just me. As a person."

Their faces soften.

"That's not nothing, it means he's noticed you," Claire says.

"But it can't be something," I reply quickly. "That's not who I am."

"You're human," Maya says. "That doesn't make you reckless. It makes you honest."

I glance down at my glass. "I just hate that a stranger made me feel more valued in five minutes than Nathan has in the last year."

We all go quiet.

Then Claire grins. "Okay, but what's his name?"

"Jack Callahan."

"Oooh," Tara sings. "Strong. Reliable. Definitely the name of a man who builds things."

"He only offered me coffee," I mumble again, more to myself.

"What color are his eyes?" Maya asks.

"Blue."

"Yep. That's it. We're done for," Claire says, sliding me her glass like a toast. "He's your emotional support neighbor."

We laugh again, and it lifts something in me—if only for a minute.

Maya twirls her wine glass between her fingers. "Do you remember when we used to rate every guy we met based on their shoes?"

"Oh my god," Claire laughs, nearly choking on her drink. "If he wore square-toe dress shoes, it was an automatic no."

"Or boat shoes with no socks. Dealbreaker," Tara adds.

"I still judge based on shoes," I say, grinning. "And Jack? Boots. Nothing fancy. But clean. Classic."

"Mm-hmm," Maya hums, satisfied. "Says a lot about a man."

"He had this calmness about him," I admit quietly. "Like he wasn't trying to prove anything. He was just... there. Real."

The girls go quiet, watching me.

"And that matters," Claire says gently. "Especially when you've felt invisible for so long."

The weight of her words settles in my chest like a truth I've been trying to outrun.

Tara tilts her head. "What do you want, Ella? Like really. Not what the kids need. Not what Nathan expects. What do you want?"

The question stuns me. I look down at the wine in my glass, at the flickering candle between us.

"I want to feel like myself again," I whisper. "I want to laugh without guilt. Sleep without pressure. And maybe... just maybe... I want someone to look at me like I'm more than what I do for everyone else."

Silence. The kind that isn't empty, but full.

Maya nods. "Then don't forget that. No matter what happens."

The clink of glasses is softer this time—less celebration, more promise.

We sit there a while longer, reminiscing about college road trips, failed first dates, and the time we dyed Claire's hair firetruck red and blamed it on a shampoo mix-up.

Eventually, we settle into a quiet comfort, the kind only lifelong friends can offer.

Later, the bar begins to empty around us, but none of us move yet.

We're not just catching up. We're remembering each other. Remembering ourselves.

When I leave the wine bar that night, the cool air kisses my cheeks, and my face still aches from smiling.

But beneath the joy, beneath the buzz of wine and memory, something deeper stirs—a quiet ache for the woman I used to be.

Not guilt. Not temptation. Just that ache, soft but insistent. A reminder of what it feels like to be alive.

And I wonder…am I brave enough to let her return?

Chapter Five

The next morning, the scent of waffles drifts through the house, cozy and familiar, carried on the soft breeze that moves through the open windows. My dad is probably in the kitchen flipping them now, probably expecting me to clean up afterward, like always. But here, I don't mind. Waking up here feels like exhaling. This place is home. The sounds, the smells... it calms something in me. It's safe. Peaceful.

My dad's always been my steady place. After the divorce, he became the one I could count on. My parents both worked too much, tried their best in their own ways, but my dad... he showed up. He didn't just provide—he was present.

Growing up, I did a lot on my own—made lunches, helped my sister with homework, filled in the gaps. Just… quiet. Hollow in a way I didn't know how to name back then. My parents were exhausted, and somewhere along the way, I learned how to carry more than a kid should. My dad didn't see it all back then. But when he did, he stepped in, and he never looked back.

The wounds from that kind of distance are subtle, but they

stick. It's strange how some cracks in the heart don't fully heal—how they shape the way you parent, the way you love. My parents were always there physically, but emotionally? Not so much. They were busy. Tired. Doing the best they could, maybe. But I had to learn to cook, clean, and take care of my baby sister earlier than most kids. If I didn't do it, it didn't get done. I became the built-in helper—the one who smoothed everything over. I don't blame them entirely anymore, but I'd be lying if I said the resentment is completely gone.

I was twelve when I realized I couldn't completely rely on them for comfort. Mornings were me waking my sister, making breakfast, and getting us both out the door while our parents scrambled through their routines, distracted and late. I'd come home to dishes, empty cabinets, and a quiet house that rarely asked how we were doing. That became my normal—keeping things together, staying small so nothing else fell apart. My dad eventually saw it more clearly after the divorce. He stepped up in a way that changed everything. I think he knew he'd missed a lot. But once he showed up, he never stopped.

But today, I want to focus on the present, on the people who show up. My dad, Reed, stands in the kitchen, humming softly as he packs a cooler with sandwiches and soda. His tan arms, weathered from years on the water, move with the ease of someone who has done this a thousand times.

"You sure you packed enough for everyone?" I tease, leaning against the doorway.

"Always do," he replies, flashing me a grin. "And if not, we'll catch enough to compensate for it."

I roll my eyes. "That's a lot of faith in our fishing skills."

"Hey now, my grandkids are going to be naturals. Just you wait."

I smile, letting his optimism wash over me. My dad has a way of making everything feel simple, even when it isn't.

Nathan wanders in, already wearing his fishing hat and sunglasses. "Let's get this show on the road. I want to snag a big one today."

My dad raises an eyebrow. "We all do. But it's not a competition, you know."

Nathan just laughs. "Sure, it isn't."

The kids barrel in, Nora leading the charge with her pink fishing rod. She's practically buzzing with excitement.

"I'm gonna catch the biggest fish ever!" she declares.

My dad kneels down, adjusting the brim of her sun hat. "I believe you will, sweetheart."

"Let's go!" he says with a joy I haven't heard all year. This really is his favorite thing to do.

We pile into my dad's truck—two tandem kayaks strapped to the trailer, a single one tied to the roof. The drive to the launch is short, the kind of backroad that winds through marsh grass and ends at a weathered dock beside the river.

By the time we unload, the sun is already warming the air. Nathan lingers near the truck, scrolling through his phone, while my dad and I carry paddles and life vests to the water's edge. "Let's pair up," my dad says. "Nora, you ride with your dad. Emmett, you're with me."

I take my own single and slide it into the water. We push off together, paddling gently downstream through a shaded bend where the light flickers like fish scales on the water.

"This is going to be amazing," he says once we reach the cove. "Alright, everyone, let's grab our fishing rods and get ready for some fun!"

Nora is the first to cast her line. Her little face scrunches in concentration. Nathan barely looks up as he focuses on setting up his own rod. I watch him, waiting for him to offer Nora some guidance, but he doesn't.

Minutes pass. Then—

"I got one! I got one!" Nora screams, jumping up and down.

Her rod bends under the weight of her catch, and she struggles to reel it in.

"Nathan!" I call, hoping he will jump in to help. But he keeps focusing on his line, muttering, "Hang on, I think I've got one too." Meanwhile, my dad paddles over and links up with Nora's kayak, steadying her rod and guiding her as they reel in a small, shimmering fish. "Look at that!" he exclaims, beaming with pride. "You did it, Nora!"

Nora squeals in delight, holding up her beautiful catch for everyone. I glance at Nathan, still absorbed in his task, and I feel mixed emotions—wishing he would share in her joy.

Later, back at the house, Nora is practically glowing as she hovers over her fish, daydreaming about our dinner plans. "I want it for dinner, Mommy," she says, her eyes sparkling excitedly.

"We'll need to clean it first," I smile, glancing at Nathan, eager to share this special moment.

He sighs. "Yeah, yeah. I'll get to it."

But he doesn't. Hours pass. The fish sits forgotten on the counter, and my frustration only grows.

"Nathan, are you going to take care of this?" I finally ask.

He waves me off. "I said I would. Just give me a minute."

When he finally looks up from his phone, it is too late. The fish is spoiled.

Tears well in Nora's eyes as she stares at the limp fish. "But I wanted to eat it," she whispers.

I kneel down beside her, wrapping my arms around her small frame. "I know, baby. I'm so sorry."

She buries her face in my shoulder, and I glance at Nathan,

hoping he'll say something, anything. He disappears down the hallway without a word, not even a glance at her. And just like that, the moment she worked so hard for is gone, and I realize for the hundredth time that he will never change, not for me and not for them. The silence between us feels heavier than any words could. I stare at the empty doorway, wondering how many more disappointments it would take before I stop expecting anything from him at all. I want to scream at him, ask why he can't see what she needs, what I need. But I don't. I just stand there, holding the weight of yet another moment he let fall.

Moments later, my dad enters, taking in the scene. He doesn't say anything, just gives my shoulder a reassuring squeeze. It is a simple gesture, but it assures me he is on my side.

After the kids are in bed that night, I sit on the porch with my dad, the salty breeze brushing against my skin. "You okay?" he asks. "How are things at home with Nathan?"

I exhale slowly. "I don't know. Sometimes, it feels like I do this whole parenting thing alone."

He's never said a bad word about Nathan, but I know he sees it too.

I would never tell my dad about the arguments and fights, how I feel unseen and like a failure, or how I can't believe I am married to a man who doesn't love me anymore.

My dad nods thoughtfully. "I get it. It's not easy. But you're doing great. They're lucky to have you, El. Don't ever doubt that." I swallow the lump in my throat. "Thanks, Dad."

He pats my knee. "And hey, Nora will catch another fish. Next time, we'll make sure she gets to eat it." I smile through the tears threatening to fall. "Next time."

We sit in the stillness of the night, the hum of the crickets and the distant lapping of water filling the silence between us.

I stare out into the dark as the weight of the day settles over me, but somewhere beneath it, there is a flicker, small but steady. Families aren't perfect. They bruise, they bend, they fracture. But the ones who keep showing up—those are the ones who matter. And maybe that's enough to hold on to.

Chapter Six

A few days into our stay in Coral Pass, the pull becomes too strong to resist and I cave. I'd been holding back, replaying my friends' advice to stay cautious. Jack's been lodged in my thoughts like a quiet hum beneath everything I do. After our brief chat at the gym, I added him on social media. Colby too. Innocent enough. But today, I give in.

I scroll through my camera roll and pause on a video from the marina, Nora reeling in her first fish off the kayak, eyes wide, laughter spilling into the salt air. On impulse, I send it.

Me: Oops, meant to send this to my dad. Unless you want to witness our chaotic fishing victory lol.

Jack: Hahaha this made my day. She looks so proud. Y'all make it look effortless.

The tension dissolves. My chest opens, air rushing in as a smile spreads, wide and real, creasing the edges of my eyes.

Me: It was anything but easy. But she loved every second of it.

Jack: That's the good stuff. Honestly, this is better than any tourism ad. Hope the rest of your trip's been good?

Me: It's quiet, which is rare. My dad's in his element. The kids are having a blast. We're heading back tomorrow morning.

There's a pause, three little bouncing dots. Then:

Jack: Glad to hear it. I picked my kids up yesterday. Spent the week with family. A lot of noise. A lot of love.

A warm ache pulses through my chest. I picture him in some coastal town, surrounded by people who know him inside out. That kind of stability draws me in more than I want to admit.

Me: That sounds perfect. Are they happy to be back?

Jack: Most of them. One of the little ones hugged me and said, "Daddy, I never want to leave you again." And yeah... my allergies flared up after that.

I laugh out loud, the sound too big for the stillness around me. His words soften something in me I didn't know was tight.

Me: Ugh, I would've melted. Kids know how to break us. How long were they gone?

Jack: In the best way, yeah. Just six days, but it felt like forever. Juggling work and the kids solo makes me wish I could clone myself some days. But moments like that? Makes the chaos worth it.

I glance out through the patio door. The backyard's bathed in the last gold of sunset, the pool catching bits of violet sky. My dad's in the rocker with a drink in hand, eyes half closed. The clink of ice in his glass blends with the hum of cicadas. It's peaceful. Familiar. But my mind isn't here.

It's with Jack.

Me: *I'm glad they're home. I couldn't even do one full day without mine. I don't know how you do it. I can barely hold it together with two—and I have help. Seriously… you make it look easy.*

Jack: *Well, thanks. And I get that. Some things are out of our control. Some things aren't. Knowing the difference is everything.*

I stare at the message, my pulse doing that fluttering thing again.

Me: *I try to control everything, but I still end up screwing it all up.*

Jack: *Or maybe you're just human. Even when you mean well, mistakes still happen.*

I don't know how to respond without saying too much. So, I don't. Not right away.

Nathan's already asleep in the chair, a soda can slipping from his hand—like showing up is the only part he plays here. The kids are still playing, giggling from the guest room floor where they've dumped out every board game they could find.

Eventually, I get them cleaned up, brushed, and tucked in. Nora asks for her glow-in-the-dark blanket. Emmett wants another glass of water. The usual. But once I settle into the recliner and the house quiets, our conversation replays in my head like a favorite song on loop.

I pick up my phone again.

Me: *I'll text you when we're back in Eastwell.*

Jack: *I'll be looking forward to it.*

Simple. Easy. And yet it feels like something passed between us, something small, but real.

Later, when the kids are asleep and the house has gone still, I lie in bed and watch the ceiling fan trace slow, lazy circles. The warmth from our exchange lingers like a soft echo, warm, slow-burning, and a little dangerous. I barely know him. But that's not the point.

The point is I feel seen. And I hadn't realized how long it's been since I felt that way.

Jack doesn't say much, but when he does, it lands, like a match struck in a dark room. Quick. Bright. Impossible to ignore.

I'm not naïve. I know better than to read too much into a few messages. But I also know what I felt, the lift in my chest, the way my skin warmed when his name appeared.

Nathan and I are a shell of what we used to be, if we were ever truly anything more than obligation and routine. It's hard to tell now.

I'm not naïve. But I also know what it feels like to be seen—and how long it's been.

I close my eyes and hear his words again.

I'm glad you reached out. Me too.

I just don't know what to do with that yet.

Chapter Seven

We came home late last night. It was well past midnight when we finally pulled into the driveway, too exhausted to do anything but stumble inside and collapse into bed. This morning, the house feels eerily quiet without Nathan. The emptiness seems sharper somehow, as if the brief reprieve of our trip had only masked the cracks for a moment. Being away softened things, or maybe it was just the comfort of distraction. Either way, Nathan's already back at work, and the silence has returned louder than before.

New toys are scattered everywhere, creating a plastic minefield of chaos across the living room floor. Usually, the mess would bother me, but today I welcome it. Their laughter fills the house, a soothing sound that momentarily drowns out the noise in my head. These days feel impossibly long, stretched thin by the demands of two kids, but I'm adjusting—mostly. Emmett's clingier than usual, not acting like he's almost four. Maybe he senses the tension that seeps through the house like a fog whenever Nathan and I are in the same room. Maybe he knows his days are numbered and he will soon be in preschool. This would be enough to wipe me out, but that's not what's draining me today. Not really.

It's Jack.

He's in my head constantly, uninvited, unstoppable. It's ridiculous, but his presence lingers like a whisper I can't quite shake. At night, he sneaks into my dreams, his warm smile, the low timbre of his voice that feels like safety, and the touch I haven't felt but imagine all too vividly. I hate myself for letting it happen, for allowing him into my thoughts. I'm married, after all.

Nathan's not perfect, but he's a good man. And yet, here I am, scrolling through my phone, fighting the overwhelming urge to message Jack.

The break has thrown me off-kilter. The routine of school drop-offs and pick-ups is gone, leaving me with nothing but time. This morning, in my scramble, I found my coffee maker, filters and coffee, but I don't have any creamer. Earlier, I peeked outside, Jack's car was gone. But I message him on social media anyway.

Me: *I found my coffee maker. It's set up and ready to brew, but I don't have creamer. Do you have any?*

Jack: *Happens to the best of us. I always have creamer. I only have the powder kind but I'm not home right now.*

His casual response sends my thoughts spiraling. I stare at the screen, cringing at my own boldness, but the thrill of his reply outweighs the shame.

Me: *I can't be picky in a pinch, and thanks anyway.*

The words feel hollow the moment I send them. And yet, deep down, I am already scheming, imagining ways I might find myself alone with him. The thought both terrifies and exhilarates me.

An hour later, my phone buzzes again.

Jack: *I'm home for the next 45 minutes. If you still need a creamer,* *let me know. I've got to shower and change for a lunch outing.*

The mention of a shower sends my imagination into overdrive. I can picture him, water streaming down his shoulders, his skin glistening under the harsh bathroom light. I shake my head, trying to push the image away, but it's too late. My cheeks flush as I type out a reply. I stare at the door for a beat too long, wondering what it would feel like to say yes. Just creamer, I told myself. Just conversation. But I stayed put. Because I knew it wouldn't stay that way.

Me: *Damn again, lol. I just got everyone ready to get some from the store.*

His response is quick but brief, a thumbs-up. That's it, a single, indifferent gesture, yet it sends my heart racing. Did he sense my inner turmoil? Could he tell how much I want to see him? I type another message, desperate to explain.

Me: *I told the kids I would buy them candy, there's no going back now. Yes, I bribed them.*

Jack: *Haha.*

I stare at the screen, my fingers hovering over the keyboard. I want to say more, to keep the conversation going, but what can I say? The truth is, I'd already talked myself out of seeing him. Not because I didn't want to, but because I am terrified of what might happen—or what I might want to happen.

☾☾☾

As I am folding laundry later that day, kids' laughter drifts in through the open window, and I glance outside to see Jack at the park, chasing his kids. The sight tugs at something deep inside me, a longing I can't quite name.

"Kids, want to go outside and play at the park?" I ask, trying to sound casual.

"Yes, Mommy!" they shout, their excitement contagious.

I throw on my favorite ripped jeans and a snug green top, not thinking too hard about why I care how I look. As we step outside, Jack catches my eye. He stops mid-run, his gaze locking with mine for a brief, electrifying moment.

At the park, I sit at an old wooden worn-out picnic table, feigning interest in the kids as they play. Jack is close enough to talk to, but I can't bring myself to say anything. My heart races whenever he glances my way, and I hate how my body betrays me.

I tuck a strand of hair behind my ear, the breeze tugging at the loose ends as I shift on the bench. "So... how long have you lived in this neighborhood?" I ask, my voice lighter than I feel.

Jack leans forward, his arm drapes casually along the table's edge. "About two years," he says, his lips quirking into a half-smile. "Give or take."

"Two years, huh?" I nod, my gaze flicking toward the kids chasing each other across the playground. "And how many are yours?"

His laugh catches me off guard, warm and unguarded, and makes me want to lean in closer. "Four." He jabs a finger toward the chaos in the distance. "All mine."

"Four?" The word slips out before I can stop it, my eyebrows lifting. "You're kidding."

He grins, already pulling out his phone. "Nope. Here, look."

He stands, stepping around the table until he is beside me, so close I can feel the heat rolling off him. When he holds out his phone, I reach for it instinctively, but he doesn't let go.

Our hands barely brush, skin on skin, but the spark is instant, sharp, electric. My breath catches, and I forget what I am supposed to be looking at for a split second.

"See?" His voice is softer now, the edge of his sleeve

grazing my arm. "This was us at the beach last summer. Long day, I didn't think we would survive, but we did."

I nod, though my focus stays on his fingers, still wrapped around the phone's edges. I pull my hand back first, pressing it into my lap to keep it steady. "Looks like a beautiful day," I murmur, but my voice feels too thin, too tight.

And when he looks at me, really looks at me, I know he feels it too.

"Where is their mom? If I am prying just tell me it's none of my business," I ask. "She burned me bad," he says, looking out across the playground. "Honestly? Every relationship I've had ended with me getting burned," he says in a tone that says that's all he will say. What does he mean burned? I wonder how many women thought they wouldn't be the ones to burn him.

Then Nathan's car pulls in, and my stomach drops. The fragile thread connecting Jack and me snaps when Nathan steps out, his presence grounds me—and not in the way I want. Sweaty hands, I smooth my hands down my jeans. A nervous habit Nathan's pointed out more than once—usually with a look that shuts me up.

The kids run to him, their laughter filling the space as he scoops them up. Nora hangs back a step, hesitating just long enough for me to notice. Her smile dims as she glances at Nathan, searching his face like she's waiting for a cue. It's barely a beat—but it's enough. My heart tightens. She shouldn't have to wonder if it's safe to run to her dad. He flashes a warm smile that doesn't quite reach me. When he finally approaches, he presses a quick kiss to my lips. It is soft, obligatory, and his voice matches it. Nora glances my way, eyes flicking between me and Nathan before darting away. I force a smile I don't feel.

"Hey, honey."

I force a smile, but my pulse hasn't slowed.

Jack stands, shifting slightly, his polite smile firm but guarded. "Hey, I'm Jack," he says, extending his hand.

"Nathan." My husband's grip is strong, a little too firm, and the air between them feels heavier than it should have. I swallow hard as Nathan turns to me, his brow furrows.

"What's for dinner?"

"Lemon-herb chicken and rice," I say quickly, smoothing my hands down the sides of my jeans. "But I don't have any lemons, so I need to go get some from the store."

Jack's voice cuts through the moment. "I've got some."

I blink at him. "Really? Can I borrow a couple?"

"Of course." He smiles. "Let me grab a few. Can you watch my kids for a second?"

"Yeah, no problem."

Jack's already heading home, and I catch myself watching, his stride easy, confident, until I feel Nathan watching me.

"What?" I ask, too sharp, too defensive.

Nathan chuckles, but it doesn't reach his eyes. "Oh, nothing." His smile stays fixed. My stomach knots—a chill running sharp up my spine.

Jack returns moments later, holding a bag of lemons as if it is the simplest thing in the world. Our fingers brush when he hands it to me, and my butterflies sing in my stomach.

"Thanks," I say, my voice softer than I intend.

"Anytime." His eyes linger long enough to make my breath hitch before he turns and returns to his kids.

I clutch the lemons like they are fragile and precious, my pulse still unsteady as I feel Nathan's eyes tracking me back to the house.

Later that evening, as I stand in the kitchen, the memory of Jack's easy smile and steady gaze haunts me. The lemon he gave me sits on the cutting board, a small, potent reminder. I slice it carefully, the sweet aroma filling the air as I prepare dinner.

The lemon-herb chicken simmers on the stove, its rich scent mingling with the soft hum of laughter from the kids in the living room. My hands move on autopilot, but my mind is miles away, circling back to Jack and the spark I can't ignore.

When I finish cooking, I plate an extra serving, wrap it in foil, then grab my phone and send Jack a quick message.

Me: *Too late to swing by for a second?*

My heart hammers as I hit send, my thumb trembling over the screen.

The silence stretches, heavier with every passing second. No reply. I walk over and stand there on his front porch, debating whether to leave the plate and disappear before I can regret it or knock and see him. But something, something I can't explain—pulls me forward, the foil-covered plate warm against my palms as if it carries the heat building inside me. Nathan's voice flickers through my head—Where the hell were you? I shove it down. Just this once. I knock.

When Jack opens the door, his smile stops me cold, easy, genuine, the kind that makes breathing impossible. He reaches for the plate, his fingers brushing against mine, and that slight touch sends a ripple through me so sharp it makes my knees weak.

"Thank you," he says, low and warm, handing the food to one of his kids. Before I can step away, he wraps me in a quick hug, casual and effortless. I don't lean in, but I don't pull back either. It's over in a second—but it leaves something behind. Something I carry all the way back to my house. I cross the front yard, my pulse still thrumming. Through the window, I catch Nora watching me from the couch, her eyes wide and searching. I force another smile—too quick, too thin—and turn away.

Chapter Eight

It's been a couple of weeks since I've seen Jack. I catch myself peeking out the window more than I care to admit, scanning for his car. He's always gone. Still, I wonder where he goes and why I care so much.

Nathan and I are hosting his coworker and his wife for dinner tonight. I haven't met them yet, so I'm scrambling to make sure everything is right. It's a chance to make friends, something I know is essential, especially for couples like us. But as I set the table, a part of me can't help wishing it were Jack instead. The thought knots something low in my gut. Guilt. I shake my head, trying to clear it. I can't think like that. I won't.

I take the trash outside when dinner ends; the plates are mostly empty. The cool air bites at my skin, but I barely notice it. My eyes drift instinctively to Jack's house, empty driveway, just as I expected. The slight pang of disappointment that follows feels ridiculous. I scold myself as I head back inside.

I grab my phone and shoot him a quick message before I can think about it.

Me: *Are you going to be home tonight?*

His response is quick.

Jack: *Later tonight, yes. What's up?*

The butterflies stir, and I chastise myself for how easily his words affect me. My thumbs hover over the keyboard, hesitating momentarily before I type.

Me: *This is probably a weird question out of nowhere... but are you a grilled chicken fan?*

I cringe, already regretting how impulsive I sound. Why can't I play it cool for once?

Jack: Of course.

Me: *We had some friends over for dinner, I made way too much food, so if you want some, feel free to stop by.*

There's a pause, and for a moment, I wonder if I've crossed some invisible line. When his response comes, my heart sinks.

Jack: *Driving up to Ashland tonight. Dropping the kids off. Probably won't be back until late.*

I chew my lip, hesitating, before typing again.

Me: *Got it. Long trip. Be safe.*

The reply doesn't come right away. My stomach knots as I stare at the screen, wondering if I've pushed too far. Maybe he's tired of my questions, tired of me. The thought stings more than it should. Finally, the screen lights up.

Jack: *I'll probably grab something on the road and crash when I get in. But thank you.*

I keep my face neutral, but my heart tells a different story. I laugh it off.

Me: *So, you're saying no to a home-cooked meal? That's a first.*

Jack: *Haha. I guess I am.*
Me: *If you change your mind, it's here. I'll probably still be awake.*
Jack: *You're the best. I don't want to be mean to a new neighbor, so if you are up, I'll have some.*

His words make me smile despite myself. My heart, which had sunk just moments ago, lifts a little. He always manages to shift the mood and find the right words, even in the most straightforward exchanges.

Me: *Not really, but ok, I'll make you a plate.*

As I finish cleaning up after dinner, I find myself nervously preparing a plate for Jack, my hands trembling slightly as I scoop the chicken and vegetables onto it. I tell myself it's nothing—again. But the story's starting to feel as thin as the wine in my glass. My heart betrays me, racing at the thought of seeing him.

About half an hour later, my phone buzzes again. I grab it quickly, my pulse quickening.

Jack: *I'm sorry, I'm exhausted. Rain check?*

His words hit harder than they should. The disappointment is quick, irrational, and sharp. Disappointment wells up in me, and I have to blink back the sting of tears. Nathan notices the change in my expression.

"Everything okay?" he asks, his tone distracted.

I nod, forcing a smile that doesn't quite reach my eyes. "Yeah, I'm fine."

I retreat to the bathroom, shutting the door behind me. The silence wraps around me, and I stare at my reflection in the mirror, wondering why I feel this way. Why does his rejection—however reasonable—sting so much? It's silly, I know. But for a moment, I thought maybe he wanted this connection too. Finally, I find the strength to message him back.

Me: *Alright, be careful.*

The words are simple and neutral. But as I send them, they feel like a goodbye, even though I know it's not.

After our guests leave, the house begins to settle. The kids are bathed and tucked into bed, one by one. Emmett is already asleep, his soft, rhythmic breathing filling the quiet of his room. Nora clutches her favorite book as I kiss her forehead, promising to return and read to her once I finish cleaning up.

After washing my face and changing into my pajamas, I head downstairs to the kitchen, still messy from dinner. The dishes are piled high in the sink, and the remnants of the dinner party are scattered across the counters. Nathan has already gone to bed, leaving me with many chores and restless thoughts.

The kitchen feels colder than usual, the air brushing against my bare skin as I lean against the counter. I pour a splash of white wine into a coffee mug. It's what was clean. I don't care. As I sip, my mind drifts back to Jack. His words, his smile, the way he makes me feel seen in a way I haven't felt in years. I stand there, mug in hand, letting the silence press in. The weight of disappointment is heavier than the glass. The wine is warm now. I forgot about it. I sip it anyway, more out of habit than need. I hear Emmett stir upstairs, his little feet padding across the hall. I wait, but he settles. He must have had to go the bathroom. The house sighs again.

The vibration of my phone against the counter pulls me from my thoughts. I glance at the screen. It's him.

Jack: That plate still up for grabs? I'll be home in about 40.

I stare at the message, my emotions flipping, hope, hesitation, irritation, a flicker of something like joy. Why now? Why wait until I'd already let the idea go?

My fingers hover over the screen. It shouldn't matter this much. But it does.

Me: *I'm still up. Full transparency: I'm in pajamas, slightly wine-*

glowy, and very much in post-hosting survival mode.

His reply comes quick.

Jack: *Sounds like the most authentic version of you.*

I laugh quietly to myself.

Me: *That's one way to spin it.*

Jack: *I mean it. You don't have to try so hard all the time.*

I stop. Reread that.

Me: *That feels like something a therapist would say... but weirdly, I needed to hear it.*

Jack: *Just a neighbor with good timing.*

Me: *Noted. Chicken's still warm if you change your mind.*

Jack: *I might swing by. Depends how wrecked I am when I get home.*

His words land softly this time—less about the food, more about the comfort it represents. The ache I hadn't admitted starts to loosen. The smile that finds my lips isn't forced.

Jack: *You're doing more than you know. Just wanted to say that.*

It's simple. Unexpected. And it wraps around me like a blanket I didn't know I needed.

Me: *Brownie points officially restored.*

The conversation stays light from there. Little jokes. A meme he sends that makes me snort into my wine. It's easy. It's safe. And somehow, it still means everything.

When the messages fade and I set my phone down, I notice my cheeks ache from smiling. The kitchen is finally clean. The night has gone quiet.

I make my way upstairs, the house humming low and still. After brushing my teeth and washing my face, I catch a glimpse of myself in the mirror. There's something softer about my reflection. Something a little more... awake.

I switch off the light and slide into bed.

The silence presses in, but it doesn't feel as heavy tonight.

His words linger.

And as I close my eyes, one question returns—steady, dangerous, impossible to ignore:

What does it mean when the only person who makes you feel seen… isn't your husband? And why do I want to hold on to that?

Chapter Nine

It's hard to believe we've been in Eastwell for nearly two months. The days blur together when you're surrounded by family—and yet somehow, there's never quite enough of them. I keep checking my phone, hoping to see Jack's name pop up on the screen. What started as casual has become something else entirely. I hope he feels the same way. It's exciting to hear from him, and he gives me a welcome break from these monotonous days.

I've been trying to keep my distance—not reach out first, stay busy. Nora's back in school, which means more time for chores—and thinking. Emmett mostly colors, watches TV, and plays with his toys. I pull the damp laundry from the washer, the scent of detergent clinging to my hands just as my phone buzzes in my pocket. Maya's name lights up the screen. I wipe my palms on my jeans and answer.

"Hey, girl," I say, trying to keep my voice light.

"Hey, yourself. What's up?"

I laugh softly. "Oh, you know. Just drowning in mom duties."

"Living the dream, huh?" she teases.

"Basically," I say, tossing clothes into the dryer. "What about you?"

"Getting ready for work. Dreading it, honestly."

I hesitate, the words already pressing against my lips. "Can I tell you something?"

"Always."

I swallow, lowering my voice. "I've been messaging Jack. A lot."

"What?" Her voice sharpens. "Why?"

"I don't know." The truth sits heavy in my chest, but I push it down. "I like talking to him."

"Ella." Her tone drops, a warning. "Does Nathan know?"

"No," I say too quickly, gripping the edge of the dryer. "But he's noticed. I've caught him watching me… watching Jack." My stomach twists as the confession leaves my lips.

I let out a shaky breath. "It's harmless. We're just talking," I say, but the words feel flimsy, like tissue paper stretched too thin.

"Sure," Maya says—and I hear the doubt sharpen in her voice. "That neighborhood's basically one giant group chat. Everyone sees everything. Watch yourself."

She pauses, her voice dropping low. "Careful, Ella. You're handing him matches and acting like the fire's his fault."

"Look, I gotta go. But seriously—keep your distance."

"I will," I say, but we both know I wouldn't.

That afternoon, as I stand at the counter stirring a pot of mac and cheese for the kids, my phone buzzes. I set the wooden spoon down on the countertop and glance at the screen. It's Jack. My stomach flips.

Jack: *Hey, you ever used the Whispyr app?*

My heart skips at the question. I try to play it cool. A secure messaging app. The kind where messages vanish.

Me: *The one with disappearing chats? You worried someone's going to leak our creamer debates and fishing takes?*

Jack: *Hey, that's premium content. But seriously... sometimes it's better to keep things between us. You got it?*

I hesitate. Guilt flickers. But curiosity wins.

Me: *I use it to message my sister. Why?*

Jack: *Add me.*

Later that evening, after the kids are asleep and Nathan's lost in another deep dive about golf gear, I scroll through my phone in bed. I open Whispyr, find his username, and hover for a second before I tap "Add." Seconds later, the notification pops up.

Jack has added you back.

His message lands instantly: a selfie. Couch slouched, beer in hand, cap low, smile lazy.

Jack: *Cheers to my favorite neighbor.*

I smile and reply with a shot of me on the couch in joggers and a hoodie, hair still damp from a shower, holding a can of hard seltzer.

Me: *Cheers back. Long day.*

The next few days blur together in soft exchanges. Nothing overt. Nothing scandalous. But under the surface, there's a hum. A quiet daring neither of us names.

Later that night, with the kids asleep and Nathan snoring down the hall, my phone buzzes again.

Jack: *What's the vibe tonight, seltzer, tea, or reckless decisions?*

I snap a quick selfie, hard seltzer in hand, hair messy, soft lighting, but dressed. Presentable. Flushed, maybe, but not exposed.

Me: *Hard seltzer. Second can. Chaos pending.*

Jack: *You look good. Like the kind of good that makes people reckless.*

Another image follows; him, reclined, T-shirt stretched across his chest, the kind of half-smile that says everything without saying anything.

Jack: *You inspired me.*

Me: *I'll take that as a compliment.*

Jack: *You've been on my mind. More than I want to admit.*

The message hits differently. It lands. Heavy. Electric. For a heartbeat, I think of Nathan. Of how far this is from harmless. But the thought passes, easier than it should.

We talk more. Not just flirtation, though there's plenty of that, but real stuff. Regrets. Dreams. Things we don't say in daylight.

When I finally fall asleep, phone still in my hand, I know something's shifted.

This isn't innocent anymore.

The next morning, another message from Jack:

Jack: *Meet in person and talk?*

I stare at the screen. My pulse quickens. It sounds casual. But we both know this isn't just a friendly meet-up.

Me: *When and where?*

Jack: *The clubhouse back porch at 11.*

I set the phone down slowly, like it might detonate. My mind floods with questions. *What would I wear? Joggers and a tee? Hair down or tied up? Would he notice if I wore lip gloss?*

I hate that I'm thinking this way.

But I am. Jack is everywhere. In my thoughts. In my dreams. In the space Nathan used to fill without even trying.

Then come the other thoughts—the ones that knot my stomach and chill my hands. Eastwell is small. The playground moms notice everything. One odd glance, one "Did you see?"—and I'd be pinned beneath someone else's story.

I imagine walking beside him. The quiet between steps. The tension.

I sit up, suddenly restless. I scroll, searching for a reason.

Maybe I take Emmett for a walk and we end up at the clubhouse—there's a playground there. If anyone sees me, it won't seem strange. Maybe I just run into Jack coincidentally. I could ask him to show me around, just to learn about the place. But even I know that's not what this is.

And maybe that's the problem.

Maybe that's the scariest part of all. Because I'm not looking for harmless.

I'm looking for what happens when no one's watching—and nothing stands in the way.

Chapter Ten

The following day, I wake with a start, my heart racing as if I haven't slept a wink. Emmett bounces out of bed, his toy firetruck sirens already blaring. "Momma, I'm hungry!" he yells. I roll out of bed, moving through the motions of breakfast, school clothes, wiping up spills, and picking up toys. But my mind is elsewhere. It keeps drifting back to the clubhouse back porch at 11.

I glance at the clock again. Time moves like molasses. It's like the whole morning is stretching out, and the weight of it presses down on me harder with every minute. I've replayed Jack's message from the night before in my head a hundred times: The clubhouse back porch at 11. I can't get rid of the blush that creeps up my neck whenever I think about it. *What's going to happen when we're alone? Or worse, what if it's more than just physical?* I spent most of the night running through possible reasons to go over there, but now my mind is fixated on something else: *Will anyone see me?* It's a public place, a place where the whole neighborhood gathers. I don't think anyone will be there at the time of day but anyone could be watching.

The thought tightens in my chest. I can picture it already—someone noticing me walking over there, their eyes lingering, wondering why I'm heading to the clubhouse alone. *What if someone sees us? What if Nathan finds out?* The thought makes my stomach twist. If Nathan finds out... everything could change. My family, my life, all of it could unravel in an instant. But it's more than that. The worst part is that part of me doesn't even want to stop. I'm standing here, knowing exactly what I'm about to do, and I'm not sure I regret it.

Nathan is already gone to work, his usual quick goodbye barely registering. He's never the one I'm thinking about anymore. My thoughts are full of everything and nothing at once, but mostly, they're consumed with how exposed I feel, how vulnerable.

I pull on my favorite jeans and a loose sweater that fits just right, loose enough to look casual, but tight enough to make me second-guess every movement. I check myself in the mirror a few times, trying to make sure I don't look like I'm trying too hard. I tell myself it's no big deal. I'm just stepping out for a minute. No one needs to know.

When I start my walk to the clubhouse, Emmett's hand grasping mine, I feel exposed. Will anyone see me walking toward Jack? The thought sends a pulse of heat through me. I swear I feel eyes on me. Halfway there, I catch sight of a woman checking her mail. She glances my way—just a flick of her eyes—but my heart kicks up anyway. I offer a quick smile, casual, like I'm on a normal stroll. She tilts her head slightly, watching a beat too long before turning away.

When I round the clubhouse corner, I spot the tiny security camera mounted above the door. I swallow hard. It probably isn't even on. Probably.

I raise my phone and notice it's 8:57. I open the gate and let

Emmett play in the fenced-in playground steps away from the gated porch on the back of the clubhouse. My palms sweat against the fence rail. My breath comes shallow, my heart thudding. Would he even show up? I can't shake the feeling that I'm being watched. My phone buzzes in my hand, and I lift it to check, it's Jack.

Jack: *I see you.*

My eyes dart around in every direction, and then my eyes lock onto his. He is standing next to the back door, leaning against the glass windows that span from the ground to the ceiling. He signals for me to come here. "Emmett, I will be right here on the porch," I call out. "Ok, mama!" he says in return as he slides mid-way.

When I finally reach the back porch gate, I hesitate for a moment. The familiar setting now feels different, like everything has changed. I open the gate and step inside, and our eyes meet. I can feel the tension between us rising.

"I didn't think you'd come," he says, his voice low, but there's a hint of relief in it.

I smile, trying to cover the flutter in my chest. "I didn't think I would either."

I step onto the porch, my heart pounding. Jack doesn't hesitate. He looks at me, his gaze almost daring, and asks, "Have you seen the inside?"

I shake my head, breath catching. "No, not yet."

"Well, check it out," he says, holding the door open for me.

I stop just shy of the doorway. My hand hovers near the frame, the space between us electric—and heavy. For a heartbeat, I picture Nathan. The morning goodbyes. The years we've built. Emmett playing just a stone's throw away. This is the edge of a line I can't uncross.

I tell myself it's just curiosity. Just a walk inside. But even I know that's a lie.

My pulse hammers as I take a breath—and step through.

The clubhouse is dim, the air thick with anticipation and nerves. I barely register the door closing behind me before he's there—his hands on my waist, pulling me toward him.

His lips crash into mine—urgent, starving, like we've both been holding our breath for weeks. I respond before I can think, my fingers tangling in his hair, pulling him closer. His kiss deepens, his other hand sliding under my sweater against my back.

His lips trail down to the curve of my neck, and I gasp—his touch sending a bolt of electricity straight through me. My hands clutch his shirt, holding him like the world might slip away if I let go.

"Ella," he murmurs into my skin, his voice low and rough and laced with want. It sends a shiver racing down my spine.

My pulse pounds, erratic—guilt, desire, fear swirling so fast I can't untangle them. I press my hands against his chest, breaking the kiss, trying to catch my breath, trying to catch myself.

The air feels thick, suffocating. I want to stay. I want to press into him, drown in this heat, this connection I've been starved for. But I can't. I shouldn't.

My body hums with want, but my mind is screaming—leave.

"I can't," I whisper, my voice barely audible. "I… Emmett. I need to get back."

Jack draws back, his hands lingering at my hips. His expression is unreadable—regret, restraint, something darker flickering beneath. "I know," he says quietly. "I didn't mean to…"

"No." I shake my head. "Don't apologize. I wanted…" The words stick. I can't make myself say them.

I glance at the clock on the wall—grasping for anything to

anchor me. "I have to go," I say, my voice firmer than I feel.

He nods slowly, stepping aside.

The walk home feels unreal—the grass damp beneath my feet, the sky too bright. My lips still tingle from his kiss, and part of me wants to turn back.

But I don't.

On the porch, I drop into a chair and stare at my wedding ring.

The weight of what I've done settles deep—hot, sharp, like a burn I can't soothe. My skin still hums with his touch. I can't breathe away the thudding in my chest.

I don't know what scares me more: how wrong it was… or how much I want it again.

The breeze shifts, carrying the faint scent of coffee and pine from the woods behind the house. It should calm me. It doesn't.

I sit there, hands clenched in my lap. Did I really just do that?

Part of me hopes I didn't. Part of me hopes I did.

I don't know what comes next.

But I know I won't forget the taste of him—the way it felt like everything I've been missing.

And that terrifies me more than anything. Because I don't know if this was a mistake… or the beginning of something I won't be able to stop.

Chapter Eleven

The next day, I'm still reeling from it. This wasn't some invisible line—I crossed a bold, red one. *What was I thinking?* I stand before the mirror, my reflection fractures behind streaks of water and smudged fingerprints. It isn't just the glass that's dirty, it's me, cracked and smudged by choices I can't take back. I barely recognize the woman staring back at me. I am not the kind of woman who cheats. I am the woman who cries herself to sleep beside a man who doesn't see her. The woman who scrubs dishes until her hands crack and her heart aches. The woman who feels invisible in her own home, even though she's the one holding it all together. Maybe it isn't cheating. Maybe it's survival—a single gasp after years underwater.

I know I'm unhappy, I know Nathan doesn't see me—but does that justify getting involved with Jack?

I splash cold water on my face and stare at my reflection again, my damp skin doing nothing to wash away the guilt that clings to me. My lips still tingle. I press my fingers to them, like I can erase the memory of Jack's mouth on mine. The heat, the urgency, it all comes flooding back, and I grip the edge of the sink, my knuckles white.

How did I let this happen?

I try to rationalize it. I try to justify what happened. I hadn't planned this. But even as I say it, I feel the cold burn of regret seeping through me, like ice water washing over the heat Jack left on my lips. Isn't that what people always say before their lives implode?

I imagine Nathan finding out—his voice sharp, his fists slamming the table, the kids crying in the background. *Would he throw me out? Take the kids? Or worse, stay but make my life hell in ways I can't imagine?*

Nathan has so many flaws, but hadn't I made a promise? Hadn't I vowed to stick it out, to choose love every day, even when it felt impossible? And isn't this the opposite of that promise?

But then I thought about all the times I had begged Nathan to see me, listen, and care. About how many nights I fell asleep feeling lonelier in our bed than I ever had before I met him. About the yelling, the criticism, the indifference that chipped away at me bit by bit until I wasn't even sure who I was anymore.

And then Jack really saw me.

He didn't just look at me, he saw me. And for once, I didn't feel heavy. I felt wanted. Whole. His words poured into the cracks Nathan left behind like resin hardening to make me whole again. His touch, though brief, reminded me I wasn't invisible after all.

I slide down to the floor, my back against the vanity, and pull my knees to my chest. The tears come quietly, slipping down my cheeks without resistance. I am caught up in something dangerous, something selfish. But it feels good—and that's what scares me the most. Because for the first time in years, I feel alive. I feel wanted. And if I let go of this, what will I be left with? Who am I, if I'm not seen, not wanted? I wipe my eyes and stand up, forcing myself to focus. I can't undo what happened, but I can stop it from going any further. I have to, for my kids, for my marriage, for myself.

I grab my phone, hovering over Jack's name in my messages. My finger trembles, but I don't type anything.

What can I even say?

I'm sorry. I can't do this.

I shouldn't have let it happen.

It was a mistake.

But none of those feels true. And maybe that is the problem. Part of me didn't want to stop. Still doesn't. That terrifies me.

My phone vibrates, snapping me out of my thoughts. It's Nathan.

Nathan: *You need to pick up more eggs, milk, and energy drinks today. Don't forget the energy drinks.*

No hello. No how-are-you. Just another list of demands, as if I'm not his wife anymore, just someone who checks off his errands. It's like he's forgotten I'm a person with needs, a person who still exists in this house, even if he's never bothered to see me.

I set the phone face down and look at myself one last time in the mirror. The woman in the mirror stares back at me, her eyes hollow and searching. Was this who I had become? Or had she always been there, waiting for the cracks to show? I didn't recognize the woman looking back. She looked tired and desperate. But beneath that, there was something else. A spark. A flicker of rebellion I didn't quite know how to extinguish.

I have to make a choice.

I don't know if I am strong enough to make the right one.

Dinner is tense, but not because of what I'd done. Nathan

is already annoyed. The kids are bickering, and Nora spilled her milk, which sent him into one of his predictable rants about discipline and respect. I stand silently, clearing plates, feeling the weight of my guilt with each movement. At the sink, each plate I scrub is another layer of regret, another piece of my soul I can't scrub clean. The dish rattles in the basin as I scrub, like I can erase more than dinner. Maybe if I keep scrubbing, I can make the cracks in my marriage disappear too, wipe away the resentment that clings to me like dried-on grime.

I look over to the dining room just in time to spot Nora's shoulders slumped, and she disappears into the living room. I follow her a few minutes later and find her curled up on the couch, hugging a pillow.

"Hey, sweetie," I say softly, sitting beside her. "What's wrong?"

She doesn't just see the tension—she feels it settling into our home, into her. She sees the cracks in me, just like I see the cracks in Nathan. And it breaks me all over again. Doesn't care. That's what I've been trying to tell myself, but I can't make it stop. Not for me, and not for her.

I pull her into my lap, holding her close as her tiny body trembles against mine. 'I care, baby. I'll always care.' But even as I say it, I feel the distance growing between us, the life I've built slowly cracking, and I can't stop it. I smooth her hair, pressing my lips to the top of her head, willing her to believe it.

But even as I said it, I felt the helplessness creeping in. Nathan's indifference isn't just breaking me—it's cracking them, too.

Later that night, after the kids are in bed, I stand in the kitchen, wiping the countertops. Nathan sits in the living room, half-watching a golf show, his phone in his lap.

"You don't have to be so hard on Nora," I say finally, not looking up from the sink.

"I wasn't hard on her. She has to understand discipline."

"She spilled a drink, Nathan," I snap, turning to face him. "It wasn't on purpose. It was an accident."

He looks up, annoyed. "She's always spilling stuff. She needs to pay attention."

"That's not true. Occasionally, yes, but not always."

His eyes bore into me, searching and probing. "You've been… off. Always on your phone. Jumpy. Quiet. What's going on, Ella?" He leans back on the couch, but his eyes stay on me, sharp. "Is there something I should know?"

"What do you mean?" I ask, trying to gather specifics.

"You jump every time your phone buzzes," he says, eyes narrowing. "You never used to do that."

Something inside me snaps. "You know what, Nathan? Maybe I wouldn't be so jumpy if I wasn't walking on eggshells whenever you're around."

He doesn't even flinch. Just grabs his phone and starts scrolling again.

I want to scream, but I grab a drink and march upstairs.

Lying in bed that night, I replay the day over and over. *Nora's disappointment. Nathan's dismissiveness. And* Jack. *Always Jack.*

What scares me most isn't the guilt, it's the hunger. The way I can't stop thinking about him. His touch makes me feel alive in a way I haven't felt in years. I know it was wrong, but that doesn't make it easier to let go of.

The door creaks open, and Nathan enters without a word, pulls off his shirt, crawls into bed, and turns off the light. As if I were furniture. As if nothing were broken.

And as much as I hate myself for what I did with Jack, a small voice whispers that maybe, just maybe, it's the first real thing I've felt in a long time.

My phone buzzes against the nightstand, and for a split second, my heart leaps, Jack. But when I glance at the screen, it isn't him.

Maya's name lights up my phone like a beacon I don't deserve. She's always listened, but how could I tell her this? How can I put words to something I barely understand myself?

The phone buzzes again, and my thumb hovers over the answer button. But what would I say? That I'm unraveling? That I'm not sure I can stop?

I let it ring out, my chest tightening as guilt crawls under my skin.

I set the phone face-down and roll over, closing my eyes.

As I am dozing off, my phone buzzes on the bedside table. I reach for it, half-expecting it to be a text from Maya. But it isn't.

It's Jack. The screen glows, his name like a secret I wasn't ready to give up.

Jack: *We need to talk.*

My stomach tightens. Talk about what? The kiss? What did it mean, or what could it mean?

My finger hovers over the keyboard, trembling. I didn't let myself think about Nathan or the kids. Not in that moment.

Me: *Tomorrow.*

The message sits there, glowing, pulsing like a silent alarm. I close my eyes, but its weight stays. Tomorrow isn't a maybe. It's the first shift of a stone on the riverbed—small, quiet, but once moved, nothing will settle the same way again. And once it's moved, even a fraction, it never settles in the same spot again.

Chapter Twelve

The next day, after the kids have eaten breakfast and are preoccupied with their toys, I grab my phone. My heart beats faster than I expect as I open the messages app and type.

Me: *Good morning.*

Jack: *Good morning. I know yesterday was a lot.*

My fingers hover over the screen, unsure of how to respond. Finally, I type back:

Me: *It was. I don't even know what to say.*

His reply comes quickly, the words cutting through me like a blade.

Jack: *Maybe we shouldn't keep doing this. It's not fair to anyone. But I don't know how to stop either, Ella. You're married. I don't want to be the reason your life falls apart. But I still want you.*

My stomach twists as I stare at the message. I blink rapidly, trying to process what I am reading.

Me: I don't understand. Are you saying we should stop talking?

There is a long pause before his response comes through.

Jack: I think we should stop talking and seeing each other.

The words feel like a punch to the gut. I stare at the screen; my vision blurs as tears fill my eyes.

My fingers tremble.

Me: If that's what you want.

Jack: It's for the best.

I set the phone down on the sofa with trembling hands, my vision blurry as hot tears spill over my cheeks. The ache in my chest spreads like a slow burn, hollow and cruel. But beneath it, there's a spark of anger, too, a desperate longing for something that should have been mine but wasn't. Why show me I'm alive just to walk away? Just then, Emmett appears right in front of me. "What's wrong, mama?"

"It's okay, I'm okay; go back and play." I say through quiet sobs. I hate that Emmett sees me like this. He didn't deserve to witness me in this state.

The warmth of our connection, the way Jack made me feel seen and alive, it felt so real, so undeniable. But now, it's gone, ripped away instantly, leaving me with nothing but the weight of emptiness. I press my palms to my face as the tears come harder, my mind circling the same agonizing question. How can something that feels so right vanish so quickly?

☾☾☾

The day passes in a blur of sadness and confusion. As I lay in bed staring at the ceiling that night, one thought consumes me: What am I supposed to do now?

☾☾☾

Morning comes too soon. The pale light of dawn filters through the curtains, but I can't muster the strength to get up. My phone sits on the nightstand, dark and silent. I resist the urge to check it, knowing there will be nothing from Jack. He has made himself clear.

I drag myself out of bed and go through the motions of getting the kids ready. Breakfast, backpacks, and goodbyes. I plaster on a smile as I drop Nora off at school, but inside, I feel hollow.

On my way back, I grab a coffee, leaning into my routine, but everything feels off; even my coffee doesn't taste the same. Back at home, the house feels too quiet. My phone buzzes in my back pocket, and my heart jumps before I even look. But it isn't Jack. Just a reminder for a parent-teacher meeting next week.

I shove the phone into my pocket and pace the kitchen. My thoughts storm with flashes—his eyes, his hands, his mouth. I can't shake the feeling that it meant something. Why is he pulling away now?

I grab my keys and drive without thinking, ending up at the park.

My phone buzzes again. This time, I hesitate before looking. It isn't him. Instead, it's Maya.

Maya: *Hey, how are you? You've been quiet.*

Me: *I don't know. Can we talk?*

Maya: *Of course. Video?*

Me: *Yes. I'm available right now if you are.*

My phone rings immediately.

"Okay, spill it," she says the moment I answer.

I don't even try to hold back. I tell her everything—the late-night messages, the glances, the clubhouse, the kiss, the silence that followed like a door slammed shut.

Maya listens, her expression shifting from sympathy to frustration. "He's scared," she says when I finish. "You both are. But cutting you off like that? That's not fair."

"He said it was for the best," I mumble, staring at the

Emmett playing on the slide.

"For who? Him? You? Because it doesn't sound like it's the best for you." She tilts her head. "Ella, what do you want?" My mind settles for an answer and lands on that first look Jack gave me outside. That's what I want. But not just sometimes. All the time.

I feel the weight of Maya's question pressing on me, like a mountain on my chest. The truth feels too heavy, too messy. I want Jack, but I'm not sure if that's enough. What if it's just about wanting someone to see me, to make me feel like I'm more than just a mother and wife? I'm afraid of what it would mean if I admit that to myself.

I blink at her. "I don't know."

"Yes, you do."

Her words echo long after we hang up. *What do I want? And what if he doesn't want it too?*

That night, I lay awake again, replaying our conversations. I reach for my phone, scrolling through old texts, lingering on the ones that make me laugh or blush. I type out a dozen messages, deleting each before sending it.

Finally, I set the phone down and close my eyes. Maybe Maya is right, maybe he's scared. But I am, too.

The following day, I wake up determined. If Jack wants to stop this, okay. I wasn't going to let him vanish and leave me holding all the feelings. I deserved an explanation.

Me: *I need to see you. Just one conversation.*

This silence is tearing me apart.

It takes him an hour to reply.

Jack: *I don't think that's a good idea.*

My heart sinks, but I'm not giving up.

Me: *Please. I just need closure. One conversation. That's all I'm asking.*

Another hour passes before his response comes through.

Jack: *Okay. Tomorrow night. Parking lot at the clubhouse. I'll be there.*

I open the Notes app and start typing things I might say, soft, rational things that make it seem like I'm fine. Like I just want to clear the air and move on.

But I don't want closure. I want answers. I want him to look at me the way he did in the gym—like I mattered. I want to ask why he ran when things got real. Why he made me feel something and then disappeared.

I stare at my reflection in the hallway mirror, trying out the words out loud to myself. They sound powerful in my mind, but weak and fragile when spoken.

I tell myself I can handle this. That I'm only asking for closure. But as I type the words, I can't shake the feeling that I'm lying to myself. I don't want closure. I want him to look at me like I'm the only thing that matters. I want him to undo this ache he left behind. I want him back. And maybe that's the scariest truth of all.

Chapter Thirteen

The next day, all I can think about is the conversation Jack and I will have later. What do I even want from this—what could I possibly say? I bury myself in busywork—scrubbing, sorting, folding—anything to drown out the message still echoing in my head: "I think we should stop talking and seeing each other."

No matter how hard I try, Jack lingers. His voice. His smile. The heat of his touch. They slip through the cracks I thought I'd sealed, settling into the quiet corners of my mind where they can't be ignored. I feel as if I will never escape the pain of this loss or the ever-present question that refuses to subside: why did he pull away right when I finally felt so connected, so happy, and so at peace?

☾☾☾

Later that night, after Nathan leaves for work, I read to the kids, tuck them in, check the doors, and slip out into the quiet darkness, heading toward the clubhouse parking lot. I freeze when I spot the lone car in the lot. It takes a few seconds for my eyes to adjust, and then I spot him—his face. I walk slowly across the grass, my heart pounding in my chest, and open the passenger door. I slide into the seat, trying to steady my breath. But nothing about this feels steady. The air feels thick inside the car, our breaths mingling in the hush between us.

When our eyes meet, my heart sways. I thought I was ready for this face-to-face moment, but my body and my heart clearly missed the memo. His eyes search my face as he reaches for my hand.

"Don't you dare try to touch me," I say, my voice shaking. "You opened this door, then slammed it in my face, and now you want to hold my hand?"

I look at him, my chest tightening. "Why did you do that to me? Why did it have to be through text?"

He looks away, jaw tight. "You want the truth?"

I nod.

A deep breath escapes him "Because I was scared. I told myself I'd never get close to anyone again. My ex-wife, she cheated. I found messages on her phone late one night and the whole thing unraveled from there."

He looks back at me then, voice low. "It hollowed me out. I stopped believing in anything real. And then you came along. You are the first person I've truly connected with since. And you are married. I don't want to hurt anyone."

His voice breaks slightly. "I didn't know how to hold on to you without feeling like I was breaking everything else in me." He looks away, breaking eye contact for the first time since I entered his car, and says, "I've been thinking about you all day long."

I blink, trying to wake myself from the daze his words have put me in. Did I really hear that—or am I only hearing what I wish he said?

This man who had pulled me in so close only to push me away was now reaching out and pulling me back in with just eight words. I take a deep, deep breath, shift my weight in the seat trying to settle the battle of emotions inside me: anger, relief, hope, and confusion.

I finally look at him. "How can you say that, Jack?" The frustration in my voice is evident, rising inside me like I am being drowned.

He turns toward me, his gaze locking with mine. His voice is low but firm, filled with something raw. "I can't stop thinking about you. About us. About everything we started. I can't, and I won't walk away from it."

A shaky breath escapes me, my chest tightening with every word. My mind races, his voice washing over me, stirring up emotions I can't control. I'm angry. Hopeful. Completely undone. Who does he think he is? I'm not some toy he can pick up, then put back down when he feels like it. Can I even believe his words after he quickly slammed the door on what we started?

I shove the anger down like clothes into an overstuffed suitcase. Before I can speak, he keeps going—pleading, unraveling, "I thought I could do the right thing and stay away. But I can't. I don't want to."

Everything around me blurs into a fog as his words sink into my soul. I feel like I'm standing at the edge of something that could consume me—or destroy me completely. My hands visibly shake, and I slide them under my legs to hide them. I say, "Jack, you said we should just be friends. You said it was for the best. I'm not some lifeboat you cling to when the storm hits."

He looks me in the eyes, steady and unwavering. "I told myself I could walk away before I ruined you too. I was lying. I was trying to protect us both, but I can't anymore. I want you, Ella. All of you."

The words knock the air from my lungs.

Wanting me is one thing. Holding on to me? That's something else entirely. I want to believe him, but fear gnaws at me, leaving me breathless.

My breath hitches. Pulse pounding, I bury my face in my hands, warm tears slipping through my fingers. It is everything I want to hear, but also everything I am terrified of. I take a moment to steady myself.

"Jack, this is dangerous. You know that, don't you?" His response takes me off guard, his tone determined, "I know what is at stake. But I can't pretend anymore. Can you?"

I close my eyes, his words echoing in my mind. Can I pretend? Can I deny how alive he makes me feel? How my heart races when he's near, how my world brightens when he looks at me? It isn't just some thrilling adventure, it is engulfing my entire being. I'm teetering at the top of a roller coaster, terrified of the drop but aching for the fall all the same.

I look up again, wiping the tears from my cheeks as I say, "No, I can't pretend."

My chest heaves under the weight. Maybe it's the wall he just tore down with nothing but words.

He must sense the weight of everything pressing down on me because his next words lift it like a hand to my chest, "Then don't. I'll be here when you're ready."

His words are simple, but they cut deep, leaving me trembling. I stare at him, emotions swirling, excitement, fear, and something else I can't name. I stand. "I have to go," I whisper. The weight of it feels like a betrayal, and I don't know if I can bear it.

I pause, my hand on the door. "Jack… if I come back, it has to be real. I can't survive another maybe."

He leans forward, voice low but unwavering. "Then I'll make it real. All of it. I'll be here. When you're ready. Not a second before, not a second after."

I want him. But on my terms. If I fall, it'll be by choice.

The door clicks shut behind me. But his words trail after me like a shadow—quiet, certain, waiting.

Chapter Fourteen

The sound of yelling pulls me from my sleep; it's muffled but unmistakable. For a second, I think it is a dream. But then I hear the faint cry of a child, Emmett, I am sure of it. I throw the covers off and swing my legs over the bed. The carpet grounds me—soft underfoot, solid beneath chaos. Moving quickly, I follow the sound of Emmett's sobs.

At the top of the stairs, the noise becomes clearer. "Daddy, I want to go play golf!" Emmett wails, his little voice cracking. Nathan's reply slams back, sharp and final. "No. I told you fifty times, no!" My heart squeezes as I descend, each step amplifying my anxiety. When I reach the bottom, I say, "Come here, baby!" Emmett runs to me, crashing into my arms. I kneel, my knees press into the hardwood as his tears soak into my shoulder. The ache of his little heartbreak mirrors my own.

I lift my eyes to Nathan, unable to hide the pain. "Why don't you take him with you anymore?" I ask softly, though I already know the answer. It is Nathan's birthday, and he'd declared today a "guys-only" golf outing with Colby. I'd hoped, foolishly, that he'd reconsider. But Nathan rarely changes his mind, especially when spending one-on-one time with the kids.

"I told you, Ella," Nathan barks, his voice hard and final. "It's my birthday. I just want to relax."

"Why don't you offer to take him another time so he has something to look forward to?" I try again, my voice calm but pleading. His face flushes, his body language screams that he is done with this conversation. "I'll take him another time," he snaps, brushing me off. Always another time. Never now.

Hoping to defuse the tension, I call the kids to the table and retrieve Nathan's birthday gift. We'd wrapped it together last night, red paper and a blue bow. The kids hand it to him, beaming. Their joy is unshakable—his isn't. Nathan tears into the wrapping, the paper falling in pieces to the floor. Inside is new golf balls, his favorite ones chosen with love. His smile is fleeting, forced. "Thanks, I like it," he says, but I know better. His disappointment hangs in the air.

Before I can dwell on it, there is a knock at the door. Nora darts toward it, and I sharply stop her, "Don't open that!" I reach the door, unlatch the deadbolt, and find Colby smiling nervously. "I wasn't sure if I should knock with all the yelling," he jokes. I force a smile. "Nathan's ready," I say, stepping aside to let him in.

Nathan grabs his golf clubs and kisses the kids goodbye. His goodbye to me is nothing more than a fleeting side hug and a kiss on the cheek. "Don't forget the barbecue at the park today," he says. His words stir something I wish I didn't feel.

"I won't forget," I reply, blushing. He'll be too drunk by the end of the night to stand—like always at these things. At least I have Jack to look forward to.

After they leave, the house settles. The kids play, their laughter filling the room as I start breakfast. I watch them bounce on the couch cushions, carefree and happy. I wonder if their resilience is a blessing or a shield. Are they so used to the yelling that it no longer affects them?

Breakfast passes quickly, and the kids clear the table without complaint. As I pull out the crock pot to start on the pot roast for the party, a thought lingers in my mind. I hope Jack will like it not Nathan, Jack. That realization burns through me more than the spices I scatter over the roast.

The rest of the day slips by in a blur of tasks, the morning's tension fades into a dull ache at the back of my mind. After setting the food to cook in the crock pot, I wrangle the kids into the car and head to the store. I move through the aisles on autopilot, picking up some rolls, the drinks Nathan requested, and on a whim some wine coolers for myself. I'd need it later, a buffer against my emotions.

Just thinking about seeing Jack tonight frays my nerves, quickens my pulse. I tell myself to stay calm and to keep my composure. I can't let Nathan notice anything unusual, not even a flicker of my feelings.

Once home, we unpack the groceries, the kids run off to play while I organize everything for the party. I busy myself, yet my mind keeps wandering to Jack. I haven't heard from him all day. What is he doing? Is he thinking about me, too? The question lingers, dangerous and thrilling, as I put away the last supplies.

By five o'clock, Nathan and Colby return worn out and half drunk. As Nathan heads upstairs to shower, I seize the chance to visit Jack without him around. I get the kids ready, grab the crock pot of chicken, and make our way to the park. My heart quickens as I spot Jack behind the folding tables by the grill, his signature black T-shirt hugging his shoulders, a backward cap framing his face, light-washed jeans, and pristine white shoes complete the look. He's turning meat on the grill, his focused expression pulling at me in ways I can't explain.

"Hey, neighbor! What you doing?" I call, my voice brighter than I intend. Jack looks up, that familiar smile—disarming, dangerous, impossible to look away from.

"Hey, lady! How's your day going?" he asks, his tone as warm as the sun dipping low in the sky.

"Better now," I say, the words slipping out before I can stop them. I catch myself, my voice thick with something I don't want to acknowledge. "What are you making?"

"Ribs," he replies, gesturing to the grill. "Two racks of regular, two honey-crusted."

"That sounds amazing," I say, my grin impossible to suppress.

"What's in the pot?" he asks, nodding at the crock pot in my hands.

"A roast—my specialty," I say proudly.

"I can't wait to try it; you know how much I love good old-fashioned cooking," he says, his eyes lock onto mine as I pass by. Our hips brush lightly, the contact from his body sends a ripple of energy through me. I know his eyes are locked onto me as I reach the doors, and I turn to meet his gaze. Our smiles stretch; too wide, too knowing. The unspoken sits heavy between us.

I set the crockpot on the serving table, plug it in, and slide our drinks into the cooler. After greeting Jack's kids, I take a moment to step back, scanning the crowd. The park is alive with chatter and laughter, the soft hum of the barbecue blending with the distant sounds of kids running around.

I pause, catching my reflection in the cooler's shiny surface, and something about it catches me off guard. The smile on my face feels genuine and effortless, and for the first time in a long while, I feel beautiful and important. It's as though I'm seeing myself from the outside, free of the weight I usually carry.

I stand there, lost in the quiet of it for a moment. But the reality hits—I've got a party to manage, kids to watch over, and Jack... I glance across the yard, my pulse racing as our eyes lock.

Later, after going home to gather Nathan, the park is alive with energy. Colby, Lauren, and their kids arrive, and laughter spills across the tables. Nathan is in his element, drink in hand, his boisterous laugh rising above the chatter. The barbecue is everything he wanted, a spectacle, a show. There are plenty of people around, some I've met, some I haven't.

I move through the space with practiced ease, greeting guests, balancing snacks, and watching the kids. Nathan looms like a storm cloud—louder, looser, unpredictable. Jack is by the cooler, chatting with Lauren and a few other neighbors. Our connection is undeniable; even when others are around, I can feel him. Every time our eyes meet, the world seems to melt away, the noise around us fading to a distant hum. It's like we're the only two people in the world. Nathan catches me staring at Jack across the yard and walks over to me.

He leans in, his whisper clipped and low, "Why do you keep looking at him like that?"

"Like what?" I say, my voice low so no one can hear.

"You know what I mean," he says, trying to search my face, but I keep looking away.

"Can we talk about this later?" I ask, trying to move the conversation to a later time.

"Sure," he finally says, turning away and returning to sit beside Colby.

By the time the game ends, I find Nathan head down on a nearby picnic table, his head lolling as he mutters something I can't quite make out. The kids, sugar-crashed and exhausted grab their blankets as I heave Nathan to his feet, dragging him back to our house. God, he's heavy, and not helping much.

"Great party," I say, my voice steady, though every muscle in my body screams for me to look back at Jack as we leave.

"Thanks for coming," he says with his signature smile.

Back home, I settle Nathan onto the couch, his snores filling the house as I clean up the remains of the evening. My phone buzzes in my back pocket.

Jack: *Meet me by the old gazebo, by the water, in an hour.*

Me: *I'll be there.*

My heart races as I stand frozen in the kitchen. I don't have to think long. Nathan is passed out, the kids are asleep, and every nerve in my body urges me forward. The thought of Nora or Emmett waking and needing me stops me cold… but then I see Jack's eyes in my mind—and I go. I grab my shoes and keys, slipping into the night like a shadow.

The park is quiet, the only sound the distant rustle of trees in the breeze. The moonlight stretches over the path, guiding me toward the water. The glow softens everything, casting long shadows as I reach the old gazebo. Jack stands there, waiting, his silhouette framed by silver light, as if the night is holding its breath. The closer I get, the more my heart hammers against my chest. I can hear the sound of my breath, shallow and quick, as I take each step toward him. The cool air presses against my skin, sharp and still, and my hands are trembling, unsure if this is the right thing to do. For a moment, I just watch him, my pulse quickening. The stillness around us feels like a world apart from everything else. It's as if the night itself is waiting, holding its breath.

When he turns and sees me, his face lights up with that smile I can't shake from my mind. "You came," he says, his voice softer than I expected.

"I didn't think I would," I admit, the words slipping out before I can stop them. My feet carry me closer, but I stop a few steps away, unsure. The air between us crackles, thick with all the things we've both been hiding.

Jack steps toward me, his presence drawing me in like a magnet. He reaches for me, his hands finding their way to my waist, pulling me closer. He whispers in my ear "I've been waiting for this moment, Ella." My breath catches as his lips brush mine, tentative at first, then deepening as we both give in to the pull between us.

The kiss is everything I've been denying, everything I've been too scared to let myself feel. His hands slide under my shirt, his touch igniting something inside me that I can't ignore anymore. The world outside the gazebo falls away until it's just us, caught in this moment that feels both inevitable and impossible.

When we pull apart, I'm breathless, my mind reeling. "Are you sure?" I whisper, my voice shaking.

Jack doesn't hesitate. "I'm sure," he says, his voice low and unwavering. "I've wanted this for a long time."

The words settle in my chest, and I feel the weight of the choice we're both making. The tension that's been building between us is finally coming to a head, and I know it's not something I can take back. But in that moment, I don't want to.

I don't want to stop.

He leads me back into the shadow of the gazebo, the moonlight casting everything in a soft glow. His hands are gentle but firm, guiding me as if he knows exactly what I need. And maybe he does.

The world outside doesn't matter anymore. It's just him and me, here, now.

Afterward, when we lie there together, tangled in the quiet

of the night, Jack's fingers trace lazy circles on my skin. It's like time slows down, and in the stillness, I realize something.

I'm not invisible. Not forgotten. Not leftover. Not just a wife. Not just a mother. I'm Ella. And maybe it's time I start choosing myself.

Chapter Fifteen

In the days following the barbecue, I struggle to keep my head above water. I feel pulled toward Jack like a magnet, drawn by a force I can't resist. My heart says one thing, but my mind is filled with guilt. I don't know what I want anymore, my life with Nathan, or this impossible, magnetic connection with Jack. This feeling is ever-present, and it's even stronger now, after we had our encounter that beautiful Sunday evening.

I stare at the calendar on the fridge, my finger hovering over the circled date. Nathan's upcoming trip. I have been counting down the days with a strange mix of dread and longing, each crossed-out box dragging me closer to the only place I feel like myself, near Jack.

But that smug satisfaction I'd felt when Nathan first announced the trip has already vanished. His words from last night echo in my mind: "That trip's been delayed. Something with logistics. We're pushing it back a couple of weeks."

Weeks.

The word slams into me like a punch to the gut. His voice

keeps echoing in my mind, making everything feel like it's moving in slow motion. I'd been counting on him being gone, and now... he won't be. The frustration I feel is suffocating. It's a weird place to be, wanting your husband to leave so you can spend time with a man who lives two doors down. I slam the marker cap onto the counter, gripping it like I can transfer all my rage into it. My escape plans were ruined by logistics. Logistics. I can't believe this is happening to me. Is the universe stepping in and planning to destroy the one thing that makes me happy? It feels like the hope I clung to after that night is slipping through my fingers, and the need to be near Jack—to feel his touch again—presses into me like a fever I can't break.

I've spent the last few days trapped in the vivid replay of our night together, each stolen glance, every whispered word, and the electrifying press of his lips etched into my memory. He has altered something in me, and the thought of never seeing him again throbs like a bruise I keep pressing.

The sun hangs just over the horizon as I step onto the back porch, phone in hand. My thumb hovers over Maya's name—then I tap. She answers before the first ring finishes.

"Hey, girl!" Her voice is bright and effortless, like a lifeline tossed my way.

"Hey," I say, trying to match her ease. "How are you?"

"I'm good! How about you?" she asks, the warmth in her tone steady.

"I'm… great," I lie, my voice trembling under the weight of the truth I've been carrying. "I actually need to tell you something."

"Tell me!" Her excitement spills through the line, a spark I'm not sure I deserve.

I swallow hard. "We went to a neighborhood barbecue at the park the other day."

"Okay?" she says, her curiosity piqued. "Was it fun?"

"Yes, it was… fun," I say, the words faltering under the strain of everything it didn't say.

"How fun?" she presses, always catching the undertones I try to bury.

"It was great… until Nathan caught me staring at Jack and decided to confront me about it," I confess, my voice tight.

"Oh, Ella," she says, her voice softening like she already knows there is more.

"And then Nathan got drunk, so drunk I had to drag him to the house and leave him passed out on the couch," I continue, the memory burning hotter as I speak. "And after that… I met Jack alone by the water."

The silence isn't judgment—it's anticipation. "And?" she finally prompts, her voice low with anticipation.

"And… I slept with him," I admit, the words spilling out with a thrill I can't suppress, no matter how hard I try.

"Oh my God!" she exclaims, her laugh bubbling up. "Well, how was it?"

I can't stop the smile from taking over. "It was amazing," I say, the memory of his touch takes over me. "Every moment… the way he touched me, how his lips felt on mine, how he made me feel so, so safe, so wanted." My voice trails off as I let the details spill, painting the night in vivid color for her.

Maya listens without interruption, her soft hums encouraging me to keep going. When I finally fall silent, her tone shifts, the excitement is laced with something heavier. "I'm happy for you, Ella. I really am. But… I'm scared for you, too, if that makes sense."

"It does," I whisper, her words settling into the quiet space between us.

We talk for another twenty minutes, her laughter easing the weight on my chest even as her lingering worry stays with me. Eventually, she has to go, work called, and I set my phone down on the counter, The chill of the counter steadies me as I stare into the dark. The ache in my chest lingers, a strange mix of longing and guilt twisted together, refusing to let go.

My phone immediately buzzes, causing my heart to leap in my chest. I grab it, my pulse quickening as Jack's name lights up.

Jack: *I hurt my ankle playing pickup basketball earlier today. It's not that bad, but I think I might've twisted it or sprained it. I can barely walk on it now. It looks swollen.*

My chest tightens. The idea of him being alone, hurt and trying to power through it, stirs something inside me. It's more than concern, it's a deep need to take care of him, to be there for him. I've never felt this way about anyone—not even Nathan.

I hover over the keyboard, my heart racing as my mind runs in circles. Do I send the message? Do I let myself care? Each second drags, and I'm left with no choice but to give in to this need to help him.

☾☾☾

Me: *Do you need anything? I can bring you something.*

His reply comes quickly.

Jack: *I'm okay. Just tired. Don't worry about me.*

A panic rises in my chest. He's brushing it off, but I know better. I know he's not okay. And whether he wants me to worry or not, I already do. I have to see him. Even if it's reckless. Even if it's dangerous.

☾☾☾

Later that evening, I stand in the kitchen stirring a pot of chicken and rice soup, but my mind is elsewhere. I picture Jack just two doors down, in pain and alone. The thought sends a pang through me. I look at Nathan sitting at the table with the kids and say, “I’m taking Jack some soup, medicine, and an ice pack as soon as the food is ready because he hurt his ankle and can barely walk.” I don’t ask—I tell him, which is rare for me. I won't let Jack go hungry and hope my soup will help him recover quicker. When the soup is ready, I ladle it into a plastic container, grab a loaf of bread, and wrap it in foil. I tell myself it is just a neighborly gesture, something anyone would do. But as I pull on my jacket and step into the cool night air, I know I am lying to myself. As I cross the front yard, I glance over my shoulder and see the river, the dim moonlight shimmering over the calm and steady surface of the water. I finally step onto Jack's front porch and knock.

He answers after my second knock, his hair a mess, his eyes shadowed with exhaustion. He looks thinner, paler. When our eyes meet, there’s a spark—surprise, maybe relief. I hope it’s something deeper.

"Ella," he says, his voice raspy, a faint smile softening his face. "What are you doing here?"

I hold up the bag containing the food, medicine and ice pack, my heart slams into the walls of my chest. "I figured you weren't eating much and probably needed some other things too. So, I thought I'd bring you something."

He hesitates slightly; his hand lingers against the door frame. “You really didn’t have to come all the way over here,” Jack says, his voice soft, filled with equal parts gratitude and something I can’t place. “But... I’m glad you did.”

"Of course," I say softly. "But I wanted to."

He limps aside, allowing me to walk in. The house is dimly lit and smells faintly of lemons and household cleaner. I set the food on the counter in the kitchen while he leans against the wall, watching me.

"You're too good to me," he says, his voice quiet after a moment.

"I wish I could do more," I reply, meeting his gaze. "I just... I had to come because I could feel you needed me." I can feel him even when I'm not close and know what he needs even when he doesn't say it.

"Sit down and let me see it," I insist, my voice soft but firm. He winces as he limps across the room and sinks onto the couch. His ankle is already swollen, a dark bruise beginning to form. My breath catches in my throat as I gently examine it. "You need to stay off it tonight. I'll get some ice, Motrin, and dinner. Just relax." Our fingers graze when I hand him the pill, a spark shooting up my arm. He doesn't pull away. Neither do I.

"Ok, ok, I will do my best," he says with a slight laugh.

I can feel this force drawing me to him, even with the heavy silence. My body and soul yearn for him in a way I have never experienced before. My eyes slowly move from his gaze to his lips, and for a second, I think he might close the distance between us.

But sadly, he doesn't. He sighs heavily instead, rubbing the back of his neck. "Ella, you shouldn't be here. You've got the kids and Nathan..."

"I don't care about Nathan," I interrupt, my voice trembling. "I just needed to be near you. Even if it's just for a few minutes."

He lets out a quiet chuckle, then takes the medicine, moving his arm up to his mouth. "You're going to drive me crazy."

"Join the club," I say with a weak smile.

The room feels like it is closing in on me, the air too thick. Finally, Jack straightens and nods toward the door. "You need to go," he says gently, "before Nathan comes looking for you."

I want to stay. I want to be close to him, to run my fingers through his hair, to feel the comfort of his warmth against mine. But I can't. I only nod, swallowing back the words I wish I could say, and walk toward the door, feeling like I'm leaving a part of myself behind. My emotions bubble up, and I leave before the tears can follow. I turn and start toward the door. Each step feels like a betrayal of my own heart.

"Ella?"

I stop, glancing back at him.

"Thank you for being you," he says, his voice soft, his eyes holding mine.

I nod again, unable to speak. The cool air stings my face as I step into the night. My craving for him hasn't eased. It settles in me—quiet, constant, like breath itself. As I walk back across the grass, the night air biting at my skin, each step feels irreversible, like I'm already too far in. I want Jack. And I'm done pretending I don't. Whatever comes next… I'll face it.

Chapter Sixteen

The shrill ring of my phone jolts me from sleep, cutting through the quiet stillness of the early morning. I fumble across the bedside table until my fingers find it, squinting at the glowing screen with one eye open. 6:04 am. My dad's name glows softly against the dim light. I swipe to answer and bring the phone to my ear.

"Hey, Dad," I mumble, my voice thick with sleep.

"Hey, sweetheart!" he says, his voice brimming with warmth and pride. Every now and then, he still calls early just to check in before work.

"How are you feeling?" His tone is light and teasing, but beneath it lies genuine curiosity.

"Honestly? I kind of feel different today. It's hard to explain, but… different."

"You sound good," he says, pausing just long enough for the words to settle in.

"I am, Dad," I reply, the truth of it sinks deeper into me. "I really am."

"That's good. You deserve to be happy." His voice is rich

with compassion, the kind that always makes me feel safe.

"Where are you off to today?" I ask, noticing the faint hum of road noise in the background.

"Almost at work," he says. "Just wanted to hear your voice."

"Thanks, Dad," I say, smiling. "Love you."

"Love you too, sweetie," he says just before the call ends.

I set the phone down, my heart warmed by his words. I don't know what it is exactly, but it does feel like a new beginning.

The phone rings again just as I lean back into the pillow. Maya's name lights up this time. I answer with a grin.

"Hey! What are you up to today?" she chirps, her voice buzzing with enthusiasm.

"Just enjoying the peace and quiet before the chaos starts," I say.

"Well, I hope today's everything you want it to be. You deserve it."

"Thanks, Maya," I say, still smiling.

In the days leading up to tonight, I've been reflecting on the past few years of my life. I'm standing at a fork in the road—one where I have to start choosing what I want instead of living for everyone else's happiness. So, I planned a small get-together, a low-key night with people who feel like home.

Nathan, of course, had plenty of notice but still chose to work. Honestly, it's better that way. He didn't even ask who was coming. Maybe he'd stopped caring altogether.

Maybe I had too.

I didn't need him here, clouding the night with his quiet disapproval. Instead, I invited Colby, Lauren, and, of course, Jack—along with all the kids.

Jack.

Today, Jack had a tattoo appointment. He'd mentioned it

in passing, explaining it was a cover-up for an old tattoo he'd gotten during his marriage. The placement on his upper arm is so personal, so vulnerable. When I asked him what he would cover it with, he replied casually, "A Phoenix."

A Phoenix.

It seemed random, but I didn't press for details. I knew he'd explain when he was ready, and I looked forward to seeing the finished piece. More than that, I was looking forward to having him at the house tonight, in my space again, without Nathan around.

By the time guests begin to arrive, the house is buzzing. The next-door neighbors, Colby and Lauren, bring their kids, filling the air with laughter and chaos. I'd already had Jack's kids with me all afternoon so he could go to his appointment without any stress. Watching all ten kids—Jack's four, Lauren's two, and my two—play together makes my heart swell in ways I'm not prepared for. For a fleeting moment, I wonder if this is a glimpse of my future, a blended, beautiful mess of joy. I force myself to push the thought away, afraid of letting myself hope too much.

Just then, a knock comes at the door.

I quickly move to it, open it, and there he is, Jack, dressed in head-to-toe black: black dress boots, black jeans, and a black polo with a single white stripe along the collar. I can't help but smile. My eyes travel from his face to the plastic-wrapped tattoo on his arm.

"Show me!" I say, my voice so eager that I can't hide it.

He slowly unwraps it with a smile, and when it is fully exposed, it takes my breath away. The Phoenix is stunning, a work of art—a black phoenix mid-rise, its wings still half-tucked, as if unsure whether to soar or stay grounded.

"It means I've been burned," he explains, his voice steady, "but I came back anyway."

I didn't need him to elaborate. I know what he means: his divorce, his struggle, his becoming a single father to five kids, and somehow making it through each and every day.

He hands me a small bottle of lotion. I don't know what comes over me, but I squeeze some into my hands and gently apply it to his arm without thinking. My fingers move over his skin with an intimate, instinctual care. With Nathan, caring felt like obligation. With Jack, it feels like instinct. After I retrieve a new piece of plastic wrap from the kitchen drawer and start re-wrapping it, I realize I didn't think twice about doing it. It feels as natural as breathing—I want to take care of him.

I look around the room, hoping no one notices. But everything is already changing—whether I'm ready or not.

☾☾☾

After dinner, the group decides to play charades. The kids pair up in teams of two while the adults split up as well. Somehow, Jack and I end up on the same team. The moment we do, my pulse quickens.

When it's our turn, Jack steps up to act out a clue. He shoots me a look, mischievous and challenging. He starts miming, and I laugh before I can help it.

"Rollercoaster!" I guess, shaking my head when he shakes his. He waves his arms and then falls to the floor.

"A bear attack? Dramatic fainting?" I guess again, and he gives a theatrical groan.

"Romeo and Juliet!" I shout, and he leaps to his feet, grinning wide.

We win the round.

He holds up his hand for a high five, and when our hands meet, he doesn't let go right away. Our hands meet—a simple touch that shouldn't feel electric. But it does. There's something in his eyes, something that lingers, and for a brief moment, we are the only two people in the room. That flicker of connection intensifies every time we speak, touch, or even lock eyes.

Later, as the kids wind down and guests begin to leave, Jack helps me clean up. It's quiet again, just the two of us rinsing cups and picking up toys.

"You know," he says softly, "I didn't think I'd have any fun tonight. But I did. Because of you."

I look up at him, startled by the honesty in his voice. I want to say something back, something that matters, but all I can manage is a small smile.

Nights like these start ordinary. And somehow, without meaning to, they change everything.

Chapter Seventeen

The party hums around me, but my eyes can't help but search for him. Jack stands by the dining table, holding an envelope like it carries more than just paper. When our gazes meet, he offers that quiet, steady smile that makes the room feel suddenly smaller, more intimate.

☾☾☾

Once the guests have gone and the house falls into silence, I find myself stepping out onto the back patio, a glass of wine in hand. The fairy lights overhead glow softly, like stars lingering past dawn. The kids are asleep, the music has faded, and it's just me, caught somewhere between a quiet joy and an overwhelming weight I can't name.

The screen door creaks open, and Jack steps outside, the envelope still in his hand. He doesn't speak at first. He just sits beside me, his silence weighted with unspoken things, before offering the envelope to me.

"What's this?" I ask, my voice barely above a whisper.

"Something I wrote," he says softly. "It's not really a gift. I just... needed to say it somehow."

I take it slowly, unfolding the flap and sliding out a single printed page. It's a poem titled For the Girl Who Carried the Weight—no name at the bottom. Just words. Words that catch in my throat before I even read the first line.

For the Girl Who Carried the Weight
She never asked to be the strong one.
She just was.
When the storms came,
she built roofs from silence and grace.
When things broke,
she was the glue no one saw,
holding the edges of a home that forgot how to say thank you.

I pause, my breath catching as I process the words. Is he talking about me? Why me? It feels like he knows me in a way no one ever has, the weight of my daily burdens, my quiet resilience, the love I give to everyone else without asking for anything in return. Isn't this what I've been silently hoping for? Maybe I don't remember what it's like to be seen, and that's why my instincts doubt it.

The words blur as tears gather in my eyes. I press the poem to my chest, a breath catching in my throat as the emotions swell. It's as if he's seen through every defense, every crack, and somehow found beauty in the broken parts of me that I thought were beyond repair.

☾☾☾

Without a word, I turn and wrap my arms around him.

This hug isn't casual, isn't playful—it's everything. My thanks. My awe. My heart, pressed against his.

Jack holds me like he means it, and for the first time in a long time, I let myself be held.

As I sink into the warmth of his embrace, something inside me shifts. It's no longer just a pull, it's a truth, one that settles deep in my chest. I'm falling in love with him. And for the first time in years, I'm not afraid of it.

Chapter Eighteen

I turned thirty last year, and something shifted. Just a number, they say—but somewhere in the months that followed, I stopped being the version of me that tolerated everything. One who isn't afraid to see what's been missing all along. This morning, for the first time in as long as I can remember, I wake up excited. Not for the usual mundane tasks that fill my days, but because tomorrow, we are all going to a music festival. Jack won the tickets on a local radio station and immediately invited us. Like he couldn't imagine going without us.

Just the thought of him makes my heart ache in ways I can't fully explain. But today, I can't let myself dwell on it. Not when tomorrow's festival looms. The show starts at 6 p.m. down by the water, and if I can just survive this day, I'll reap the benefits soon.

Nathan's coming, of course. So are Colby, Lauren, and Jack. It's a whole carload, an awkward mix of people that already feels heavier than it should. I can already feel the tension humming under the surface between Nathan and me, the way silence builds between people who've run out of things to say. Even when he tries, like with the blender he bought me as a surprise gift, it only highlights how far we've drifted.

I try not to let it get to me. He doesn't know me anymore. How could he? We built this life together—brick by crumbling brick, patching over cracks we never fully acknowledged, but somewhere along the way, the foundation split, and now, here we are. Yesterday, he took me to get a new pair of cowgirl boots after I begged him. The brown leather with green stitching is beautiful in a way I didn't expect. But then he bought himself two pairs, and it hit me: even when he's doing something for me, it's still about him.

I force myself out of bed, even though every bone in my body protests. My muscles ache like I've been carrying the weight of this family on my back for too long. Maybe it's just part of getting older. It could be the endless grind of giving so much and getting so little in return. Or perhaps it's because my heart is quietly, relentlessly aching for someone else. Jack.

I shouldn't think of him like this, but I do. His eyes light up when he talks to me like he's actually seeing me, not the faded version of me this house has worn down. He listens in the ways Nathan didn't anymore. Maybe never did.

I shake the thoughts away as my feet hit the cold floor. It's dangerous, thinking about him like this. Wanting him the way I do. I pull on my clothes quickly, keeping my mind on the day ahead and off the ache in my chest that has nothing to do with being older and everything to do with Jack.

As I step onto the stairs, the muted laughter of the kids drifts in from the back porch. The sound is muffled by the glass door that separates their world from mine, a thin barrier that feels thicker than it should. I glance toward the kitchen as I pass, already knowing what I'll find. Or rather, what I won't.

Nathan didn't make breakfast. Of course, he didn't.

I sigh, not even bothering to feel disappointed anymore. Instead, I let my mind wander to the same useless dream I've had for years that maybe something will change one day. That one day, I'll wake up to a reality where I'm not the one carrying this family on my back. But then I shake the thought away, forcing a bitter laugh at my own absurdity. Small victories.

Pushing through the back door, I step onto the warm asphalt of the porch. The kids turn to me, their faces lighting up as they shout in unison, "Good morning, Momma!" It's so in sync that I wonder if they rehearse this when I'm not paying attention.

"Good morning," I reply, smiling despite myself. "Where's your dad?"

"Next door," Nora says, her voice matter-of-fact.

Colby's house. Of course. I know he's not with Jack. They're more acquaintances than friends, which is fine by me. I didn't need Nathan bringing our tension into Jack's orbit.

"Are you guys hungry?" I ask, already knowing the answer.

"Yeah!" they chorus, their enthusiasm cutting through the morning haze that clings to my mood.

"Let's make pancakes, okay?"

"Yay!" they shout, already bounding inside ahead of me. I follow them into the kitchen, feeling the familiar pull of my role as their everything, their cook, their caretaker, their constant. It's exhausting, sure, but it's also the one thing that makes me feel like I still have a purpose, like I still matter.

The front door creaks open and slams shut, followed by the kids' unmistakable chorus of "Daddy!". Nathan's back.

I glance over my shoulder as he rounds the corner into the kitchen. His boots click against the floor, a sound that felt more like a warning than a comfort these days. He strides toward me with that familiar confidence, wrapping his hands around my waist and pulling me close. Before I can step back, he presses a kiss on my cheek.

"Want to turn that off and sneak upstairs with me?" he murmurs, his voice low and commanding, more of an expectation than an invitation.

I didn't even flinch, but my eyes flick to him sideways, searching his face for something familiar. The man I married. The man I used to want. But I find nothing, just the weight of his presence and the pull of his demand.

Once upon a time, I wouldn't have hesitated. In fact, I've never turned him down, not once in all the years we've been married. Whenever he reached for me, hinted, or asked, I gave him what he wanted. What he needed. It didn't matter if I wanted it too—his needs always came first.

But now? Now it's different.

Something shifts inside me, like I'd stepped off the well-worn path we'd been walking for years and chosen another. A path that didn't include bending to his every touch or melting under the slightest bit of attention he decides to throw my way.

For the first time in my life, I feel the pull of my own gravity, the weight of my own desires. And it doesn't point toward him anymore. It only points to one man, and he lives two doors down. Of course, I can't betray myself and show my cards just yet, but I have a feeling that one day, maybe soon, I'll have everything in order and make my move.

"No."

The word cuts clean through the moment—sharp, sure, and mine. It hangs between us, a small but powerful declaration of something I'd never allowed myself before: defiance.

For a moment, I savor the way it feels, to stand up for myself, saying no without guilt. It is like rediscovering a part of me I'd buried long ago, a spark of power, not just as a person but as a woman who deserves more.

Nathan's face twists, and he doesn't hide the irritation simmering beneath his skin. Without another word, he turns on his heels and stalks toward the garage, muttering something low and guttural. As he disappears through the door, his parting shot came just before it slammed shut.

"Don't forget my parents will be here in two hours."

My stomach drops. Crap. His parents. I have completely forgotten they are coming to watch the kids while we go to the festival tomorrow.

I exhale sharply, already running through a mental checklist. The house isn't in terrible shape, but Nora's room still needs to be prepped. Luckily, that is an easy fix.

I turn to her, my voice calm but firm. "Nora, go make up your bed, put your dirty clothes in the hamper, and make sure the rest of your room is clean."

At seven, she is more than capable of handling most of what I ask of her. She's always eager to please, and I can't help but notice how she's starting to mirror me, maybe she's beginning to understand how much I carry, even at her young age.

"Okay, Mama!" she chirps before darting off.

I smile faintly, knowing I'd still need to go behind her to double-check everything, but her help eases something I didn't even know I was holding. Every little bit counts, and I can't help but feel gratitude for her sweet, eager heart. She has no idea how much she lightens my load or how much I hope she'd never feel the kind of weight I carry now.

☾☾☾

A couple of hours later, after breakfast is cleaned, dishes are put away, counters wiped down, and Nora's room is double-checked, Susan and Dan finally arrive. The sound of the kids' shrieks of joy echoes through the house as they run to greet their grandparents.

I force a smile as I follow behind them. Susan never just visits—she arrives, takes over, and suddenly it's her house, her rules. There is something about how she moves through my house, her presence loud and uninvited in ways that aren't always tangible but are impossible to ignore. She has a knack for stepping on my toes as a mom, correcting me in small, pointed ways or taking charge of situations I didn't need help with.

She doesn't have to say anything—just being in the room with her makes me feel like I'm failing some invisible test. I can't decide if it is intentional, her way of asserting some authority, or if she is just wired to take over, her maternal instincts unable to adjust to someone else running the show. I used to work hard for her approval. Now I don't bother.

I do what I always do—I bite down on my pride and stay quiet. It's easier to stay quiet, especially in front of the kids. But the tension settles between us like a thick fog. If I had a dollar for every time I bit my tongue in this house, I could've bought my way into a better life by now. For Nathan. For the kids. For the fragile peace that is barely holding everything together.

"Hi, Susan. Dan," I say, my voice light and polite as I greet them at the door. Susan breezes in like she owns the place—hugging, fixing, taking command like it's her name on the mortgage.

I stand back, watching how she effortlessly takes over the room. I have to remind myself to breathe, as it feels like her presence consumes all the oxygen.

Just two days. I repeat it like a prayer. Two days, and I can go back to pretending this house still feels like mine.

Chapter Nineteen

The next day, after lunch and a trip to the park to let the kids burn off some energy, I retreat to the bathroom to start getting ready. The sound of the water running fills the space, white noise that drowns out the chaos of the house behind the locked door. For a rare moment, I am truly alone.

I stand in front of the mirror, studying my reflection. At first, I barely recognize the woman staring back at me. But as I examine myself more closely, something within me shifts. I see my undeniable beauty, in the shine of my blonde hair, the soft blue-gray glow in my eyes, and even in my body.

My body.

The weight of motherhood I've carried for so long is finally starting to lift. Maybe it's the endless movement of motherhood, or maybe, just maybe, it's something more. A different kind of change, a shift I can't quite name but feel deep in my bones.

I run my hands down my sides, tracing the curves I've been too busy—or too tired—to notice. For the first time in years, I don't pick myself apart. Instead, I stand taller, straighter, feeling a quiet kind of pride. Then, unbidden, a thought of Jack slips into my mind, and a smile stretches across my face.

Was it him?

Is he the reason I'm starting to see myself differently? Beginning to believe I can be more than a mother, a wife, a tired woman drowning under the weight of it all. He makes me feel alive again, like someone worth attention, worth noticing.

This realization hits me in gentle waves, washing over me and leaving its mark deep within. I smile at the woman in the mirror, really smiling for the first time in a long time.

Once in the shower, the hot water cascades over me, soothing and scalding all at once. The heat sinks into my muscles, loosening the tension I carry every day, but it does more than that. It transports me. For a brief moment, my mind drifts to Jack, his touch lingering on my skin, his body pressed against mine in the stillness of his room. I can almost feel him, almost hear his breath.

But I shake the memories loose, forcing myself back into the present.

After my shower, I reach for the lace I've tucked away for tonight, the kind of lingerie Nathan's never noticed but Jack would. I slip it on, the delicate fabric whispering against my skin, before retrieving the white dress I've chosen days ago. It's not just a dress; it's a declaration—a weapon

I step back into the bathroom, the steam clinging to the mirror like a veil, and flip on the fan to clear it. As the fog clears, I see my reflection, a woman prepared for battle. I pull out my makeup bag, my hands steady as I begin the ritual. My war paint, then the white sundress. Tonight, I don't just want to see Jack. I want him to really see me. And I want him to lose the battle I'm hoping he's waging inside himself.

Just then, Nora skips into the room, her little feet barely making a sound as she hums a tune only she knows. She stops, her curious eyes scanning me as if she's solving a mystery. "Why are you getting ready, Mama?" she asks, tilting her head like she always does when she senses something worth uncovering.

"I'm going to a festival tonight," I say, smoothing the fabric of my dress, trying not to sound too excited.

"Is that why you're so happy?" she asks, her perceptive gaze cutting straight through me.

"Yes, that's why," I reply, unable to keep the tiny smile from my lips.

"Did Daddy buy you tickets?" she asks, her tone innocent but her curiosity sharp.

"No, baby," I say softly.

Her little brow furrows, the wheels in her mind already turning. "Then how did you get tickets?" she presses, her voice a mixture of wonder and determination.

"Jack won them on a radio show," I say, my tone light, hoping it will satisfy her.

"He did?" she shoots back without hesitation.

I hesitate, my breath catching for a moment. "Yes, he got really lucky to be the 15th caller," I say finally, hoping to deflect her curiosity.

Her expression shifts, and her wide eyes narrow slightly. It isn't a look I recognize, and it lingers in the space between us. I wonder what thoughts are circling in her little mind, what questions she is holding back, and whether she is piecing together a puzzle I didn't realize I'd set in front of her.

☾☾☾

By 5 p.m., my phone buzzes with a text.

Jack: *Ya'll ready?*
I smile, my heart quickening as I type back.
Me: *We'll be outside in 10 minutes.*
His reply comes swiftly.
Jack: *See y'all then.*

Ten minutes later, we step outside, and there he is.
Jack.

His eyes find mine instantly, locking on like a magnet to its match. For the first time, there is no pretense, no mask to shield the truth. The desire in his gaze is raw and unguarded, and it hits me with a force that steals my breath away.

I feel it. I see it. And in that moment, everything else fades into the background.

The ride to the festival is alive with energy, the kind that buzzes beneath your skin and makes you feel like anything is possible. Music blares from the car speakers, everyone singing along, and laughter spills out of the open windows. For a little while, the tension melts away, replaced by the shared excitement of the night ahead.

As we stand in line waiting to get in, I notice something curious, the way the other women check out Jack when he isn't looking, the way they whisper to each other. Jealousy rises within me, unexpected and uninvited. I'm standing next to my husband and I'm upset that other girls are checking out Jack.

Once inside the smell of barbecue, the sound of laughter, the buzz of neon signs overhead, it all makes the world feel far away. It's like stepping into a memory you hope will never fade. We grab some food, snap pictures, and let the festival's atmosphere swallow us whole. But I keep finding my eyes drifting to him.
Jack.

His dark jeans fit him perfectly, casual but tailored in a

way that draws the eye. He's wearing a fitted charcoal T-shirt that clings to his frame just enough, and a light gray hoodie hangs from one shoulder like he tossed it on without thinking. On his feet, clean sneakers, simple, understated. He looks effortlessly good, like he always does. Not trying. Just being. And that's the thing about Jack, he could belong anywhere. He has this unshakable ease, this quiet confidence that turns any space into his own without making a sound.

And in that moment, surrounded by the swirling energy of the festival crowd, I'm not just looking at him, I'm imprinting him. Every glance, every motion, every quiet pause. Because no matter how much I try to pretend otherwise, Jack isn't just a part of tonight. He's the gravity pulling me through it. The thing I can't look away from.

☾☾☾

Later in the evening, the buzz of the festival hits its peak. Drinks are flowing, laughter has turned to dancing, and inhibitions fade into the thrum of music and conversation swirling through the field. I've had one too many adult beverages, and my head swims in that loose, reckless way that makes everything feel possible. Dangerous, but possible.

"Nathan, I need to go to the bathroom," I murmur. "You are a big girl, I'm sure you can find them," he says. I find the bathrooms, with ease as it's the longest line around. After exiting, I glance up and spot Jack making his way toward the beer tents. I wonder if he came looking for me, or another drink. I watch him for a moment, his shoulders cutting a clean line through the crowd, the soft evening lights catching the back of his shirt.

Then, without thinking, I move.

I loop around the back of a row of food trucks, weaving

through spilled light and shadows until I'm just behind him. My heart hammers in my chest as I reach out and wrap my fingers around his forearm. He stops, turns—and the moment our eyes meet, his expression shifts from surprise to something else entirely.

I pull him gently but insistently behind a tent, into a narrow passage where the shadows are thick and the music sounds distant.

He doesn't speak. He doesn't have to.

His hands find my waist as my back presses lightly against the tent wall. His body is close—too close—and not nearly close enough. His mouth meets mine in the next breath, and the kiss is different this time. It's deeper. Hungrier. Reckless in the way it devours hesitation.

"I hoped you'd follow," I whisper, breathless against his lips.

"I always will," he murmurs, his voice rough, his forehead resting against mine.

The crowd hums just beyond the fabric wall, oblivious to the storm unraveling in the shadows.

His hands slide down, steady and sure, fingers brushing over the hem of my dress. When they meet skin, I suck in a sharp breath. My head tips back against the tent, and my eyes flutter closed. I shouldn't want this. But I do. God, I do.

This isn't just want—it's need. Raw, electric need that burns through me like a fuse lit too close to the end.

His lips find the hollow of my throat as his hand roams, and I melt into him, every nerve alight. The noise outside muffles into a distant echo as we lose track of everything but the heat between us. There is no past. No future. Only now.

Then my phone buzzes. His follows. Again and again—relentless.

Reality forces its way back in.

We freeze, breathless.

"They're looking for us," he says, pulling back just enough to meet my eyes.

"I know," I whisper, my fingers still twisted in the front of his shirt.

He tucks a strand of hair behind my ear, his expression softening. "What should we do?"

I swallow hard, pulse still racing. "You go grab the beers. I'll walk back first, give it a minute or two. If we show up together, it'll be obvious."

He nods, pressing one last kiss to my cheek. "Be careful."

"You too," I say, stepping back into the light.

I weave through the crowd alone, giving myself time to steady my breathing and smooth my dress. When I return to the group, Nathan is pacing, his jaw tight.

"Where were you?" he asks, eyes narrowing.

"I got turned around after the bathroom," I say calmly. "There was a crowd by the merch tent, and I must have looped the wrong way."

Nathan glares at me, unconvinced. "You've had too much to drink, Ella."

I shrug, feigning nonchalance. "Maybe. It's a festival. That's kind of the point."

Just then, Jack returns, two cold beers in hand. "Here we go," he says, handing one to Nathan with a casual grin.

Nathan eyes him, then me. "You ran into her?"

Jack nods. "Just as she was coming back. Figured I'd grab the drinks while she made her way over."

Nathan doesn't respond, but his jaw twitches. He turns away.

But I stay there, still and unshaken. Because something has shifted. Something inside me is no longer willing to settle. Not tonight.

Jack catches my gaze from across the field, and that look subtle and steady, is all the confirmation I need.

Whatever happens next, we've crossed a line.

And there's no going back.

Chapter Twenty

It's been nearly a week since I last saw Jack, since that unforgettable moment at the festival. The ache of missing him is almost unbearable now. I crave his scent, his smile, and most of all, his touch.

The late afternoon sun hangs low in the blue spring sky, casting a golden glow over Whispering Oaks' community clubhouse. Laughter echoes across the open field, the sound of burgers sizzling mingling with the air. A banner flaps lazily above the welcome tent, reading "Whispering Oaks Spring Fest – All Ages Welcome!" We received a flyer in the mail for a community center volleyball get-together, a makeshift tournament with no real rules, just fun.

The community center here is really amazing, volleyball courts, an Olympic-sized swimming pool, a recreational center with couches, TVs and grills along with a full size gym. As we make our way around back, I see many people I don't recognize, some just talking and others playing volleyball. When it is our turn, I step onto the court, the sand is firm beneath my feet, packed down from kids running and neighbors gathering. Jack and his oldest daughter are on one side of the volleyball net, while Nathan and I team up on the other. I use the word 'team' loosely—let's be honest, we haven't been one in a long time.

I'm not exactly dressed for competition, but comfort wins over style here. Tight black shorts cling to my legs, paired with a black sports bra and a spaghetti-strap white tank top, now soaked with sweat and sticking to my skin in the heavy air. My hair is pulled into a low ponytail, stuck stubbornly to the nape of my neck with every serve, every jump, every stolen glance at Jack from across the net.

I can't stop watching him, not just his volleyball skills, though God, he's good. It's the way his body moves. Effortless. Controlled. He once mentioned, almost casually, that he played in beach leagues in California growing up. But it's only now that I realize how much of himself he's poured into it.

I notice how he toys with Nathan, sending arching lobs and quick spikes that leave Nathan stumbling and me chuckling behind my hand. But when he plays against me, his shots are different, gentler, deliberate. Even from across the net, it feels like he's watching over me.

Emboldened by the moment, I reach for the hem of my white shirt and pull it over my head, leaving just the sports bra against my skin. The breeze kisses my skin, briefly cooling me before Jack's gaze finds me. Three months ago, this kind of confidence would've felt foreign. But now, I'm starting to see myself the way Jack sees me—not just a wife or a mom, but the real me. It isn't obvious, but I feel it, the way his eyes linger just long enough to send a slow heat spreading across my chest. It isn't the sun warming me anymore. It is him.

It has been years since I played volleyball, but the burn in my legs and the rhythm of my heart pounding in my chest feel incredible. Or perhaps it isn't just the exercise. Maybe it is Jack's effect on me. I'd do just about anything to be near him now.

Sweat trails down the back of my neck, teasing its way over my chest, pooling at my stomach. My body is working overtime to cool itself, though I'm not sure if it is because of the sun or the way Jack keeps looking at me; his gaze trails after every serve, every laugh.

When Nathan decides to take a break and Colby jumps into the game, Jack doesn't hesitate. He trots over to my side of the net, his smile easy, his presence magnetic. He says nothing about why he switches sides but doesn't have to. I know. He wants to be closer to me. And honestly? I want that, too.

He lets me take most of the plays, but I can feel his eyes on me the whole time. He isn't just watching—he is studying. The way I move, the way I jump, the way I exist in the space between him and the ball.

Nathan has essentially quit the game entirely, beer in one hand, making gestures with the other, deep in conversation with Lauren on the sidelines about forty feet away. Jack edges closer, his voice muted and low but intentional. "On your next volley, try cupping your hands like this," he says, demonstrating the motion with a soft flick of his wrists.

"I'll try that," I reply, although a devious plan is already forming in my mind.

The next serve from Colby comes sailing toward me. I turn to hit it but deliberately mess it up. The ball flies awkwardly, bouncing into the sand and rolling away. I look at Jack, feigning confusion, silently hoping he will step in.

"Ella," he says, a smile tugging at the corner of his mouth. "Try keeping your wrists together. Anticipate the ball and guide it with your forearms. Like this." He demonstrates again as he hits the ball back over the net, then nods to Colby for another serve.

I adjust. The volleyball whizzes toward me again, and I cup my hands and mistime the hit on purpose. The ball rockets sideways, nearly clipping a woman mid-laugh. I lift my hand, a silent apology. When I turn to look at Jack, the intensity of his gaze sends a jolt through me. Our eyes meet, and at that moment, it feels like his eyes are speaking in some ancient language. A language built on hidden nuances and subtle gestures.

He takes another step closer, reading me perfectly, as if he understands what I am doing. "Let me show you how," he says, his voice soft and deliberate. "Colby, send one more this way."

"You got it," Colby calls back, still clueless to what's really unfolding.

Jack is suddenly there, millimeters away, the space between us dissolving, his body against mine. "Turn like you're getting ready to hit the ball," he says, his voice a quiet command that isn't controlling but undeniably seductive. I catch the flicker of movement in my peripheral vision—Nathan, beer in hand, glancing up from his conversation just as Jack steps in closer. His gaze lingers for a second too long, brow furrowing, before he turns back to Lauren.

I turn back to Jack, my heart racing faster than I know is possible. The world around us seems to blur into the background, and for a second, I wonder if everyone else can feel it, too, this invisible cord pulling us together, this risky, reckless tether.

He leans in, so close I can feel his breath, warm and deliberate, against my skin. My stomach flips, nerves sparking like live wires. Then, just above a whisper, he murmurs, "Your hair smells amazing."

I let out a nervous, reserved laugh. "I'm sweaty and gross

right now."

"Not to me, you're not," he says, his tone low, unapologetic.

The air between us is electric, and in that moment, I don't care who is watching. All that matters is us.

Emmett's cries snap me out of my trance. My head jerks up just in time to see him fall in the bounce house nearby. He's sprawled face-first on the floor, while the other kids jump around him, tossing his body like a rag doll.

I don't even think twice. I sprint to him, crawling inside the bounce house. By the time I reach him, his cheeks are streaked with tears, his lip trembling as I sit him up. Gently, I brush the grass off his arms and knees, checking for any real damage.

"You okay, baby?" I ask softly, kneeling to his level.

"Yes, Mama," he whimpers, though the steady stream of tears down his cheeks tells an entirely different story.

I press a kiss to his forehead and smile. "Hungry?" I ask, my tone bright, hoping to distract him.

His face lights up in that wild, unfiltered way only kids know how. "Yes!" he said, the tears forgotten as fast as they had come.

I help him to his feet, wrapping an arm around his small shoulders as we start toward the table piled high with food. Glancing back, my eyes find Jack. He is watching us intently, a soft smile tugging at his lips. For a moment, the air between us feels heavier and warmer. Then I turn back to Emmett, grateful for the distraction his little hand provides as it clings to mine.

Moving through the chaos, I make plates for the kids and swat at flies like a woman on a mission. Eventually, I get everyone settled in their places, where we eat, laugh, and joke like nothing else mattered.

When it is finally my turn to make a plate of food, I realize Nathan has disappeared into the clubhouse for another beer. Typical. Jack appears beside me at the table, quietly fixing his own plate. I don't think much of it until his hand brushes against the small of my back as he passes by, lingering just long enough to jolt through my entire body.

I freeze for half a second, my breath catching in my throat. Glancing around, I confirm no one has seen it, but my heart didn't get the memo, it's racing like I've just run a marathon. Jack acts like nothing happened, but that fleeting touch scorches—lingering beneath my skin long after it's gone.

As the night continues, the darkness creeps in, and the Florida mosquitoes swarm with a vengeance. The string lights flicker above us. Volunteers fold chairs and collapse tents. I'm still cleaning. Nathan goes inside to use the bathroom, but he never comes back out, leaving me, as usual, to clean up after everyone, alone. I'm not the least bit surprised. This is how it always goes.

I gather plates, fold chairs, and round up the kids. Jack sent his kids home with his oldest and stayed behind. He appears out of nowhere, grabbing chairs and stacking them neatly without a word.

"You don't have to do that," I say, trying to sound firm but failing.

He shoots me a look, one eyebrow raised. "I insist."

I don't argue. I can't. Something about how he moves, purposeful and deliberate, makes me feel adored and appreciated.

When we reach the table to cover the leftover food, his hand brushes against mine as we work the foil over a plate. The touch is brief but electric, and his eyes are already on me when I look up.

My pulse surges. The space between us hums with

everything we can't say. Time seems to pause and I think he is going to kiss me. I want him to.

But he doesn't. He just stares into my soul, and in that breathless silence, I know I'm already his—even if I never get to say it out loud.

Chapter Twenty-One

The shrill buzz of my phone alarm jolts me awake at 6:25 a.m. My body groans in protest as I turn off the alarm, and every muscle aches in a way that feels unfamiliar. That volleyball match a few days ago did more damage than I realized. So, what they say about getting older is true. It's not just a shift in your mindset, but in your body, too.

I wince in pain as my feet hit the floor. My legs wobble beneath me, as if drained of strength. Stretching before and after the activity would have been a good idea. Lesson learned. I grab my favorite sweatshirt and pink sweatpants from the top drawer, quickly pull them on, and step out of the room.

Nathan is home, probably sitting in front of the computer researching golf trips or scrolling on his phone. The thought brings a twinge of frustration, but it is a familiar feeling by now. I've stopped expecting him to help with the daily chores of raising this family. Expectations only lead to disappointment.

I check Nora's room first, and it is empty. With a tired sigh,

I shuffle down the hall to peek into the Emmett's room, which is just as quiet. The stairs loom ahead of me, a daunting reminder of my legs' soreness.

I grip the railing and start down cautiously, carefully negotiating each step with my aching muscles. When I finally reach the bottom, I feel a strange sense of accomplishment, like I conquered an Olympic event instead of a simple staircase.

The house is eerie and quiet. The table displays the morning events and breakfast pancakes, from the looks of it, but no one is around. Plates and syrup-streaked dishes sit abandoned, waiting for me to clean up. Then, I see the note stuck to the refrigerator in Nathan's handwriting:

"I got the kids ready early. I'm taking Nora to school. I'll be back soon. Hopefully, you get to sleep in."

For a moment, I stare at it, half expecting to wake up and realize this is a dream. I pinch my arm—nope, still awake. Gratitude should come easily, but instead, my mind spirals. *Had Nathan noticed the way Jack and I had connected during volleyball? Did he see the glances, the unspoken tension?*

Nathan works nights now, which means he is home during the day. It's a blessing on paper—but in practice, just one more person for me to manage. Still, he'd taken all the kids with him, which is a relief.

The sound of tires on asphalt pulls me from my thoughts. I glance through the window and see Jack pulling into his driveway. My heart speeds up as I grab my phone and open Whisper.

"Not at work yet?" I type quickly.

His reply comes almost instantly. "In a few minutes, I will be."

The corners of my lips tug upward. Without thinking, I type, "Can I stop by real quick?"

"Come on!" he replies.

I slip on my sandals, adrenaline dulling the ache in my legs as I hurry out the back door. The damp grass clings to my toes as I cross the yard and step into Jack's house without hesitation.

With a spoon in his right hand, he is standing in his kitchen, taking a bite of oatmeal. His eyes widen slightly at seeing me, but his surprise doesn't last long.

I don't stop. I round the corner, my heart hammering, and walk straight to him. Without a word, I pluck the bowl from his hands and set it on the counter.

I wrap my arms around his neck and press my lips to his, pouring all my longing into the kiss.

For the first time, I didn't wait for him to make the first move, and he didn't seem to mind. His arms search my body and find their way to my waist, pulling me closer and grounding me in the moment. All the stored tension, all the unspoken feelings, it all overflows in that kiss, and for once, I didn't think about what would happen next—only now—only him.

Our bodies move in perfect rhythm like we've been lovers in some past life. His fingers trail along the edge of my pants, igniting a fire under my skin with every slow, sensual touch. The world feels smaller, quieter—just the two of us caught in this stolen moment.

When we finally break our bodies apart, his intense and unyielding eyes search mine. "Can I see you tonight?" he asks, his voice low, rich, and filled with something that makes my stomach flip.

"Yes," I whisper, trying to catch my breath.

A happy smile spreads across his face. "Good," he says, his tone smooth as velvet. "Because I'll have a surprise waiting for you."

"A surprise?" My voice betrays me, curious and eager.

"I have to head off to work," he says, a mischievous smile gracing his face, his hand lingers on my waist as if he didn't want to let go, "but I'll be waiting for you tonight."

"Can't wait," I murmur, my lips curving into a smile I can't hold back.

Before I can move away, his hand slides to my backside, giving it a playful squeeze as his lips claim my mouth again. The kiss is more profound this time, forcing a sound from deep within me I don't recognize, a moan so raw, so primal, it feels like it came from somewhere locked away.

When I eventually force myself to leave, I walk out the back door, my heart racing. Crossing the yard feels dreamlike, like I'm not walking but floating, weightless, unburdened, as if the grass beneath me is a magic carpet carrying me all the way home.

The day slips by in a blur of chores. My interactions with Nathan are the same as every other day: hollow exchanges about bills, schedules, and the kids. It feels like we aren't even living a shared life anymore, just two people existing in the same house, trapped in a routine we'd fallen into the day we said, "I do."

When Nathan heads to work, I clean up the scattered toys and settle the kids in front of a G-rated movie. Usually, I'd feel drained by the end of the day, but tonight is different. I move through the motions with a slight smile on my face. Something is waiting for me. Something from Jack. A surprise.

As I tidy up, the possibilities swirl in my mind. Is it a gift? Flowers? Something completely unexpected? With Jack, it can be anything—he has a way of making the mundane feel exhilarating, of turning the ordinary into something extraordinary.

It is just after ten when the kids are asleep. I hop in the shower, allowing the warm water to wash away the day's tension. Afterward, I take my time, apply lotion to my body, spray on some perfume and put on my clothes.

Once I finish, I grab my phone and type a quick message.

Me: *Ready for me?*

He replies immediately.

Jack: *Yes.*

My heart races with anticipation. Me: On my way

But after I retrieve my keys from the little hook near the back door, my phone rings. It is Nathan.

"I'm getting off early tonight," he says. "I was thinking we could watch a show together like we used to."

I swallow the lump of disappointment rising in my throat. "About what time will you be home?" I ask, trying to keep my tone neutral.

"Probably an hour or two, maybe a little more," he says casually.

The words hit me like a smack to the face, and a million thoughts race through my mind. Why me? Why tonight? Why now?

I didn't give myself any time to think about it. I slip out the back door into the night and walk to Jack's. He is waiting for me to arrive; his face lights up as I step inside.

"Jack," I say, my voice cracking slightly.

"Hey," he replies, his excitement diminished when he sees the conflict in my eyes.

"I can't stay long," I disclose, guilt threading through my words. "Nathan will be home early tonight."

His expression falls for a moment, but he quickly masks it. "Do you at least have time to see the surprise?"

"Yes," I say, the anticipation from earlier bubbling up again.

"Close your eyes," he says, reaching for my hand.

His warm touch ignites a delightful shiver down my spine

as he guides me through the living room, creating a moment full of connection and joy. I trust him completely, every step heightening my curiosity.

"Keep your eyes closed," he says, his hand extending and settling on the small of my back. The warmth of his touch grounds me, even as anticipation lifts me off the floor.

I let him guide me, step by step, through the darkened room, my breath catching every time I imagine what might be waiting.

The silence between us isn't awkward—it is electric. Every second stretches, heavy with emotion and mystery.

"Open your eyes," he whispers in my ear.

I open them.

My breath catches.

A string of soft flickering tea lights line the hallway, their golden glow dancing against the white walls. The effect is stunning. The house feels transformed, sacred somehow, as if the moment has been carved out of time just for us.

I blink, awestruck. "Jack… what is this?" I whisper.

"Go see," he says softly, the excitement in his voice barely contained.

I follow the lights slowly. At the end of the hall, the guest bedroom door stands open. I step forward and peek inside.

The room is glowing. Dozens of candles cover every surface—flickering on the windowsill, dresser, nightstands, even the floor. Their golden light bathes the space in warmth, casting soft shadows that move like breath. The air carries a whisper of something sweet—vanilla, maybe rose—and underneath it, unmistakably, him.

On the bed, a dark blue duvet lies beneath a scattering of folded notes. I step closer, drawn to the tenderness in the gesture. Each slip of paper is marked with one word—Beautiful. Brave. Desired. Enough. Words I hadn't heard in years. Words I didn't know I still needed.

It looks like they were placed one by one, deliberately, with care. My breath hitches as I take it all in, and my chest tightens with something I can't name—something too big for words.

I turn to him slowly, tears already rising in my eyes.

"Why?" I whisper, my voice breaking like glass.

He doesn't hesitate. "Because you deserve the best a man can give," he says, voice low and sure, like it is the only truth that matters.

That is when the dam breaks, and the tears stream down my face.

I reach for him, my hands cupping his face as I kiss him with everything I have—every unsaid word, every aching question, every part of me that has been waiting to be seen and chosen.

We sink onto the bed of notes, the candlelight painting us in gold. The room, the world, everything outside of this moment fades into silence.

And as his gaze holds mine, something inside me shifts. For the first time in years, I see myself clearly—radiant, wanted, whole. Not just a wife. Not just a mother.

Me.

The woman I thought I'd lost is still there, waiting to be found. In his eyes, I remember her. Wrapped in candlelight and Jack, I realize—I'm finding my way back to myself.

Chapter Twenty-Two

The chill of the kitchen tile stings my feet as I make my way to the refrigerator, reaching for the usual breakfast items: bacon, eggs, and sausage. My eyes stop on the calendar, and I freeze. Nathan's off to a two-week technical conference in Scottsdale. His company's been planning it for months. I circled the date on the calendar weeks ago, then erased it, and circled it again, unsure of what the time away might bring.

A smile tugs at my lips, but a flicker of sadness follows—soft, uninvited, and lingering. I pause, standing there, trying to untangle the feeling and its source. It isn't sadness; I'm not upset about him leaving. If anything, it means more time with Jack, or at least the hope of it. No, the sadness is for the kids. They will miss their dad, which stirs something I haven't felt in a while.

I can't recall the last time Nathan and I shared a real, happy moment. Did we ever have those moments, or was I just fooling myself? Had I ever really felt loved by him? Or had we been stuck in this lifeless cycle longer than I wanted to admit?

The soft thuds of little feet upstairs interrupt my thoughts, grounding me in the present. One thing about our house, you can hear everything. Every creak, every step, every sound between the walls and floors.

The kids descend the stairs, their tiny footsteps growing louder as they race to find me. Behind them, heavier footsteps follow, Nathan's.

I shake off thoughts of Nathan leaving, of Jack, of everything that feels too tangled to unravel right now. Instead, I focus on the task in front of me: making breakfast, keeping the morning moving, and getting everyone ready for the drive to the airport.

He's been trying lately, dropping the kids off at school, folding laundry now and then. The silence between us hasn't changed—but it doesn't cut as deep. We still don't talk much, but the shouting matches that had defined so much of our marriage have disappeared.

Maybe my happiness, the joy I'd found with Jack, has rubbed off on him. Perhaps he isn't blind to the newfound light in my reflection, the radiance I can finally see in myself. Maybe he is starting to see it, too.

☾☾☾

Later that evening, the ride to the airport is short, but the weight in the car is heavy. The kids are already sad, their quiet sniffles the only sound breaking the silence. Nathan drives without speaking, his fingers tapping the wheel in a steady rhythm. When we pull up to the curb, he pops the trunk, and we all climb out. I help the kids unbuckle while Nathan grabs his bags from the back. The scrape of suitcase wheels on concrete sounds louder than it should.

As he closes the trunk, Nathan glances at me. "So, what are

you going to do while I'm gone?"

I arch a brow. "Oh, you know... just keep the kids alive, juggle school drop-offs, dishes, laundry. Same as always."

He doesn't respond, just gives a tight nod and turns toward the terminal.

When Nathan says, "It's time for me to go," the kids start crying, and he pulls them into his arms. Their small bodies cling to him, faces buried in his shirt. Guilt pinches my chest—not because I'll miss him, but because they will.

I wonder if, when they're older, they'll remember this version of us. The quiet unraveling. The marriage already broken, even if none of us had the words for it yet. And then he turns to me. He reaches out, wraps his arms around me, and before I can process what is happening, he kisses me. A deep, deliberate kiss, something he hasn't done in a very long time.

I freeze, unable to move. It doesn't feel like love. It's not love—it's a performance. A rehearsal for an audience I'll never belong to. His lips press into mine, but they don't stir anything inside me, not warmth, not longing. Just the hollow ache of knowing what love really feels like… and this isn't it.

Because I'm not his anymore. And deep down, I know, I belong to someone else.

Back at home, after the kids settle in, they ask to video call their dad. I help them get set up, stepping quietly out of the room to give them space. But I linger just outside the doorway, listening.

Nathan's voice comes through the speaker. "Alright, alright, love you guys. Be good for your mom. I'll bring back something cool. I have to go now, I'm boarding the plane."

He sounds distracted. Disconnected. Like he's already gone.

Afterward, I change out of my dress and put on a pair of

snug blue jean shorts and a soft t-shirt, something more comfortable for the evening. I get the kids into their favorite comfy clothes and start making dinner. The sound of my phone buzzes on the counter breaks through the quiet hum of the house, pulling my attention. Jack's name lights up the screen, sending a quiet thrill through me.

Jack: *Is he gone? How are you and the kids?*

His message catches me off guard. I want him to be relieved that Nathan's gone, and I expect it, but there's something more underneath. He isn't just focusing on his relief; he cares about how the kids and I feel.

Me: *Yes, we're doing okay. It's a lot for the kids, you know?*

I stare at the screen, unsure of what else to say. My feelings are a chaotic swirl I can't entirely untangle.

Jack: *Maybe you can come over after the kids are asleep, and we can talk about it.*

Talk. His words linger in my mind. I don't want to just talk; I want to feel him, lose myself in his touch, warmth, and presence. My fingers tremble as I type.

Me: *I definitely will!*

Later, as I tuck Nora into bed, she tilts her head and asks, "Mommy, why are you so happy lately? You smile all the time now." The question lands like a stone in my stomach. I kiss her forehead and smooth her hair, heart fluttering. "Just happy to be with you," I whisper. But her words follow me out of the room like a shadow. She sees more than I give her credit for. More than I want her to.

Afterward, I slip into the shower, the kids finally settled after stories and double-checks. The scalding water rushes over me, but my mind is elsewhere—on Jack, and on the two weeks ahead of us, full of possibility. For the first time in forever, it feels like I can have all of him.

And tonight, it's my turn to surprise him.

When I finish my shower, I smooth lotion over my skin. The soft scent of lavender clings to the air. I slip into a dark plum bra and panty set—simple, but powerful. I didn't buy it for him. I bought it for me. I didn't plan on wearing it tonight. I just... knew it was time. Something about tonight felt different.

I stand before the mirror and stare—not just at how I look, but at how I feel. Sexy. Confident. Alive.

I pull on a hooded sweatshirt and comfy pants, hiding the secret underneath. Then I reach for the back door, fingers curling around the cool handle. I've stepped through this door a hundred times like it meant nothing. But now? It feels like a line I keep choosing to cross—out of one life, into another.

I check on the kids one last time, their soft breathing drifting through the house like a lullaby. Then I step out into the dark.

The grass brushes my ankles, and the warm summer air wraps around me like a secret. I feel like a prowler in the night—slipping away from my life, my responsibilities, the version of myself I no longer want to be. But it all fades as I cross the yard to Jack's house.

The soft glow of his kitchen light spills onto the patio, a beacon pulling me in. Before I can knock on the door, it opens, and he stands there framed by the light. He says nothing, just steps aside, his gaze unraveling every doubt in me.

Inside, he pulls me close—his arms wrapping around me in a way I haven't felt in years. At that moment, the weight of my mixed emotions disappear. He's my home now, where I feel safe, alive, and fully seen. Without a single word, I grab his hand and lead him up the stairs. The house is silent. His kids are away for the summer. It's just us now—Jack and me, alone.

When we finally reach his bedroom, I turn to him. I kiss

him deeply, the energy between us spilling into the room, thick and consuming. "Wait here," I whisper, pushing him gently to sit on the bed.

I shut the door to the bathroom behind me and peel off my hoodie and sweatpants. In the mirror, I see her again—the woman I thought I'd lost. Radiant, full of life, beautiful. Jack has unlocked something in me that has been buried for so long. The smile reflected what my soul told me: I am becoming me again.

I turn off the bathroom light and step back into the room. The fan brushes my skin, sending a chill—not from cold, but from the vulnerability of standing bare before him, nothing hidden.

His eyes find mine—intense, unwavering. Slowly, his eyes scan my body, taking me in. By his look, I can tell it isn't just my body he sees; it is my heart, my mind, and my soul. His intense expression tells the story and says everything words can't: excitement, yearning, desire, and an unspoken hunger that mirrors my own.

I stroll toward him through the dimly lit room, my eyes lock on him, watching how his breath grows heavier with each step I take. I want, no, need him, all of him, forever. When his strong arms pull me close, his hands move over my body, his touch sensual, igniting something deep within me. Our lips collide again, and between kisses he breathes, "You're intoxicating."

His words unravel the tension inside me, melting my body into his. With a newfound surge of confidence, I push him back onto the bed, tug his shirt over his head. I kneel down and unbutton his pants, slip them down to his ankles, and off. I want to feel all of him, every inch, to pull him closer until there is no space between us. I want his warmth, strength, and presence to consume me. I want us to become one.

For the first time, I wonder what would happen if someone found out. Not just about the affair, but about the way I feel. This isn't casual anymore. This is real.

Later, around 2 a.m., we move down the stairs—his touch still etched on my skin, warmth blooming in my veins. The intimacy of our moment wraps me like a blanket. But we hear a loud bang from the first floor that sounds like a door slamming. It shatters the quiet moment, freezing us both in place.

My heart settles in my throat as Jack instinctively moves closer toward the noise, his arm brushing mine as he gently nudges me back behind him.

"Stay here," he whispers, his voice low and confident.

My hand tightens on the railing, and every muscle in my body tenses as I watch him move methodically down the stairs. His shoulders are square, his posture protective, and he radiates strength and vigilance. The silence stretches unbearably, and my senses are fully aware, broken only by the hum of the air conditioner.

"Jack?" I call softly, my voice trembling and barely audible over my heart pounding in my chest.

"It's okay," he replies, his tone steady but still alert. He disappears around the corner, leaving me alone in the dim light of the staircase. My mind is in overdrive, conjuring every terrifying possibility, each worse than the last.

When he finally reappears at the stairs, his expression has changed, the tension melting into something softer, almost sheepish.

"Dishwasher," he says, laughter threading through his voice. "Sounded like it choked on a spoon."

Instant relief hits me all at once, rushing through my body in a surge and bubbling up as laughter I can't hold back. The absolute absurdity of the moment shatters the tension in the room, and soon, we are both laughing so hard tears are spilling from our eyes.

"I thought I was going to have a heart attack," I say, wiping at my cheeks, still shaking from both fear and disbelief. Jack grins, shaking his head. "I thought we were about to face a full-blown home invasion." He takes a step closer, his smile softening as he reaches for my hand. "Guess I'll have to do better next time."

His words stir something deep within me, reaching far beyond the laughter. It fills the empty spaces I'd forgotten to notice, places I didn't know I needed someone else to fill. "You did just fine," I murmur, my voice quiet now, touched with vulnerability.

At that moment, I understand something I haven't before. To Jack, I am not just someone he wants. I am someone he cares for, someone he would protect without hesitation. And in that realization, I feel safe in a way I haven't felt in years. With him, I am more than cared for; I am cherished. And I know, without question, that he will do anything to keep me safe.

Chapter Twenty-Three

For almost two weeks now, my nights have followed the same rhythm—kids to bed, doors locked, heart racing, and two doors down to Jack. Every day, I ask myself if I am doing the right thing, and I tell myself to stop. My brain wants me to stop, but my heart won't let me. Each night, I find myself wrapped in his arms, growing closer and closer to him. I hope he feels the same way.

Tonight, the room feels warm, not just from the heat of his body or the electricity in his touch, but something more, like our hearts radiate out and raise the bedroom's temperature. The warmth around me presses in like a weighted blanket—heavy with meaning, but somehow still comforting.

As I lay tangled in the sheets, pillows strewn across the floor, my skin hums with lingering warmth, my breath still unsteady. I turn to him, watching the slow rise and fall of his chest, the beads of sweat on his forehead. With each encounter, we move together more effortlessly, trust weaving between us like an unspoken promise. Every time feels more natural, and just when I think it can't get better, it does. The silence between us stretches, thick with meaning. Not uncomfortable. Not yet.

I turn my head to look at him, the fingers of my left hand tracing over his chest down to his belly button. Who is this man? Why has he come into my life? Why am I falling so hard? He looks so satisfied, so at ease, unguarded in the dim light of his bedroom. It is a rare sight, one that makes my chest tighten unexpectedly.

When he finally rolls in my direction, our eyes meet, and in that moment, I feel like I've known him far longer than a few months. It is as if he'd always been there, woven into the fabric of my life, even though I know that isn't true. I have trouble imagining my life before him as if he'd always been present.

"You're quiet," I murmur, letting my fingers draw lazy circles over the rise and fall of his chest, needing his silence to end before it fills the room with worry. "What's spinning around in that head of yours?"

"I was married for six years. We dated for two before that," he says, his voice low. "But I never felt this. Not like this."

He pauses, and I feel his heartbeat shift under my hand. "I don't know what it says about me… or about her. But with you, it's like I can finally breathe."

Jack takes a breath, his gaze searching mine, the weight of his truth hanging between us. Then, with all sincerity, he says, "I love you."

His voice wavers, soft but sure—and I hear everything he's not saying, too. He isn't just saying it, but he is hoping I don't run from it.

No one has ever said it like that, not with tenderness, not with truth.

His words fill the room with a vibrant energy, shattering

the silence with an impact that vibrates deep within me.

My body freezes, my breath catches in my throat, and for a moment, I'm not sure if I've heard him correctly. But the look on his face, the vulnerability in his eyes, leaves no room for doubt.

"What?" I manage to whisper, my voice barely audible.

Jack exhales deeply, sits up, and runs his hand through his hair. "I mean it," he mutters, more to himself than to me.

"Did you mean to say that?"

"I did."

His words press against my mind like a heavy weight, unwilling to let me breathe. I sit up, clutching the sheet like armor, like maybe fabric could protect me from words I'm not ready to face. Thoughts race around in my mind, a tangled mess of shock, fear, and something I can't quite name.

"Jack..." my voice trails off, unsure what to say. I didn't anticipate him ever saying this or ever crossing this line.

"I know," he says quickly, his voice tinged with a slight frustration, though it seems more directed at himself than towards me. "I shouldn't have said that. I didn't mean to put that on you."

My heart aches at the conflict etched across his face. I can see the pain and the uncertainty but also the truth. I know he means it, but I don't say it back. And I can sense that it hurt him. Maybe I feel that way, too; perhaps I do love him, but it scares me more than anything. I must leave now.

"I need to go," I say suddenly, the words tumbling out before I can stop them.

He just stares at me, his expression shifts from regret to hurt. "Ella…"

I cut him off before he can continue. "I just... I need some time to think," I say, easing myself out of his bed and gathering my clothes. My hands tremble as I get dressed. I do not look at him, unable to face my emotions.

By the time I turn back around, fully dressed, he stands only a few feet away, arms crossed over his chest, his jaw clenched like stone. It feels like time stands still, and we just stare at each other for a moment. The air between us is thick and heavy, with the weight of unspoken words.

"I'm sorry," I reply softly, my voice cracking under the pressure.

Jack shakes his head, a nervous laugh escapes his lips. "Don't apologize. I shouldn't have put you in this position."

I want to say anything to ease the tension and make sense of the whirlwind of emotions threatening to consume me, but I can't muster the strength. I open my mouth, but no words come out. So I just turn and leave the room, my heart pounding as I descend the stairs and slip out the back door into the cool night air.

Back home, I pace. I wash my face. I check on the kids even though I already know they're fine. The silence is unbearable. I sit on the edge of the couch, phone clutched in both hands—but I don't text him. I can't. Not yet.

What if I broke something? What if that look in his eyes was the beginning of goodbye?

He loves me.

I replay the words, the way his voice cracked, the weight in his eyes. My hands tremble—not from cold, but from the quiet wreckage of what just happened. As much as I want to bury it, I know part of me feels it, too. Something deep. Something I'm not ready to name.

I glance at the watch on my left wrist, it's 2:24 a.m.. The house is completely silent, the kids asleep, the faint white noise of the air conditioner in the background. Usually, the quiet soothed the turmoil inside, but tonight, it feels oppressive, the weight of my choices pressing down on me.

When the emotions finally subside, I feel disappointed in myself. I want to call Jack, to explain, to make him understand that I didn't run because of him but because of me. What would I even say? That I am scared? That I can't handle the depth of what is happening between us?

At that moment, my phone buzzes on the counter. I hope it isn't Jack. How will I handle this? I pick it up slowly, almost deciding to just ignore it. It is him.

Jack: *Midnight snack? Potato skins.*

I quickly type back, a smile already forming on my face.

Me: *What?*

Jack: I'm making some potato skins. Want some? I am hungry and figured you might be too.

I can practically smell the melted cheese and bacon before I even reply.

My phone is still in my hand when the message comes through. I read it twice, heart twisting. Maybe this is how he reaches for me, through humor, through warmth, through snacks at midnight. I hesitate for a second, hovering near the door. Not because I don't want to see him, but because I already know I'll fall a little harder the second I do.

Me: *Yes, I want some.*

Shortly after, he texts back:

Jack: *Omw!*

Minutes later, he appears on my back porch, quietly opening and closing the metal screen door, a white dinner plate in his hands. "Here," he says with a tiny grin, his face soft and different from how it had looked in the bedroom just twenty minutes earlier.

"Thanks," I manage to say.

"Ella, it's okay. Really," he says quietly. His hands cup my face, and he kisses me softly. Then, without another word, he turns and starts out the door, leaving me alone to face my thoughts.

I freeze on the porch, my feet rooted to the concrete, watching him walk away. Something stirs deep inside me, aching with a longing I didn't know I had. It comes from a place in my heart I haven't touched in years—ache, fire, and surrender.

"Jack! Wait," I call out, the words escape before I can stop them. He stops immediately, turns back toward me, and steps through the screen door again. Our eyes meet as I set the plate on a nearby plastic picnic table. His arms reach for me, and mine for him. He pulls me close and kisses me hard and deeper than ever before. I look into his eyes, and my walls shatter.

The words scare me even as they leave my lips. But the second they're out, I know; I mean them.

"I love you too," I whisper, pulling him close as the truth settles between us.

Chapter Twenty-Four

In the days following, after Jack and I admitted the truth that we'd been avoiding, the pull between us only deepened, and the tension inside me grows with every hour. Nathan's trip ends soon. I should be counting the hours, dreading his return—but all I feel is panic. Panic that the blur of these past two weeks with Jack is about to break apart. Panic that everything I've tasted, everything I've let myself feel, is about to end. But with every stolen moment, the weight of what I'm risking grows heavier, pressing down like a storm I can't outrun.

The kids' laughter fills the house, but each burst stings like a needle, the guilt so sharp it steals my breath. They don't know that their world is teetering on the edge of something irreversible, on the brink of shattering. The foundation they trust—the one I built with Nathan—is on the verge of cracking

Late one afternoon, as I watch the kids play in the yard, Nora runs over to me, her tiny arms wrapping around my waist, her head pressing into my stomach. "I love you, Mama," she says, her voice so pure, so untainted by the world. Her love is pure. Undemanding. But I feel like a stranger in my own skin, like I've cracked something open I can't glue back together. If she knew the truth, would she still run to me like this? The weight of my choices pressing down on me, suffocating.

That last night with Jack keeps creeping into my thoughts, stealing my focus. It is becoming something I can't control. Nathan is coming back any day now. *Would he sense what has changed in me? Would he see through me, through my walls, and find the truth?*

Every night, I tell myself it will be the last time. The last time I let myself fall so completely into this. But the promise to myself is always shattered, undone by the pull, the desire, the ache of my need for him. No matter how many times I swear I'll stop, I find myself back in his bed, caught in a force I can't resist.

During the daytime, though, it is different. In the sun's harsh light, my doubts come creeping in, sharp and accusatory. How can I be sure he loves me? Why am I doing this? Why am I risking everything? These thoughts play on repeat in my head, louder each time, demanding answers I don't have.

I think of Nathan folding laundry and reading to the kids, something he'd begun to do in the days before he left, and those questions twist inside me. How can I keep betraying this life we'd built? But when night falls, the doubts soften, fading into whispers in the corners of my mind. And as the stars appear, these whispers are swallowed entirely by the magnetic pull toward Jack. It's as though I can't breathe unless I'm with him.

Jack looks at me like he sees all of me, the parts I keep hidden, the ones I forgot existed. When I am in his arms, the weight of my world lifts, replaced by a safety I haven't felt in years. He sees me in ways Nathan never has. With Jack, I am not just a wife or a mother. I feel beautiful, desirable, and alive.

And yet, even as I radiate under his touch, guilt lingers at the edges of my mind, a constant shadow threatening to shatter the fragile bubble we've created.

It is the kids' faces that haunt me most. They have no idea what is happening to me. Sometimes, their innocent words pierce through me, sharp and unrelenting. While playing at the park this afternoon, Nora runs over and asks, "Why are you so happy, Mommy? Did Daddy do something nice?"

Her question catches me off guard, and I can't find my voice for a moment. How can I explain that my happiness isn't coming from her father? That it isn't born from the family we've made together but from someone who stands just outside of it. Instead, I smile and say, "Mommy's just having a good day." The lie tastes bitter on my tongue.

Nathan had started trying before he left. He helped around the house, cooked dinners some nights, and even played with the kids more, without me asking. At first, I dismissed it. Too little, too late. The cracks ran too deep for a fresh coat of paint to matter. But the timing nags at me.

Where was this effort when I was crying myself to sleep day after day? Where was he when I needed him—not as a co-parent, not as a roommate, but as a partner? Now, after I've finally found something real, something that makes me feel alive again, he wants to change? It feels like he is only trying because he senses I am already slipping away. And I hate that. I hate that he waited until I was gone to notice I was missing.

The thought leaves me hollow. If Nathan is changing because of Jack, is it really change, or just a desperate attempt to hold on to something he thought he'd already secured? And if that is true, am I stealing something from him…or did he throw it away long ago?

The thought of Nathan finding out terrifies me. Not for me, but for the kids. They adore their father, even with all his flaws, and the idea of tearing their world apart feels unbearable. But on the other hand, the fear of losing Jack is just as consuming. He's not just an affair or a fleeting escape. He is more than that. He sees me in ways I don't even see myself. That connection, the way he understands me without me explaining, is as essential as air. Would I dare give that up?

Every day feels like a tightrope walk, balancing two worlds, trying to keep them from colliding. In contrast, my heart and my mind pull me in opposite directions. At home, I do what I have to do, cook meals, help with homework, fold laundry. I pour myself into being the mother my kids need and the mother I think I still am. But as the clock ticks closer to bedtime, my resolve always crumbles. My hands tremble as I tuck the kids in, knowing that within the hour, I'll be slipping out the back door again.

One evening, just before Nathan left for his work trip, I stood at the kitchen sink, washing dishes, when I felt him standing behind me. He wrapped his arms around my waist. I stiffened, instinctively rolling my eyes, unable to hide my irritation. The gesture was so out of character it startled me. "You've seemed different lately," he said, his voice soft, tinged with curiosity. "Happier." I forced a smile, my heart pounding in my chest. "I guess I've just been feeling good lately," I said, praying he wouldn't ask any more questions. His arms lingered longer than I hoped, and when he finally let go, he walked away. But his words stayed with me. Was he noticing the cracks? Could he feel me slipping away from him?

That night, as I stand by the back door, I don't open it. Not yet. My hand just rests on the knob, caught between two lives. I don't know how many more times I can walk through it before something—someone—breaks. As I walk to Jack's house, the guilt is heavier than ever. I tell myself it will only be for a little while, that I'll keep things simple. But when Jack opens the door, pulls me close, I lose all sense of control. All my resolve shatters in his arms. The doubts fade, replaced by warmth and a passion I can't deny.

"You seem distant tonight." Jack's voice carries a note of concern as we lay together, our legs tangled beneath the sheets. The soft glow of candlelight casts shadows on the walls.

"I'm fine," I lie, brushing a hand against his cheek. But he doesn't buy it.

He always knows when something is off. "You don't have to pretend with me," he says, his voice soft but unwavering. "Talk to me. I'm here for you."

I hesitate. The words catch in my throat, refusing to surface. How can I possibly explain the war raging inside me? How can I make him understand the guilt, the fear, the way my heart feels torn in two every time I leave for his house? But Jack has a way of looking at me that makes it impossible to hide, and so, for the first time, I let the truth spill out.

"I'm scared, Jack," I whisper. "I'm scared of losing my family and what Nathan and I have built. And I'm terrified of hurting the kids. I don't know what this means for us."

He cups my face gently, his eyes searching mine.

"I'd never want to take you away from them," he says. "But I can't pretend I don't want you. All of you. All the time."

He pauses, his eyes darkening with something deeper.

"Every time you leave…" He exhales, as if the weight of it is crushing him. "...I feel like you're slipping further away."

He shifts beside me, and after a long silence, adds, "There's something else I should probably tell you."

I look over at him, wary. "What is it?"

“I got promoted. Regional Finance Director. But it’s in Bayridge—three hours west.”

The air leaves my lungs.

"When?"

"A couple months. Maybe less. I wanted to tell you sooner, but I didn’t want to scare you off."

I sit up slowly, the words heavy in my chest. "So everything’s changing. Again."

Jack nods. "Yeah. But I’m not walking away from you. I just didn’t want this to hit you out of nowhere."

The words settle like lead between us—not an accusation, but a truth I’m not ready to face. Why now? Why does everything feel like it’s slipping through my fingers all at once?

I’m terrified. I know he means what he is saying, but I am scared of what this might mean. My life has become a tangled mess of lies, secrets, responsibilities, and expectations. And I’m not sure if I can ever untangle it enough to give him what he deserves.

How can one heart stretch between two lives? There is a war inside me, one between my head and my heart. I feel like I am being torn in two, one side holding on to being the dedicated mother and wife and the other longing to be with Jack. I want to believe I can have it all and keep my family intact while still holding on to the part of me Jack has awakened. And deep down, I know—the moment of truth is coming. The question is, when the time runs out, and the dust finally settles, who will I be holding—Jack, Nathan, or the woman I used to be?

Chapter Twenty-Five

Since Nathan returned, I've been choking on silence, buried alive inside the life I'm supposed to want. He's been home for a few days, and with every passing moment, I'm reminded of the weight of pretending…pretending I'm happy he's back, when all I feel is the strain of wearing this mask. I'd gotten used to slipping into the night to see Jack. Now, losing that freedom hits like a jolt to my system. The house isn't mine anymore, it's a cage. With Nathan home, it feels as if I am shackled to the walls of our life. I don't feel like I can breathe. Every moment with him is a performance, draining, exhausting, hollow.

It's like walking a tightrope, balancing the lie of our marriage while burying my truth beneath it. I can't look down; I can't afford to fall. If I do, everything will crash down.

Nathan doesn't notice the cracks in our relationship, or maybe he doesn't want to. He slips back into his old routines, smiling, engaging, as if nothing's shifted. But I see it now, the cracks in the veneer I once believed were solid. But I know better.

But there are moments, quick glances at my phone, the way his eyes linger when I come in late—silent questions hanging in the air. I can feel it—a shift. He's watching me more closely. That suspicion grows sharper when he leaves for work earlier than usual this evening, claiming he needs to go to the gym. He'd tried to touch me the night before, and I turned away. It was subtle but not lost on him. I know the truth. He is angry, angry because I denied him intimacy. He took it like a wound he refuses to speak about. Nathan always deflects blame, never acknowledging his part in the disintegration of our marriage. In his eyes, everything is my fault, my responsibility. And for years, I have believed it. I used to think it was because I'd failed as a wife. As a mother. This idea propels me to work harder to meet his expectations of me. But now, I am beginning to see things differently, and more clearly. The fog is starting to lift, and I am beginning to see myself differently.

My last encounter with Jack took our connection deeper than I ever imagined. It's like we're two halves of the same whole, and his love forces me to confront emotions I've buried for years—emotions I don't know how to process, but can't ignore anymore. Although it had started as a subtle undercurrent inside me, it has become a tidal wave, crashing through the walls I'd built around my heart. The intensity of what I am feeling for Jack terrifies me but also awakens me. Awakens me to who I really am deep down. Every stolen glance, every secret message, every midnight rendezvous only fans the flames of my desire for him. The danger never deters me; it fuels me, rocketing me toward the life I dream of.

☾☾☾

Later that night, the house is quiet again, the rhythmic

sound of the television in the background and kids fast asleep. I stand in the kitchen, my phone in hand, staring at the message I just received from Jack.

Jack: *I miss you and need to see you.*

My heart races as I read his words. I know it is reckless. Nathan has just returned to work, and it will only take one slip-up for everything to come crashing down. But the thought of being near Jack, of feeling the warmth of his body against mine again, is impossible to resist.

Me: *Give me about 10 minutes.*

I pull my sweatshirt over my head, fix my hair in the downstairs mirror, grab my keys, and slip out the back door. The warm night air engulfs me as I cross the yard, my heart pounding harder with each step. I scan the backs of the other houses, praying no one will see me. The risk is enormous now, and if anyone sees me, it will surely get back to Nathan, but the pull toward Jack is stronger than my fear.

When I arrive, Jack's already waiting, parked in a secluded spot near the park. His expression—relief laced with raw desire—hits me the second he sees me. He leans across the center console and pops the door open from the inside. No words. Just urgency.

As soon as I'm inside, his hands cup my face like I might break apart in front of him. His kiss is immediate, urgent, hungry, full of the tension we've both been carrying for days. It cracks something open. Everything unravels, and in its place is something undeniable. Something I can't ignore anymore.

I shift closer, drawn to the heat rolling off him. My pulse hammers. Then I see it—my hand, resting near his. The ring catches the light. Silent. Accusing.

I don't hesitate. I slide it off. No flourish. Just finality.

The soft clink as it lands in the cupholder sounds louder than it should. It's not just off my hand—it's off my heart.

Jack doesn't say anything, but I see his eyes flick to where the ring vanished. There's something in his face—something that says he saw. That he understands.

And then we're kissing again, like time is against us. Like this is the last chance we'll get.

I barely register the shift from the front seat to the back. Suddenly, I'm pressed against leather, breathless and exposed. His touch surges through me, short-circuiting thought, thickening the space between us. Our bodies tangle, and the car fills with whispers, soft laughter, skin on skin.

It's reckless. It's dangerous. And it's utterly addictive.

Time halts around us. For those precious moments, there is no Nathan, no house, no responsibilities, only Jack and me, clinging to each other as if the world might fall apart if we let go. I only consider myself and what I want, need, and desire.

A sudden spotlight slices across the windshield, blinding us.

"Jack, a light!" I say, panic rising in my throat. "Get dressed, fast."

I dash across the backseat, my heart racing as I scramble to put my clothes on. The seconds feel like hours. I freeze when I hear the low thud of a car door slamming shut. A flashlight beam suddenly lights up the backseat window. We scramble, fumbling with our clothes, my breath shallow as the beam passes by. My heart pounds in my ears.

The knock is soft but final. Tap. Tap. Tap. Each one feels like a gavel. My lungs forget how to work.

"Everything okay here?" The security guard's voice cuts through the tension. Jack rolls down the window.

"Yes, we're just talking," Jack says quickly, his voice calm but with an edge of forced ease.

The guard grins slightly, clearly unconvinced. "Alright, well, if you're still here when I get back, I'll need to see some

ID and write a report."

With that, he turns and walks away, leaving us in a nervous silence.

Jack and I just look at each other, my heart pounding through my chest, the adrenaline still coursing through me from the close call. And then, we both burst into nervous laughter. The tension in the car starts to melt away, the kind of laugh that feels too loud in the silence, but it's a relief—almost like our bodies needed a way to release all that fear and anxiety.

Jack kisses me, and it settles my nerves, the laughter still lingering between us like a shared secret. "I love you," he says, his voice still a little shaky.

"I love you too," I return, my eyes still locked on his. And in that moment, with our hearts still racing from the near miss, the fear fades. It's just him and me, our voices quieting into the space we've carved between us. The weight of everything we've just been through lingers, but for now, it feels like we're safe.

"That was close," he says breathing heavily. "Yes it was," I say. "Where did he go?"

"He's probably making his rounds, but will be back soon," Jack says.

Then my phone buzzes on the floor, a sharp jolt back to reality. I freeze, dread pooling like ice in my stomach as I reach for it, the screen lighting up in the darkness.

Nathan: *Where the hell are you?*

Panic shoots through me, my pulse races like a sprinter at the starting line. "What's going on?" "Nathan just messaged me. He's home. I have to go," I whisper, trying to maintain composure but scrambling to gather my things.

I spring from the car, lean back in and kiss Jack on the lips. "See you later," I say as our eyes meet. "Be careful," he says quietly, his tone laced with concern.

I turn and head toward the back of my house. When I get to the back door I peak inside. The hallway light is on. A pair of boots sit near the entryway, Nathan's. My stomach drops. He never leaves them there. The faint scent of his cologne still hangs in the air, sharp and unmistakable. My breath escapes me when I look up and see Nathan pacing in the living room. His arms are crossed, his expression fierce, and he clutches his phone in one hand.

"Where were you, Eliana?" His voice is cold, suspicion hanging off every word.

He only calls me that when he is really mad, and how he says it makes me feel like he thinks he is above me, like a parent. He wants a reaction, a mistake—but I won't give him either.

I reach deep inside myself and force a smile. I focus on steadying my breath and answer. "I went for a walk." Not a total lie—I did walk, at least to Jack's car and back.

He takes a step back, eyes narrowing slightly, homing in on me, and I feel the weight of his scrutiny. "Ella, are you cheating on me?"

My stomach is in knots.

Panic slaps me hard.

The ring. My fingers reach for it instinctively, but grasp only emptiness. My heart skips.

I left it. In Jack's car. In the cupholder. A choice I didn't even realize I was making until now.

And if Nathan notices?

That small, shining circle could destroy everything.

A single, damning detail away from everything unraveling. "You really think I'm cheating?" I snap, forcing calm into my voice, even as my stomach knots.

Nathan's eyes tear through me, searching for cracks in my

story. Finally, he locks eyes with me. "You are not to go out walking the neighborhood at night," he says sternly.

I stand there contemplating what to say. A fire rises inside me, scorching my insides and spilling out: "You don't own me, Nathan. You never did. I just didn't see it—until now."

The look on his face is priceless. I've waited so long to say something like that—to finally speak my truth. I don't know what came over me.

He just stares at me with a deer in headlights kind of look and scoffs. "I'm going to bed. We will talk about this tomorrow." He turns and starts to walk away, muffles over his shoulder, "Who are you?"

I step into the bathroom and catch my reflection. The woman staring back is a stranger. Who have I become? What am I turning into? There's a spark inside me—quiet, but growing. It feels ancient and new all at once.

I leave the bathroom and make my way to the kitchen, leaning against the counter for support. Relief floods me, but my legs tremble under everything that's just unfolded. In my mind, the keys on the bedside table linger, a silent reminder of how close I came to being found out.

I grab my phone, fingers shaking as I type. My heart pounds. I know he's probably worried—hell, so am I.

Me: *Is my wedding ring in your car?*

Jack: *Yes. How can I get it to you?*

Me: *I'll grab it in the morning somehow.*

Jack: *I was wondering if you were ok.*

Me: *Oh yes. I told him I was walking the neighborhood. Don't worry—it's handled.*

Jack: *Wait, you told him you were out walking at this hour?*

Me: *Yes, I mean, what I said was technically true.*

Jack: *Lol. You're crazy.*

His words tug at my heart, pulling a smile and a soft laugh

from me.

Me: *Crazy for you. Goodnight, Jack.*

Jack: *Goodnight.*

When I finally crawl into bed, I stare at the ceiling like it holds the answers I can't find inside myself. The weight of it all settles on my chest, heavy and unmoving. I can't keep this up much longer—not like this. The lies are stacking, the cracks widening. But no matter how much I try to convince myself to stop, the thought of giving up Jack feels like trading oxygen for air. He doesn't just make me feel alive—he reminds me that I still am.

Chapter Twenty-Six

For nearly a week after almost getting caught by the security guard—and then Nathan—things feel suffocating. Jack and I keep our distance, choosing safety over desire for as long as we can. Each day seems to grow heavier; the pull in Jack's direction becomes impossible to ignore like gravity is conspiring against me. My thoughts spiral. I reach for my phone—Maya. She's always been my anchor in moments like this, not just for spilling the drama of my life, but to help me find my footing when my mind is caught in the whirlwind of Jack.

I scroll to her name and tap the screen. She picks up almost immediately.

"Hey, girl!" she says, her voice bright and familiar.

"Hey, how are you?" I ask, grateful to hear her voice and feel her energy.

"I'm great! Just chilling before work tonight. What's new with you? Still seeing Jack?" Her question lands with the ease of someone who already knows the answer.

"I am," I admit, a nervous laugh bubbling up. "And... we

almost got caught hooking up in his car. A security guard walked up."

"What? Are you serious?" Her tone sharpens, concern cutting through the static. "Ella, be careful. You might need to lay low for a bit—you are so lucky."

"I was," I say, the memory still fresh. "I actually thought we were caught, and Nathan started calling my phone when he got home. I made it home after he was already there."

"Wow," she says, her voice thick with disbelief. "How did he react? What did you tell him?"

"I told him I was out walking," I say, my tone light, trying to downplay it.

"So… you told him you were walking?" she repeats, disbelief giving way to concern.

"Yes," I admit with a slight giggle. "It's not like I lied—I did walk. To Jack's car and back."

"And Nathan?" she asks, not letting me off the hook.

"He wasn't happy, of course. He scolded me, then walked off to bed. But…" I pause, cringing at the memory, "I left my wedding ring in Jack's car."

Maya sighs—the kind that straddles a laugh and a lecture. "So, a lot has happened since we last talked, huh? I'm guessing you and Jack are keeping your distance some now?"

"We are," I say, though the longing in my voice betrays me. "But I hope to see him soon. It's been almost a week."

"Ella…" Her tone softens, a mix of caution and care. "Please be careful. You don't need Nathan furious, the kids finding out, or more arguments in your house."

"I know," I say, though the words feel hollow. "I'll be more careful. But…No matter how I try—I can't stay away from Jack. I have to see him."

"I get it," she says, her voice understanding but firm. "But please, please be more careful."

We stay on the phone a while longer, shifting to lighter topics. Maya tells me about a guy she's been dating and how good things are going between them. They've been on a few dates, and he's even been staying over at her house. Her happiness is infectious, and as we laugh and share stories, I feel a swell of pride for her. She deserves every ounce of joy she is finding.

When we hang up, my heart feels lighter, my thoughts quieter. Maya has that effect on me—like she can still the chaos, even for a little while.

But the calm never lasts. The pull toward Jack is relentless, growing stronger with every passing hour. It feels like an eternity, and I think I might crumble under the weight of it. The ache in my chest is constant, unrelenting, especially in the stillness of the night when the house is dark and suffocatingly quiet. Sleep evades me, thoughts tangle in a restless loop. I can't focus, can't breathe. I just want to see him.

The quiet of the house presses in. The kids' soft breathing, the hum of the fridge—none of it soothes me anymore. When Jack's text buzzes through the silence, it's like breath after drowning.

Jack: *I need to see you. Meet me at the gazebo.*

I didn't think. I didn't hesitate.

Me: *Give me 20 minutes.*

The kids were already asleep and had been for at least an hour. We'd spent the evening watching an animated movie and stuffing our faces with popcorn after dinner. Lately, they have been more needy than usual, as if they can sense the growing tension between Nathan and me. At one point, all three of them piled on top of me on the couch, snuggling in so tightly that I thought I might not make it out alive. I wanted to hold onto that moment, their warmth surrounding me, but it didn't stop the ache. It didn't stop the pull toward Jack.

The second my feet hit the porch, my heart kicks up. The anticipation is unbearable. I promise myself I won't stay long. I will be in and out before Nathan even has a chance to beat me back home.

When I arrive, Jack stands looking out over the water, his head tilted upward. What is he doing?

As I get closer, I follow his gaze. The moon. The full moon. Its bright, otherworldly glow lights up the night sky, casting everything in silver.

"Wow," I whisper, completely mesmerized.

Jack doesn't speak. He turns, pulls me into him, his arm locking around my waist. In one fluid motion, he kisses me under the moonlight—wild, perfect, and spontaneous, like something out of a dream. Before I know it, he's spinning me toward the wooden structure, but not before I steal one last glance at that moon, storing it somewhere deep inside me.

The moonlight brushes his cheekbones in silver as the scent of the river rises around us—earthy and damp, layered with the faint sweetness of blooming honeysuckle and the musk of wet stone. Inside the gazebo, tea light candles flicker around a blanket he's laid out just for us.

"Jack… what's this?" I whisper.

"I like surprising you," he says with a chuckle.

Before I can catch my breath, his lips find mine. The kiss is hungry, desperate—no room for doubt or second-guessing. I don't care.

We don't make it one step further. My pants are down before I register the motion; my underwear quickly follows. The unmistakable clink of his belt buckle hits the wood floor. His lips crash into mine again, wild and urgent, as his hands move over me like he's trying to memorize every inch.

The blanket beneath us is soft but coarse around the edges, like it's soaked in sunlight and forgotten memories—

grounding me, anchoring me, even as the rest of the world slips away. Our bodies sync beneath the full moon's glow.

A bark snaps us back. "Jack—there's a dog," I whisper. "Someone's coming, hurry," he responds. We both quickly slip on our jeans and slide out of the gazebo into the bushes close by. We are snickering like school kids. My senses heightened, I peer over the bush to see a man with a dog on a leash. Must be out for a late-night walk.

Then my phone buzzes in my pocket.

The sound echoes sharply in the dark silence, snatching me back to reality. I freeze, dread pooling like ice in my stomach as I reach for it, the screen lighting up in the darkness.

Nathan: *On my way home. Be there in 10.*

Panic grips me. My hands shake as I quickly type a response.

Me: *Okay, drive safe.*

"I have to go," I whisper, my voice frantic as I start putting on the rest of my clothes, my fingers fumbling as I pull on my shirt.

Jack stands there, watching me with a calmness I can't understand. "He's on his way," I repeat, panicking.

Jack nods. His voice is steady, but his eyes betray the tension. "What about the guy with the dog," he says, grabbing my jacket and handing it to me.

He moves first, checking for options. I wait, hovering in the dark space, holding my breath as I hear him step around the bush. When Jack returns, his expression is tense. "The man isn't far away and if he catches us," he whispers. "It could be trouble"

"Distract him," I whisper. "I have to leave—now."

Jack's jaw tightens as he thinks. Then, with a calm I can't comprehend, he says, "Wait here."

"What are you doing?" I hiss, grabbing his arm.

"Trust me," he says firmly, his tone leaving no room for argument.

From the safety of the bush, I watch nervously as Jack approaches the man. He greets him casually, striking up a conversation as if it was the most natural thing in the world. I can't hear what they are saying, but soon the man laughs, putting his phone away and giving Jack his full attention.

Then Jack calls out, "Have you seen the view from down there! You've got to see this—it's amazing, especially when the moon is full."

The man walks alongside Jack and within seconds, their laughter carries faintly through the night air. Jack keeps talking, animated and relaxed like a seasoned actor, keeping his audience captivated.

I don't wait to see more. I slip out from behind cover, moving quickly and quietly as I glide across the grass. My heart races as I reach my back porch and grab the doorknob, ready to slip inside. But just as I am about to open the glass back door, I see the front door swinging inward.

Nathan.

I peer through the back door glass and freeze as he steps into the front door. No cover. My mind scrambles for a story.

I sit down quickly in a nearby chair, pulling out my phone and pretending to be mid-conversation. This isn't who I was. But maybe that's the point. Maybe I didn't want to go back to who I was. Soon, I hear the back door deadbolt unlock, and Nathan peers out. Oh my god, I forgot I locked the back door when I left. Did he notice?

"Hey, what are you doing out here?" Nathan asks, his voice laced with curiosity.

He steps out slowly, his eyes scanning the porch. "Maya again?" he asks, but his voice is too calm, like he's testing me.

"It's getting late for girl talk, don't you think?" he asks, too casually, but his eyes linger a beat too long. "You two sure talk a lot lately." With that, he returns to the house, the sound of the refrigerator door opening soon follows.

I let out a shaky breath, my hands still trembling. I stay there for a moment longer, pretending to finish my fake conversation, the night air cooling my burning skin. My heart pounds as I finally stand up and slip inside the house, locking the door behind me.

That's when I realize—I'm not wearing any underwear. My stomach twists briefly before I smile, suddenly remembering they were probably on the floor of the gazebo. I'd risked everything tonight. One wrong move, and it wouldn't just be Nathan—I'd lose the kids, my standing, maybe even Jack. And yet, here I was, grinning like a girl who got away with something. How long could I keep doing this? Did I leave them on purpose? Maybe I did. Whoever I am now, I like her.

Grinning, I text him.

Me: *I left my black lace underwear for you.*

His reply is almost immediate.

Jack: *I found them, and I'm keeping them as a souvenir.*

The thought of him keeping them sends a jolt through me—a reckless thrill I don't want to fight. I smile to myself, my cheeks flushed. I'm not thinking about everyone else anymore. Just me. Just him. But deep down, I know—the clock is ticking, and secrets don't stay hidden forever.

Chapter Twenty-Seven

The midday sun paints the buildings in gold, its warmth soaking into my skin as I cross the lot. I haven't been to a bookstore in so long I can't remember. After dropping Emmett off with a friend, I head to meet Jack at a quiet used bookstore downtown—his idea. Emmett's questions were relentless on the drive. "Mama, why are you so happy?" "Where are you going?" His curiosity was sweet but persistent. I told him I was happy, because he is such a good boy, and that I am going to meet a friend. It isn't a lie, but it isn't the whole truth either.

We planned this meet-up a couple of days ago. I was initially taken aback by his request but then I relented mainly because I wanted to see him. We are driving separately and meeting in the parking lot. After I park and exit the vehicle, I see him. He makes his way toward me, and I find myself counting every step. After a quick hug and kiss on the lips, we stroll across the lot together. He moves like it's just another day, like this moment isn't layered with everything we're not saying. But for me, every step feels like it could tip the balance.

After almost getting busted two different times in one week, Jack and I have been laying low again. Nathan has grown more suspicious and started ratcheting up the questions and scrutiny. This is causing problems again; the arguments have returned, and his help with household chores has been withdrawn. I am not surprised at all, and deep down, I knew it would happen. He doesn't even try to initiate intimacy anymore, and I begin to notice he is spending a lot of time in the bathroom recently. He has gone back on the day shift and requested it so he would be home at night and able to watch me more. His questions have become more prevalent, asking me who I am messaging, who I am talking to, and where I am going.

Jack opens the door with that crooked grin, his hand finding the small of my back like it belongs there. He nods toward a reading nook near the philosophy section. "Looks like the perfect hideout." He is a true gentleman. In his presence, I always feel like a woman-cherished and loved. As soon as we enter, the scent of old paper and wood polish greets me as I step inside. The bookstore is cozy and dimly lit, with narrow aisles, books on shelves that stretch from the floor to the ceiling and worn carpets that soften each footstep.

I've never been to this bookstore before, and the quiet thrill of it makes me feel almost giddy. We don't buy anything right away—we just drift. Jack guides me toward a tucked-away reading nook behind a row of worn hardcovers. He pulls out a chair for me at a small table nestled between shelves and settles across from me, scanning the room before he sits. I know he's checking the exits, the sight lines. It's instinct for him—to protect, to stay alert. And somehow, that vigilance calms me. In his presence, I feel like more than just a mother or a wife. I feel like a woman again—seen, safe, and cherished.

"What do you want to drink?" he asks, motioning toward

the small café counter tucked near the front.

"A chai latte," I say, a little too quickly. "Half sweet, if they can." The excitement in my voice sneaks out before I can temper it. He just smiles and stands, brushing his hand across my shoulder as he walks away.

I'm the one who takes care of everyone else. This—someone seeing me, noticing me—it knocks the air from my lungs. I'm the one who fills the cups, who wipes the spills, who moves through life with hands full. But with Jack, I get to exhale. It's unexpected, and I feel the gratitude settle deep.

He returns a few minutes later with two steaming mugs and a flaky pastry balanced on a napkin. "Thought we could share this," he says, sliding it toward me.

I take a sip, the warmth settling into my chest. Across from me, Jack leans back in his chair, fingers curled around his cup, his smile easy and unguarded. It feels so normal, like we've done this a hundred times. Like we're just two people enjoying a quiet afternoon.

Except we're not. Not even close.

My stomach flips. What if someone walks in? What if one of Nathan's friends—or worse, one of mine—spots us in this quiet corner of town?

My eyes scan the room, landing briefly on the café barista, then the door. My fingers toy with the edge of the napkin beneath the pastry. "Do you think anyone will see us?" I ask, my voice barely above a whisper.

Jack's gaze holds mine—steady, reassuring. "We're just having coffee," he says, his tone calm, but the corner of his mouth curves with that quiet, knowing smile. The one that says we both know it's more than that. "No one's going to look twice."

But the nervous buzz under my skin doesn't fade. This is the first time we've stepped out of the shadows—no dark houses, no late-night drives. Just daylight, coffee, and the possibility of being seen. It's electric. It's terrifying.

For a moment, the clink of mugs and the rustle of paper take up the silence. I tear off a piece of croissant, even though I'm not really hungry. I steal a glance at Jack, who's sipping his coffee with that same relaxed posture—like he belongs here, like we belong here.

He catches me watching and raises an eyebrow. "What?" he says, playful.

I shake my head, a smile tugging at my lips. "Nothing. It's just… this feels surreal."

Jack leans in, elbows braced on the worn table like he's settling in for something real. "Good surreal or bad?"

My smile softens. I look down at my coffee, the steam curling between us. "Both."

We fall into a rhythm then, passing soft remarks and inside jokes between bites and sips. The kind of ease that usually takes years feels natural with him.

"Next time, you're choosing the spot," he says, his voice easy but laced with something deeper—a quiet promise wrapped in a smile.

After we finish our drinks, we don't leave. Instead, we drift deeper into the aisles, our fingers brushing spines as we pass. It's quiet in the back, and there's a sense of privacy even in this public space. Jack follows a step behind me, his presence warm at my back. I pause at a shelf stacked with vintage paperbacks, running my hand over the cracked cover of a faded romance novel and until I stop suddenly, and he walks right into me, his chest against my back, hands slipping around my waist and gliding across my bare skin.

"You'd look good reading that," he murmurs, nodding toward the book in my hand.

I glance over my shoulder, eyebrows raised. "A book?"

He steps closer. "Yes. Naked. In my bed. Reading that to me."

I blush, turning back to the shelf under the guise of reading blurbs. "You're unbelievable," I mutter, but I'm smiling. I can feel it tugging at the corners of my mouth no matter how hard I try to suppress it.

We wander slowly through the aisles, trading quiet jokes and sharing titles we remember from childhood. There's a lightness between us, a sense of being outside our regular lives. For a moment, the weight of everything else lifts. Then, like a record scratch in a perfect song:

"Ella?"

The voice sends a spike of panic through me. I turn slowly, dread coiling in my stomach. Lauren stands in the aisle, clutching a tote bag and eyeing us with pointed curiosity. Her gaze flicks from me to Jack, and lingers.

I paste on a smile. "Hey, Lauren! What are you doing here?"

"Picking up a birthday gift," she says casually, though her eyes never leave Jack. "Didn't expect to see you two together."

Jack straightens from where he's been leaning against the shelf, his smile smooth, unreadable. "Hey, Lauren. Long time."

I swallow hard, trying to keep my face neutral, but inside, something shifts. A pinprick of doubt. How does she know him like that?

"You two know each other?" I ask, my voice thinner than I want it to be. I hate the crack in it, the way it gives me away.

Jack answers quickly, smoothly. "We've crossed paths a few times in the neighborhood and at the gym."

Too easy. Too rehearsed. My pulse stutters. I feel it everywhere.

Lauren's gaze snaps to mine, her smile now pure ice.

"Small world."

How often did they cross paths? What kind of paths? I can't stop the questions racing in my mind. They rise fast, like a tide pulling at everything solid inside me.

For a moment, the air between us is thick enough to drown in.

"Well," she says, hoisting her bag higher, "don't let me interrupt your... literary outing."

Jack chuckles, but there's no warmth in it. "Books and caffeine. The usual."

Lauren nods, slow and deliberate. "Sure. Good to see you, Ella." Her eyes scan Jack like she's flipping through old files, "Jack." Then she's gone, disappearing behind a shelf like a threat left unsaid.

I let out a breath I hadn't realized I was holding, but the tightness in my chest stays.

"Think she bought it?" I whisper.

Jack doesn't answer right away. His jaw is tense, eyes scanning the aisle like we're under surveillance.

"She didn't need to say it—she knows," I murmur.

He finally speaks, voice low. "She knows everything. Let's just hope she keeps it to herself."

That night, I lie in bed replaying the afternoon, not just how Jack looked at me, but how I felt: seen, wanted, whole.

Lauren.

The way she said his name. The way her eyes cut between us like she already knew. My stomach knots all over again.

How well does she know him? Did something ever happen between them? Would he tell me if it had?

The questions come in waves, unsettling everything I thought felt safe. And yet… even now, even with the unease buzzing beneath my skin, I can't shake the way he made me feel today. For a brief moment, I stepped outside the fog of my life. I felt like myself again, or maybe someone new. Someone braver.

But the fear is real. It presses against the inside of my ribs like it wants to get out.

We're falling deeper into this, into each other, and the stakes are climbing.

My phone buzzes on the nightstand.

Jack: *Was it worth it?*

I grip the phone tightly, staring at the message. So simple. So devastating.

My thumbs hover for a moment before I type:

Me: *It always is.*

I set the phone down, the screen casting a faint glow across the ceiling, then fading to black.

In the silence, Lauren's voice echoes back to me. The look in her eyes said everything her mouth didn't.

We are playing with fire. And fire always burns.

Chapter Twenty-Eight

Nathan's heavy footsteps downstairs jolt me awake. The front door creaks open, followed by muffled voices on the porch. My heart pounds as I strain to catch any discernible words. As my eyes adjust, the morning light filters through the blinds, casting shadows on the bedroom walls. I wonder who he might be talking to. Usually, I'd lie here a while longer, preparing myself for another routine day, but not today. I have to see what's going on. Then it hits me, Colby or Lauren. I jump up, throw on my clothes, and peek out the bedroom window. I can't see anyone under the covered front porch. I push my ear to the glass and hear two distinct voices, Nathan and Colby.

Whatever they're talking about is definitely making Nathan angry. I can hear the rise in his voice as the conversation wears on. I take a deep breath, knowing the tea is being spilled about Lauren seeing Jack and me at the Book store. I sit on the edge of the bed and close my eyes, preparing myself for what's coming. My heart races like a drum, yet my mind remains stone-calm, like a rock resting at the riverbed, untouched by the rushing current. What's happening to me? Usually, I would be jumping out of my skin. I stand and stroll to the bathroom, wash my face, the warmth of the water refreshing me, and brush my teeth and hair. I can hear the kids stirring from their beds and walking across the hardwood floor, their little feet making sounds. I hear the front door slam and Nathan yelling at the kids—though I'm sure they did nothing wrong, but he takes out his anger on whoever is around; it doesn't matter who you are. "Ella!" His call carries up the stairs, reaching me like a threat.

I take one last look at myself in the mirror, smile, and leave the room, ready to face him. Something sharp and resolute is rising up inside me.

Nathan doesn't look up when I enter the kitchen. His face is buried in his phone, scrolling through the latest news or some golfing forum. I grab a coffee mug, pour myself some coffee, and stand across from him, waiting for him to acknowledge me. I set my mug down with a deliberate clink when he doesn't.

"Did you yell for me?" I ask, my voice cutting through the silence. The kids went to the back porch to play.

"Yes, yes, I did. I had an interesting conversation with Colby on the front porch." He starts with an edginess in his voice that is all too common.

"What did Colby say?" I ask, my voice light and non-confrontational.

"Lauren told him she saw you and Jack yesterday at the bookstore downtown." He looks up at me when the words leave his mouth, scanning my expressions for any change.

He slams his phone down, rising abruptly. "Do you have an explanation for why my wife is having cozy bookstore dates with another man?" His voice booms as he steps closer, towering over me before I can respond.

"So what? I bumped into our neighbor while I was browsing. We chatted for a few minutes, and then he left."

"It's not nothing, Ella; you are out late into the night, walking, and now you are out with him in broad daylight; what the fuck is going on? His voice reaches levels that must have carried through the walls, probably all the way to Jack's house.

"Are we going to talk about this, or are you just going to yell at me?" I scream, echoing through the room and bouncing off the walls. Nathan takes two steps toward me, his fists balled up, raising his voice higher. "You better stay away from him, do you hear me?"

In that moment, Emmett bursts through the back door, his small frame trembling as he positions himself between us. "Daddy, don't yell at Mommy!" he cries, his voice quivering with fear and determination. A sharp ache blooms in my chest, like glass splintering beneath the surface, as I watch our four-year-old son step between us, his tiny frame trembling with courage.

"It's okay, Emmett." I kneel and wrap my arms around him, trying to calm him down. It feels like the walls of my world are cracking, the seams pulling apart with every breath as if the center of everything I've held together is finally starting to unravel.

"We need to talk!" My voice slices through the air calm and steady, like a blade honed sharp with purpose. Nathan's head tilts slightly, caught off guard by my tone—it's not the voice he's used to hearing from me.

"Talk about what exactly? You running around behind my back?"

"We need to talk about ourselves, about this, whatever we're doing." I motion between them, my hands trembling slightly, but my voice is steady.

Nathan sighs, setting his phone down. "Ella, it's too early for this."

"It's never the right time for you, is it?" I snap, surprising even myself. "You're always too tired, too busy, too...something."

He stares at me for a long moment, his expression unreadable. "What do you want me to say? That I'm sorry? Fine. I'm sorry. Is that what you need to hear?"

"No," I say, shaking my head. "What I need is for you to care. To actually want to fix this instead of brushing it off like it's just another chore on your to-do list."

Nathan sits back down in his chair, crossing his arms. "You think I don't care? I'm working to provide for this family, and you're sitting here acting like that doesn't matter."

"It's not enough, Nathan!" The words burst out of me before I can stop them. "You think just paying the bills is all it takes? What about being a husband? A father? What about actually being present?"

The tension in the room is suffocating, and the silence that follows my outburst is heavy with truth. Nathan shakes his head, muttering something as he stands and walks out of the kitchen. Moments later, I hear the front door slam and the engine crank up, tires screeching against the concrete and peeling off down the road.

I collapse into the nearest chair, the weight of the morning pressing down on me. Emmett's shoulders droop as he retreats, and Nora lingers at the doorway, her wide eyes silently pleading for reassurance I can't provide. I see it now—etched into their posture, their hesitations. The weight they carry isn't just from the noise of the morning; it's from the silence that follows, the kind that lingers long after the yelling stops. Nora peeks her head through the back door, her eyes wide with worry.

"Momma?" she asks softly.

I force a smile, my heart breaking at the sight of my daughter's concerned face. "It's okay, sweetheart. Go play with your brother. I'll make breakfast soon."

Nora nods hesitantly before retreating to the back porch and the plastic playhouse outside. A deep, shaky breath escapes me, and I run a hand through my hair. The fight with Nathan is just the beginning. I can't keep living like this, trapped in a marriage that feels more like a prison sentence than a loving partnership.

☾☾☾

Later that day, Nathan still isn't home. I reach for my phone, my fingers flying across the screen, the words flashing across my mind, and I can't type fast enough.

Me: *I can't do this anymore. It feels like I'm suffocating.*

His reply comes the moment I hit send... like he's been waiting for me.

Jack: *My kids just came in from the park. They said they heard yelling and saw Nathan screech his tires as he left your house earlier.*

Me: *Lauren told Colby she saw us at the bookstore. Of course, Colby told Nathan. And then Nathan lost it, we had a full-blown screaming match. It seems to always be something. I don't think I can keep pretending I'm happy in this marriage. I need to figure a way out.*

Jack: *If you need anything, I'm here to help. I'll do whatever I can to assist you.*

The idea of someone focusing on me makes my chest tighten, but in a good way. He feels like my anchor—not one that holds me in place, but one that keeps me from drifting away. I am tempted to take him up on the offer, but I know deep down that I need to do this on my own. I need to find the

strength now before I lose everything.
Me: *I need to figure out a plan. Divorce from him will not be easy.*
Jack: *I've been through it before, so you don't have to do it alone.*
Staring at his message, I feel warm tears streaming down my face. My mind starts racing. The thought of leaving Nathan, of starting over, of upending the children's lives feels both crazy and terrifying. But the more I think about it, the more I realize I can't stay, not for Nathan, not for the kids, not for anyone but myself.

Chapter Twenty-Nine

The blinds on the kitchen window are slightly open, letting the soft warmth of the morning sun fill the room. But the sunlight does little to melt the tension between Nathan and me. The silence is suffocating, so quiet, you can hear a pin drop or the clatter of dinner plates as I put away the dishes from last night. I can feel Nathan's gaze on me from across the room, his presence is a weight on my skin. Heavy. Unrelenting.

"Where are you headed today?" he asks sharply.

I stiffen, surprised by his words, but I don't turn to face him. "Just errands," I reply curtly. "Grocery store, maybe the bank."

Nathan's chair scrapes loudly as he stands abruptly, his boots thudding against the hardwood.

"You're always out these days," he mutters, accusation threading his voice. "These 'errands' of yours sure take their time."

I spin around, temper flaring. "If you have something to say, Nathan, just say it."

"I'm not implying anything. But what's so pressing that you're never home when I am?" he snaps.

My hands clench into fists at my sides. I'd anticipated his suspicions would escalate, but forewarning doesn't ease the sting. "I'm running errands for this family—for you, for the kids. Don't twist it into something it's not."

Nathan steps closer, his frame looming. Always the intimidator. "I don't like it," he states flatly.

"You're out all day. It doesn't sit right," he remarks.

My heart races, fear and anger rise. My face warms. My hands shake. He towers over me, but I don't flinch. "You don't get to dictate where I go or how long I'm gone," I snap back, my voice shaking despite my resolve.

His jaw tightens, his hands flexing at his sides. "We'll see about that." And with that statement, he just walks away, leaving me wondering exactly what he means.

☾☾☾

By the afternoon, I'm ready to escape the house and take the kids to the park near the gym. I gather the snacks, and drinks. When I reach for the keys on the counter, they're there, right where I left them. But when I get out to the car and turn the ignition, nothing happens. Just silence. My stomach twists.

I pop the hood and stare at the engine. A cable is pulled free, dangling like a threat, car battery missing. My breath catches.

"Nathan!" I yell, storming back into the house.

He doesn't even look up from the couch. "Something wrong?"

"You disabled my car."

He shrugs, scrolling through his phone. "I needed to talk to you. Thought this would get your attention."

"You can't be serious," I say, my voice trembling with fury. "The kids and I were going to the park. You sabotaged our car?"

"You're not going anywhere until we talk."

"You don't get to trap me here!" My voice cracks. "You don't get to decide when I can leave."

His voice drops, cold and smug. "You want freedom? Maybe you should've thought about that before sneaking around with Jack."

That's it. I grab my phone with shaking hands and dial.

"911, what's your emergency?"

"My husband disabled my car to stop me from leaving," I say, my voice steadier than I feel. "I'm home with my kids. I don't feel safe."

Nathan bolts upright. "Ella, what the hell are you doing?"

"I'm done," I say flatly. "You don't get to control me anymore."

Within twenty minutes, the police arrive at the house. The sight of the patrol car in the driveway sends a ripple of relief through me, though my hands still shake as I open the door to greet the officers. I explain the situation calmly, though my voice cracks more than once. The kids burst in from the back porch, their laughter fading when they spot the police in the living room. They freeze, their wide eyes darting between the officers and us, confusion etched on their faces. Nora breaks the silence, her voice tentative. "Why are the cops here?"

I open my mouth and close it again. Every word I reach for slips like water through my hands.

"They're just here to help."

I kneel slightly to meet her eyes, but the words won't come. My throat tightens like something heavy has settled there. I don't know what to say.

Nathan stands in the living room, his arms crossed and

jaw clenched. "This is ridiculous," he says as the officers question him. "I wasn't holding her hostage. I just wanted to talk." The officers exchange a look before one of them turns to me. "Do you have somewhere safe you can go for now?"

I hesitate, my mind racing. I think of Jack, the quiet refuge he'd offered many times before. But I can't say his name, not here, not now. "I'll stay here with the kids," I say finally. "I just need the battery put back in my car."

The officer nods and turns to Nathan. "Sir, you need to hand over the keys. Now."

Reluctantly, Nathan grabs the car battery from the garage and puts it back in the car with the officers watching.

"Sir, you need to grab some things and leave for the night," the officers say to Nathan. "Ok," Nathan says finally.

The officers stay until Nathan gathers a few things, gets into his car, and drives away. I thank them quietly, my hands still trembling as I lock the door behind them.

The moment the door clicks shut, I collapse against it; the emotions stored inside explode through the surface like a dam finally breaking after holding back too much for too long. I'd crossed a line I couldn't uncross, and the weight of it crushed me. What if this was it? What if he kicked me out? What if I had to leave with nothing but the kids and a suitcase? My heart thunders with fear, not just of Nathan's anger but of what comes next. There is no pretending anymore. No rewinding time. A part of me has hoped it wouldn't come to this, that I could stay and somehow survive it. But now? I'm not so sure I can. And what scares me more? I'm not sure I want this marriage to survive.

After the kids are in bed that night, I sit on the couch staring at my phone. I want to call Jack and tell him everything, but my body is weak, my hands numb, unable to lift the phone. I feel raw, exposed, like a wire stripped of its insulation.

My phone buzzes, and my heart leaps at seeing Jack's name on the screen.

Jack: *You okay?*

I hold the phone, thumb poised but paralyzed. What do I even say?

Me: *No, But I'm getting there.*

His reply comes almost immediately.

Jack: *I'm here if you need me.*

Me: *Don't worry, I'll figure this out.*

A single tear slips down my cheek as I read his words. For the first time in what feels like forever, I believe that things can change. That I can be free.

Chapter Thirty

Nathan and I have spent much of our time apart in the last few weeks. His boss forced him to move out; the last thing the company wants is for any negative attention. It's allowed me some much-needed space, a chance to breathe, and, most importantly, more time with Jack. I start counting the hours between texts, memorizing the way he says my name like it might be the last time. Every minute with him is a page I fold into my heart, something I'll reread just to breathe. There's an unusual pit in my stomach, hollow and breathless. I have known of his move to Baybridge and the new job for months. And with each day, the thought of him leaving squeezes tighter, like grief I can't escape. I try my best not to think about it because when I let those thoughts creep in, tears appear, streaming down my face, leaving me feeling raw and vulnerable.

I sit at the kitchen table, staring blankly into the room. A hot mug of coffee rests in front of me, untouched. The steam curls up, the scent of almond creamer soft in the air. I wrap my hands around the mug, needing to hold on to something. My thoughts spin, looping through everything I am trying to hold together and everything I can feel slipping away. Things with Nathan have unraveled completely; the more he tries to control me, the more I want out. But how can I tear our family apart? What will happen to the kids if I leave him? And now, Jack, the only thing that makes me feel whole, is leaving for Baybridge tomorrow.

A sharp pressure coils beneath my breastbone, squeezing so tight I can't tell if it's grief or just the air leaving my lungs. I decide to push those thoughts aside, to bury them deep where they can't hurt me right now. But even though I try my best, the thoughts seep back in, looming and inescapable.

Nathan called earlier this morning. His voice was softer than it had been in weeks. The house no longer vibrates with shouting, just the hollow thump of footsteps and the clink of silverware against porcelain. But he hasn't given up. He called to speak to the kids, his tone light and cheerful when they answered, but I knew what was coming the moment they handed the phone back to me.

"Ella," he said, his words heavy even through the phone. "I want to come home, Ella. For the kids… for us. Being away is killing me."

My fingers tighten around the phone, my breath grows shallow as if the walls are closing in around me again. My mind immediately darts to Jack, how he looks at me like I'm the only thing in the world that matters and how much I feel alive and at peace in his presence. But Nathan's voice carries a different kind of pull entirely, the sound of commitment and not wanting to repeat the mistakes that my mother made.

"Let me think about it… okay?" I reply, trembling. The pain isn't for me but for the kids.

After I hang up the phone, I stay at the table, frozen in place, trying to understand what I am doing. How can I do this to the kids? Could this thing with Jack and me last after he moves? Am I willing to break apart my family for a love I wasn't sure would endure?

The kids playing in the living room bring me back to the moment. Their laughter is infectious, a small comfort to the storm raging inside me. I'd always sacrificed my happiness for them. Always. Isn't that what I'm to do as a mother? But when Nathan called, I'd heard the pain in his voice, and when the kids spoke to him, I saw the light in their eyes. Can I really deny them the chance to have their family whole again?

The thought twists like a knife in my chest. I push the mug of coffee away and stand, pacing the kitchen as if movement will still my thoughts. But movement doesn't help.

☾☾☾

Later that afternoon, Jack calls, almost sensing something is wrong. His warm voice is a stark contrast to the tension that has filled my morning. "Hey baby," he says, and just those two words feel like a lifeline.

"Hey," I reply, my voice soft but strained. He senses my pain immediately.

"What's wrong?" he asks, concern threading through his words.

I hesitate. I debate internally whether to tell him about Nathan's call earlier. Jack and I have never hidden anything from each other, and I'm not about to start now.

"Nathan wants to come back home," I finally admit.

There is silence on the line, a heavy pause I can't quite describe. "And what do you want?" Jack finally asks, his voice steady but guarded. I feel like he is bracing himself for an answer he doesn't want to hear.

"I am not sure," I say, the words coming out in a rush. "I

don't know what to do. It feels like I'm split right down the middle. The kids are so happy when he calls, and I keep wondering if I'm strong enough to face what comes next alone. But then there's you, and when I'm with you, I feel like I can breathe again. Like I'm finally alive again."

"Ella," Jack says, his voice firm but gentle. "These are tough decisions; you don't have to make them now. Take the time you need. Just promise me you'll choose what's right for you. Not for him. Not even for me."

His words settle over me like a blanket, but I still twist the edge of my sleeve, tugging threads loose between my fingers.

☾☾☾

After dark, with the kids asleep, I walk outside and sit on the back porch. The bright full moon is low, and stars scatter across the sky, their light faint but constant. The cool night air blows through the screened-in porch, brushing across my skin. I think about the phone call from Nathan, the pain in his voice, Jack's impending move, the life I have now, and the one I want in the future. It's like I'm standing in the middle of a storm, hands full of fragile things, none of which I can drop, but all of which feel too heavy to hold.

My phone buzzes beside me, pulling me from my thoughts. It is Jack.

Jack: *Come over?*

I stare at the message, my fingers hovering over the keyboard. I freeze. What if this is wrong? What if saying yes now means I won't be able to say no again?

I already said goodbye once. I shouldn't need more. But I do. Maybe I need one last night to remember who I can be.

Me: *I'll be there in 10.*

When I arrive at his house, Jack is waiting on the porch,

sitting in a chair. He doesn't say anything; just opens his arms, and I walk into them and sit in his lap without hesitation. At that moment, the world fades away. It all disappears; there is no Nathan, no move, and no difficult decisions. Only Jack and me, and the steady rhythm of his heartbeat against mine.

His arms are wrapped around me, making me feel safe and allowing me to let go of the weight I am carrying. His hand rubs across my back in slow, soothing circles, and I just close my eyes and try to burn this moment into my memory. "You don't have to say anything," he whispers, kissing my head. "Just let it go and let me hold you." He holds me tighter, but his body isn't relaxed.

"I've been packing," he says quietly. "Every time I put something in a box, it feels like I'm leaving pieces of you behind."

I don't know what to say. I press my forehead to his.

"I thought this would be easier," he whispers. "I thought if I didn't make it harder for you… maybe I could survive it, too."

We sit there intertwined, his arms around my body for what feels like hours; no words, just two souls supporting each other. "Am I heavy?" I finally say, breaking the silence. "No, you're perfect." His voice is low and supportive. I turn my head toward him, my eyes lost in the hazel of his eyes, and then I kiss him. Finally, he leads me into his house, his hand slipping to intertwine with mine. The lamp in the living room provides a soft glow of light that stretches across the room, and the lit candle on the table smells faintly of pine and something distinctly Jack.

"Do you want to talk… or just be here with me?" he asks as we sit side by side on the couch, his voice hesitant, as if he doesn't want to push me away.

All I can do is shake my head no, unable to find the words

to explain what is swirling in my mind. I just lean into him, my head resting against his shoulder, "I'm scared," I finally admit, breaking the long silence.

"I know you are," he says gently. "But no matter what happens, you're not alone. You'll never be alone."

My throat tightens, lips pressed hard together—but the pressure builds, and suddenly the tears come hot and fast, no permission asked. "I don't ever want to let you go," I choke out, my voice trembling.

His arms only squeeze me tighter, his voice thick with emotion. "You never have to," he says. "No matter where I go, you're with me, Ella. You're in my heart, Ella. And no distance, no goodbye, will ever change that."

I lift my head to look at him; his face blurs through my tears. His eyes hold a quiet determination, a promise that feels like an anchor in the storm.

"I love you," I whisper, the words tumbling out before I can stop them.

A slow, bittersweet smile spreads across his face. "I love you too," he says simply, like it is the most natural thing in the world.

As we lie together that night, the reality of his departure feels more overwhelming than ever. But we push the sadness aside for a few precious hours, holding on to each other as if we can freeze time. When I finally leave, the first rays of dawn break across the horizon, painting the sky in soft shades of pink and gold, I touch the ring on my finger, spin it backward—as if I could turn back time then quietly slide it into my pocket, like a secret I'm not ready to let go.

Chapter Thirty-One

I wake to the groan of heavy tires on concrete and a low mechanical hum outside my window. My eyes, barely open, instinctively dart toward the sound. I jump out of bed, my heart pounding, and pull back the curtain to see a rental truck idling in front of Jack's house. This is it, the day I've dreaded for weeks. The sight hits like a punch. My throat clenches, eyes burning. I blink fast, but the tears win—hot, insistent streaks racing down my cheeks before I can stop them.

I collapse face-down on the bed, the grief flattening me like gravity turned cruel. The muffled footsteps in the hallway pull me out of my spiral. Nora bursts in, her small face etched with concern.

"Momma, are you okay?" she asks, her voice soft but insistent.

I can't bear for her to see me like this. I force myself to take a few deep breaths, my face buried in the damp comforter. After a moment, I turn my head and wipe the tears away with the sleeve of my sweatshirt.

"Yeah, I'm okay, honey," I manage to say, forcing a weak

smile. But the worry in her eyes tells me she isn't convinced. "Go get ready for school," I add, my voice firmer now.

She lingers for a moment before nodding and retreating down the hallway. The second she is gone, I push myself upright, my legs shaky beneath me. I drag myself into the bathroom, splash cold water on my face, and stare at my reflection. My eyes are puffy, red at the corners. Hair tangled. Lips pressed tight like they're holding in everything I haven't said.

I force myself into the routine: wash my face, get dressed, make breakfast, pack lunches, and check on Emmett. It all blurs together, a mechanical sequence of tasks meant to distract me from the ache in my chest. But nothing works. Every bite of toast I hand out, every sip of coffee I take is weighed down by the knowledge that this is the last day Jack will be here.

After breakfast, I find myself at the living room window, staring out at the moving truck like it is some kind of monster. The movers work quickly and efficiently, carrying out pieces of Jack's life and loading them into the truck. Every box and piece of furniture feels like a part of me is being packed away. With each one, he disappears a little more.

The pain twists beneath my ribs, like a vice tightening one click at a time, until I have to press a palm to my chest just to stay upright. I hurry the kids out to the car, desperate to leave, before I see him. I don't think I can keep the tears buried if I see his face. But as I buckle the kids into their seats, our eyes meet across the yard. His gaze is heavy, filled with the same pain that is tearing me apart. I stare at him for a moment; my breath catches, before I pull myself away and retreat into the sanctuary of the car.

As I back out of the driveway, my hands trembling on the wheel, I tell myself this can't be the end. It can't be. But the weight of his departure presses down on me, threatening to crush me completely.

☾☾☾

When I return home after dropping off Nora, the scene is no better. Boxes litter Jack's driveway, movers call out numbers, and he stands on the porch with a clipboard directing the chaos. I go inside, my body numb, and collapse onto the couch. Emmett plays at my feet, laughing and giggling, a distant hum muffled beneath the static of everything I'm trying not to feel. He tries to snap me out of it with hugs and toys. I fold and refold the same hand towel like it's a task that might fix something.

☾☾☾

By late afternoon, I finally gather the courage to step outside and water the plants lining the flower bed. I glance over at Jack's driveway. The movers are finishing up, their voices cutting through the stillness.

"Only a few boxes left," one of them says, the words echoing painfully in my ears.

Soon, the truck's back door slams shut, the clipboard is signed and returned to Jack, and the engine roars to life. The truck rumbles down the street, carrying him away piece by piece. I turn, but my feet feel buried in cement. My arms hang like anchors, and every step toward the house feels like I'm walking away from something I'll never get back.

I try to distract myself by throwing myself into chores with a robotic determination, laundry, dishes, vacuuming, but none of it works. The day passes in a blur, and before I know it, I am back in the car, picking up Nora from school. As we drive down our street, I see him standing on his porch, pacing, his hands stuffed into his pockets. He looks lost, the empty house around him mirroring the emptiness in my chest. My heart breaks a little more at the sight of him. All I want is to run to him, to tell him he isn't alone. But I can't. Not with the kids watching.

☾☾☾

Later that evening, as I am cleaning up from dinner, my phone buzzes on the kitchen table. I grab it, my heart skipping a beat when I see his name.

Jack: *It's all packed. The house feels hollow.*

I stare at the screen, my fingers trembling as I type back.

Me: *I know. I was watching.*

The dots appear immediately, and I hold my breath, waiting.

Jack: *I don't know what to do with myself.*

I set the phone down, gripping the table's edge as tears blur my vision. I don't reply. I can't. How can I comfort him when I can't even hold myself together?

I rush to the bathroom, locking the door behind me as the tears come pouring out. They bring me to my knees on the cold tile floor, my hands pressing to my face as I fight to hold back the sobs. I can't do this. I can't watch him leave. Tomorrow, he will be gone, and I will have to pretend that it doesn't matter.

My phone buzzes again in my pocket, and I almost ignore it. But something makes me pull it out.

Jack: *Can we see each other tonight? Just for a little while?*

My thumb hovers. Every part of me screams yes—to run, to collapse into him, to make this night last forever. But something heavier holds me back.

Me: *I can't. I want to, but I can't.*

The dots appear, disappear, and then reappear.

Jack: *Don't shut me out, Ella. I need this memory. I need you.*

The tears come harder as I type back without thinking.

Me: *And I need you..*

I stare at the screen long after his message disappears, the weight of his words settling over me like a stone.

☾☾☾

Later that night, the silence in the house is unbearable. The kids are asleep, and the only sound is the faint hum of the refrigerator. My thumb hovers. I type, then delete it. Then type again. The glow of the screen lights up the dark like a lighthouse I can't seem to reach. I can't let him leave like this. Not without one last moment together.

I type out a message before I can overthink it.

Me: *Are you awake?*

His reply is almost instantaneous.

Jack: *Yes.*

Me: *I'm coming.*

I grab a few of the snacks we'd always joked about sharing on a date night and slip out the back door. The night air is cool, the faint scent of rain lingering in the breeze. My heart pounds as I make my way to his house. When I open the door, he is waiting for me, his arms wrapping around me as I step inside.

We don't need words. In that embrace, everything we feel is laid bare. I pull back, my eyes meeting his. I see tears glistening for the first time, and they shatter something inside me.

"I'm here," I whisper, my voice trembling.

His lips find mine in a desperate and tender kiss. We lie on the floor with his old Bluetooth speaker between us, letting song after song echo off the walls of the empty room. Each track feels like a page from our story. The music wraps around us like a memory we're too afraid to speak aloud. This is our last night, and we cling to it with everything we have, letting the moments last as long as they can.

We don't talk about tomorrow. We just hold on to tonight, to each other, like it's all we've ever had.

Chapter Thirty-Two

They say time heals, but mine isn't keeping pace with the clock's steady ticking. Sometimes healing looks like chaos; sometimes, it looks like silence.

It has been almost three months since I last felt Jack's touch, saw his face, and kissed his lips. Some nights, I wake from a dream, thinking I'm in his bed, and instinctively reach for him, my hand drifting to the cold side of the sheets. But I'm not the same woman I was when he left.

A lot has changed since that night.

Nathan moved the rest of his stuff out a week later, no dramatic exit, just a slammed door and a muttered excuse about staying with a friend until things calmed down. But things never really calmed down. They just shifted. The house feels different without him—quieter, yes, but also tense in the way that only comes after a storm. The kids ask questions I don't always have answers for. I make up answers anyway.

I stay steady. For them, and maybe for myself too. I keep the routines intact, morning rushes, bedtime stories, packed lunches like muscle memory. But underneath all of it, I am beginning to breathe differently. I started working nights at a local bar & grill called The Rusty Anchor. It's not glamorous, but the steady rhythm of pouring drinks and taking orders gives me a sense of purpose. The regulars have become familiar faces, and the clatter of dishes and hum of conversation fill the void that Jack left behind. Slowly, quietly, I am finding pieces of myself in the in-between moments.

My life feels upside down, yet for the first time in years, I am finding my footing—alone.

I can't risk going to see Jack, not with Nathan watching my every move. Even though we are separated and I am preparing to file for divorce, his suspicions are already too sharp. I can't give him solid evidence of the affair, so I stay away. If he finds real proof, it will only make things more complicated for me and, more importantly, for the kids. I won't let that happen. I am their shield from the world and all the chaos happening around them.

Most days, I persevere through the chaos, holding it all together because I don't have a choice. There is no Nathan, and for now, there is no Jack—just me and the kids. And maybe that is enough. I tuck the kids in at night, then stay up an extra hour with a book in my lap and silence around me—not lonely, just... mine. The emptiness I once felt has begun to shift into something steadier—a quiet strength I didn't know I had.

Jack and I video-call most nights, sharing pieces of our days and weaving hope into the distance between us. He is still my anchor, but I am learning to stand on my own. Last night, everything shifted. Jack told me he was coming to see me. My heart soars. For the first time in weeks, I feel something other than exhaustion or anxiety, I feel hope.

Nathan had already arranged to take the kids to his mom's for a few days. Afterward, I'd drive down and let them spend time with my side of the family, but for a few precious days, it would be me and Jack. There's a flutter in my stomach, half excitement, half nerves, that just won't settle.

☾☾☾

Today is the day. Nathan is picking up the kids at 3 p.m., and Jack is supposed to arrive before I leave for my evening shift at the restaurant. I check the clock again, even though only two minutes have passed. My stomach twists, and I press a hand to it as if I can settle the fluttering from the outside. The house is already tidied up, the kids' bags packed and ready by the door. I move through the motions, packing lunches, folding laundry, straightening throw pillows, but my mind is entirely elsewhere.

I imagine his car pulling into the driveway, his smile lighting up when he sees me. I picture the moment he steps through the door, how it will feel to wrap my arms around him again, breathe him in, and finally feel grounded after months of floating. My pulse quickens. I glance in the mirror, smooth my hair, adjust my clothes—then do it all again.

But underneath the excitement, there is a sliver of fear. *What if Nathan catches wind of this? What if seeing Jack stirs up even more trouble?* My shoulders tense at the thought. Nathan isn't the type to let go quickly; I know he's been looking for reasons to make things harder on me. But then I catch myself in the mirror again, and this time, I don't look away. I stare into my eyes, seeing the woman who has held it all together and made it this far. I'm not going to let fear stop me, not anymore.

The sound of the clock ticking feels louder as the minutes creep by. I recheck my phone and reread Jack's last message: "I'll be there soon."

For the first time in months, something feels right. Jack is coming back, but I am not just waiting to be rescued. I am ready to face this next chapter, not as someone broken, but as someone who has learned how to rebuild herself. Maybe, just maybe, this visit can be the start of something better.

The hours leading up to Jack's arrival feel endless. My hands tremble as I grip the steering wheel, my foot pressing a little too hard on the gas pedal as if speeding will somehow bring him closer. The anticipation sits heavy in my chest, twisting and tightening with every passing mile. I'd hoped he'd meet me at home, but plans had shifted. His trip took longer than expected, now I'll have to meet him in the parking lot at work right before my shift starts.

My stomach churns as I pull into the lot. I park and lean back against the seat, willing myself to stay calm, but my foot taps relentlessly against the floorboard. Time has never felt slower. Why does it always drag when you are desperate for something good?

Then, his car turns the corner. My heart jolts awake, thundering so loudly that I wonder if he can hear it. As he pulls up beside me, my hands ache to touch him. The moment his door opens, I can't wait any longer. I burst out of my car, and I am in his arms before I can think.

Relief washes over me the second he holds me. His arms wrap around me tightly, grounding me in a way I haven't felt in months. It is as if every fear, every doubt, and every sleepless night has been silenced the moment our bodies meet.

"I've missed you so much," I breathe, my voice catching as I bury my face in his chest.

"I've missed you too, babe," he murmurs, his voice soft and steady, a sound I hadn't realized I'd been starving for.

I don't want to let go. I don't want to walk into work and leave him standing there. "I only have a few minutes," I whisper, hating every second that ticks by.

"I'll take what I can get," he says, pressing his lips to mine in a kiss that makes me forget where we are and what time it is.

When I finally pull away, my heart feels heavier than before. I don't want to leave him, but reality is knocking. I reach for my bag, readying myself for the shift ahead, when he slips something into my hand.

A key.

"I rented a cottage on the outskirts of town. I'll text you the address. I'll be waiting for you," he says, his eyes searching mine.

The thought of him waiting for me, of us finally having this night, gives me enough strength to walk through the bar's doors and do my job. But my mind never leaves him.

☾☾☾

By the time my shift ends, it is almost 2 a.m. The restaurant's floors are still tacky beneath my shoes, the scent of liquor and bleach clinging to my clothes as I step into the sharp night air. My pulse races as I drive toward the hotel, the key card resting on the passenger seat like a promise.

I grip the steering wheel, breath catching as I approach the hotel. Am I risking too much? Maybe. But the thought of Jack, the way he makes me feel, outweighs the fear. I'm not being reckless. I am choosing something good, something I need. After a short drive, I arrive at a cottage tucked beneath old pine trees, its porch light glowing like a quiet invitation. As I stepped inside, the scent of fresh pine and the warmth of a crackling fireplace welcomed me. The soft glow of string lights cast a golden hue over the rustic furnishings, creating a cocoon where time seemed to pause, allowing us to simply be.

I set my purse down and cross the room in seconds, climb onto the bed and into his arms. He stirs, waking just enough to pull me close, his warmth sinking into me like a balm.

"I smell like a bar," I whisper, knowing I'll need to wash the night off me.

"You smell like something I've missed for far too long," he murmurs, his lips brushing against my neck, igniting something that's been dormant for far too long.

I laugh softly, but the moment feels too fragile to last. I slip from his arms and head for the bathroom. I turn on the shower, the sound of rushing water and steam fills the small space. Before stepping inside, I steal one more kiss—the kind that leaves no question about what will come next.

I stand in the shower, warm water cascading over my body, but my thoughts are elsewhere. Why isn't he in here with me? "There's a woman waiting in his shower, warm water cascading over her, and still... no Jack."

Raising my voice just enough for him to hear.

Within moments, I feel the draft of cool air as the shower curtain slides open, and there he is, stepping in beside me. I turn to face him, wrapping my arms around his neck and pressing my lips to his. The warmth of his touch melts away the last of my irritation.

Water streams over us, cascading down our bodies as his hands find my skin, gentle but filled with hunger. He kisses me deeply, and I feel everything else fall away. The tension and noise of the world dissolve in the warmth, leaving only us.

We move together naturally, our hands exploring, our mouths searching. There are no words, only the language of touch, breath, and desire. His fingers trail down my spine, sending shivers through me despite the heat of the water.

It starts slowly, like a dance, until the rhythm builds

between us, urgent and inevitable. The steam wraps around us as tightly as our bodies do, blurring everything but this moment. We lose ourselves in each other, in the rush of need, the pull that has always been there.

When it's over, we stay close, our foreheads resting together, breath mingling in the warm mist. My heart feels full and heavy all at once as if this moment is both a beginning and an ending.

Jack steps out first, drying off and disappearing into the bedroom. I linger a moment longer beneath the water, letting it cascade over me, trying to steady my breath and soak in the last bit of warmth clinging to my skin.

When I finally emerge, a towel wrapped snugly around me, the cool air kisses my skin. He's already in bed, stretched out beneath the covers, propped up on one elbow. His eyes follow me with quiet intensity, a slow burn that sends a shiver through me.

I pause in the doorway, leaning casually against the frame, letting the silence deepen between us. The air feels heavy, charged with all the things we've never said, and everything we're still afraid to.

I have missed this, missed him. Missed us.

Months of distance seem to melt away as I cross the room and slip beneath the sheets. He doesn't speak. He doesn't have to. The way he looks at me says it all. He knows what I want, what I need.

And he gives it to me without hesitation.

Our bodies tangle together, sheets kicked aside, pillows forgotten. The space between us ceases to exist, and I feel whole for the first time in months. I love him, and I let my body show him how much.

Afterward, we lay tangled in the sheets, the air thick with warmth and the fading echoes of passion. My fingers trace lazy circles on his chest as his hand brushes against my back.

"I can't believe you're here," I murmur, my voice barely above a whisper. "I missed you so much; it felt unbearable sometimes."

"Me too," he says, his voice softer than usual. "There were nights I wanted to drop everything and drive here to see you. But I knew you needed space—to figure things out."

I prop myself up on my elbow, meeting his gaze. "I did need space. But I needed you, too. I didn't know how to balance it. I still don't."

"You're doing more than you know," he says, brushing a damp strand of hair from my face. "You're stronger than you know, Ella. You've always been strong."

Tears sting at the corners of my eyes, but I blink them back, not wanting to lose this moment to emotion. "It doesn't feel that way most days," I admit, my voice tight.

He tilts my chin up, his gaze steady and full of quiet conviction. "Then let me remind you."

My breath catches. I lean into his touch, my eyes falling closed as my heart aches with the weight of everything between us. The vulnerability in his voice steals the air from my lungs. For the first time in months, I feel safe—not just in his arms, but finally, in my own skin.

He doesn't give me time to second-guess. His lips find mine again, and everything else falls away.

"Close your eyes," he says.

I obey, smiling as I hear him rummaging through a bag. The bed dips when he sits beside me, and his voice is soft when he whispers, "Open."

I open my eyes and see a box. A velvet box.

I sit up slowly, breath caught, as I take it from his hands. When I lift the lid, the air leaves my lungs.

Inside lies a delicate silver necklace—a crescent moon

engraved with three simple words: I found you. It shimmers softly in the dim light, fragile and grounded, like a promise.

Jack's voice is low, steady. "The crescent moon is the first moon of a new cycle. It symbolizes new beginnings."

I want to respond, but my lips won't budge. My throat tightens.

He unclasps the necklace and fastens it around my neck. The cool metal tingles against my skin, anchoring me to this moment—to him.

"I missed you," he says, voice tender.

I stand before the mirror, fingers brushing the pendant where it rests at the base of my throat. I see more than a necklace—I see a woman who was broken and rebuilt herself. I touch the metal and stand taller. Not because he gave it to me, but because I finally feel like I deserve it.

Chapter Thirty-Three

Jack stays in town for a couple of days, which pass by in a blur, and then I head to my dad's house to see the kids and visit. For their sake, Nathan and I spend a few days together. It's civil, even lovely, but of course, he pulls me aside at one point to say he wants to come home and be a family again. Watching the kids light up with joy just having us all in the same room feels like taking a punch straight to the chest. Their happiness has always been my priority, but lately, I'm starting to recognize my own needs and how vital they are.

I tell Nathan no—for now. But in the quiet that follows, doubt creeps in. *Is it the right decision? Can Jack and I make a long-distance relationship work? Does he truly love me? As a mother, aren't I supposed to sacrifice my wants for the sake of my children? What if I'm the reason their family falls apart? What if divorce leaves them broken?*

☾☾☾

After I return home, the guilt weighs heavier than ever.

The kids need stability. They need their father. Can I do this alone? Right before the guilt drowns me, my phone buzzes. It's Nathan. He never misses a chance to call and talk to the kids.

"Ella, I miss you and the kids," he says the second I pick up.

"The kids miss you too," I reply, nodding as if he can see me. "I want to come home," he adds quickly. "We need to keep our family together."

"I'm not sure, Nathan," I say, closing that door before he can wedge it open. But even as I hang up, the echo of his words lingers. What if this is a mistake? What if he doesn't deserve another chance—but the kids do?

I pick up my phone and dial Maya. The phone feels heavy in my hand like calling her makes it real. She answers on the first ring.

"Hey, girl," she says with a slightly concerned tone.

"Hey," is all I can manage.

"What's wrong?" she asks.

"Nathan wants to come back," I say, my voice cracking.

"What about Jack?" she asks.

"He is waiting for me, but can it even work?" I ask her.

"No one will ever know if something can work unless you try it," Maya retorts.

"I know, but as a mother, am I not supposed to put my kids' needs above mine?" I say.

"I don't know, I'm not a mom, but I do know how happy you have been with Jack," she says, then quickly adds, "You have become more of yourself in the last few months, and maybe Jack is the reason for that."

"I know that's true; I do feel stronger now!" I say back.

"You've come so far, Ella. Don't you owe it to yourself to see where this goes?" she says.

"Well, yes, probably, but I think Nathan deserves one more chance," I try to convince her.

"Sounds like you already know what you're going to do," she says. "Just make sure you are doing it for you, and make sure you let Jack know," she adds right after.

"Okay, I will. Thanks, girl." As I hang up the phone, my chest tightens, and I feel like I can't breathe. I decide to sleep on the decision so I can settle my nerves.

☾☾☾

The decision feels made by the next day, though it feels less like a choice and more like a surrender. I grab my phone and text Jack quickly.

Me: *We need to talk when you have time.*

His reply comes almost immediately.

Jack: *Okay, I'll call on my lunch break.*

I feel the pit in my stomach, heavy and unyielding, as I read the message and put the phone down.

Me: *Okay.*

All morning, I wait by the phone, emotions swirling like a storm I can't escape. This is going to be a tough conversation, but I can't keep Jack out of the loop—we tell each other everything.

Around eleven, I decide to take the Emmett down to the river. They can burn off some energy at the park while I focus on my conversation with Jack. When we arrive, the water is restless, waves breaking and rolling into foamy whitecaps stretching across its surface. Overhead, dark clouds gather, creeping in above the buildings on the opposite shore. By eleven-thirty, Jack's video call comes through. I answer and settle onto the edge of the nearby park bench, sending Emmett back to the slide to play.

"Hey," I whisper, my voice trembling. "Can we talk?"

"Hey, Ella," Jack says, his voice soft and steady. "Of course."

I clutch the phone tighter, closing my eyes to keep the tears at bay. Finally, I take a deep breath and look at him. His eyes search mine, and I can see the worry, the sadness already taking hold.

"Jack," I start, my voice barely audible. "I've been thinking a lot about everything, about us, the kids, what's best for them."

He nods, his jaw tightening like he's bracing himself for what's coming. "Okay."

"I think... I think I need to try to make things work with Nathan," I say, my heart breaking as the words leave my lips. "For the kids."

His shoulders sag slightly, the hurt flickering across his face before he quickly masks it. "I understand. I know you're doing what you have to. You're in a tough spot, Ella. I don't blame you," he says quietly.

"You're not mad?" I ask, surprised by his calmness.

"No," he says, meeting my gaze. "I've always known how much your kids mean to you. I can't imagine how hard this decision must be. But if you think this is best for you and them, I won't stand in your way."

I expect something else—anger, jealousy, hurt. Instead, there's understanding. His kindness makes it worse. Tears slip down my cheeks, and I wipe them away.

"I don't want to lose you," I whisper.

"You're not losing me," he says, his voice steady. "I'll always love you, Ella. Always."

"I don't deserve you," I say quickly.

His eyes meet mine as he says, "You deserve more than what you've been given. Don't forget that."

My chest aches at his words, their sincerity catching me off guard. I stare at the screen, my vision blurring with warm tears.

We sit there for a long time, wrapped in the silence of our shared sadness. When we finally say goodbye, there's no anger, no fighting—just a deep, aching sorrow.

Nathan comes back that afternoon. I hear the sound of the car engine just outside before I see him. He steps out of the car, duffel bag slung over his shoulder and suitcase in his hand, looking like someone I should have known but don't anymore. The kids don't hesitate. They run to him, their laughter slicing through the tension in the air. I stand in the doorway, gripping the frame like it can hold me together. He stops at the bottom of the steps, his eyes barely meeting mine.

"Hey," he says, his voice quieter than I remember.

"Hey." The word falls flat. I can't force myself to make it sound like more.

He walks past me, the smell of his cologne brushing against me like a ghost. I don't turn around as he sets his bags down in the living room or when I hear the zipper of one suitcase open.

Dinner is normal. Too normal. The kids' laughter echoes around the table, but I can't feel it. I can't reach the joy they're swimming in. After we put them to bed, I sink into the couch, staring at the wall like it might tell me what to do next. Nathan sits at the opposite end, the space between us feeling more significant than the couch.

"I missed you," he says, his voice breaking like he isn't sure he should say it out loud. "I'm sorry. For everything."

I turn my head, searching his face for something familiar, something I can cling to. But I see someone trying to put shattered pieces back together without knowing where they belong.

He moves closer, his hand finding my thigh. "I want this to work. I want us to work," he says, brushing a strand of hair from my face.

I let him take my hand and lead me to the bedroom. I let him kiss me and touch me, and I give him the pieces of myself that feel borrowed, not mine to offer. It's mechanical—like brushing my teeth, folding laundry, or scraping food into the trash. Something you do because you're supposed to, not because it sets your soul on fire.

Afterward, I lie there in the dark, my back to him as his snores fill the room. Tears slip silently down my face, soaking the pillow. Guilt creeps up my throat, and I sit there, heavy and suffocating.

How can a woman feel guilty for sleeping with her husband?

Because it isn't about Nathan at all.

But it isn't guilt for what I've done with Nathan. It's guilt for what I feel for someone else. For Jack. For the way his words echo in my mind, steady and sure.

"You deserve more."

I think about how he looked at me when I told him Nathan was coming home. There's no anger, no accusations, just understanding. He let me go even though I can see it breaks him. And maybe that's what love is: letting someone figure out who they are without trying to control the answer.

I start to imagine a life that isn't built on obligation, a life where love doesn't feel like chains but like wings. Maybe love isn't about who needs me most—but about who sees me the clearest.

And maybe Jack is right. I do deserve more. And this time... I won't forget.

Chapter Thirty-Four

Nine days later, the walls I built just to survive finally collapse.

Why didn't Jack fight for me? Why do I want him to fight when I'm the one who told him to let me go? Maybe he thought honoring my choice was the only way to love me right. His silence wasn't indifference—it was the kindest pain I've ever known. Finally, someone who hears me. Who respects my choices. My life.

Being with Nathan feels like drowning in slow motion—each quiet dinner, every forced smile, a new weight dragging me down. Like a cinder block tied to my ankle, pulling me deeper into the darkness of my old life. The kids seem happier, but I'm disappearing piece by piece. The life I've chosen isn't a life I can live anymore.

This morning, I pack a bag, load the kids into the car, and drive south, the highway stretching endlessly ahead. My dad's house isn't the answer, but it's a place to breathe, think, and exist without Nathan's expectations pressing down on me. I have to attend a friend's wedding back home this weekend anyway, which gives me the perfect excuse to escape.

Halfway through the drive, the weight in my chest becomes unbearable. I grab my phone and hit Maya's number, balancing it on speaker as I keep my eyes on the road.

She picks up on the second ring. "Ella?"

Her voice is warm and steady, like always—but suddenly, the dam breaks. "I can't do this," My voice breaking.

"Oh, honey. What happened?"

"Everything. Nothing. I don't know." I swipe at a tear rolling down my cheek. "I left, Maya. I packed up the kids and left. I'm going to my dad's."

"Good," she says without hesitation. "You needed to get out of there. What about Nathan?"

I swallow hard. "I tried, Maya. I did. But I can't keep pretending. It's like I'm suffocating. And Jack—I can't stop thinking about him."

She's quiet for a moment, and I picture her sitting cross-legged on her couch with a glass of wine, thinking carefully before she speaks.

"You don't have to pretend anymore," she says finally. "You deserve to be happy, Ella. And if Jack is your happiness—don't let go this time. Don't let fear keep you in a place you don't belong."

Her words hit hard, knocking something loose inside me.

"What if I already lost him?" I whisper.

"Then you find him again." Her voice softens. "You've got this. And you're not alone."

Our conversation drifts to other subjects—her and the girls and everything going on in their lives. The call ends just as I pull into my dad's driveway, but Maya's words echo as I step out of the car—steadying me like a prayer. My dad opens the door before I can knock, stepping onto the porch like he's been waiting for me. All I can do is rest in his arms and fight back the tears that want to come out.

For the first time in days, no one is asking anything of me. The silence is strange, but it feels like peace.

Things with Nathan have started unraveling again—fights simmering just below the surface, spilling out in sharp words and slammed doors. Why did I think things would change? My heart is somewhere else, with someone else. And nothing I do can change that.

I don't say anything. I can't. I just stay in my dad's arms for a few minutes. His arms hold me together as I fall apart inside.

"What's wrong?" he asks, his voice low, soothing.

"I can't talk about it." My words come out broken, trembling.

He doesn't push. "I'm here when you're ready." And I know he will be.

The day passes in a blur. I settle the kids in with my dad and stepmom, get ready, and drive to the rehearsal dinner. Laughter and music swirl around me—too bright, too loud, against the storm inside. I should be happy for my friend, but I can only think about Jack.

During the maid of honor's toast, the happy couple leans into each other, and the bride's fingers trace her groom's jaw like she's memorizing him. The way he looks at her—like he's already home—makes my stomach turn over. For a heartbeat, I imagine Jack standing in a suit across from me, eyes soft and steady, like I'm the only thing he sees. That could be us. It should be. I press a napkin to my lips and pretend it's not because I'm jealous of the way she's seen. The toast is about soulmates—how the right person makes you feel more like yourself than ever before. The words strike like lightning, ripping through the wall I've tried to build around my heart. My eyes flick to the bride and groom, their hands intertwined, eyes locked like they're the only two people in the world.

I ache. Not with jealousy, but with longing—for something I know exists because I've tasted it. I see Jack's eyes in my mind, the way he looks at me like I'm everything. Like I matter. This could be our wedding—our joy—our beginning.

Instead, I'm here—watching someone else's life unfold while mine falls apart.

When I return to my dad's, the house is quiet. The kids are asleep, and Nathan has called to check on them, sparing me the tension of hearing his voice. I step onto the back porch, sinking into a lounge chair by the pool. The faint trickle of water fills the silence, steady and calm, but my mind refuses to settle.

I pull my phone from my pocket, my fingers trembling as I scroll to Jack's contact. My thumb hovers over the screen. I practice what I might say in my head, but it all sounds wrong. What if he's moved on? What if I've waited too long?

I press it.

The line rings. Once. Twice. Three times.

No answer.

I stare at the phone, thumb hovering, then type out a message: "Call me when you can." It sits there unsent for a moment before I hit send. The silence that follows is deafening.

The breath I've been holding shatters in my chest. Tears blur my vision as I drop the phone onto the table. What am I even doing? Have I pushed him too far? Have I lost him for good?

The sobs come fast and hard, shaking my whole body. I need him. I ache for him. But what if wanting him now is nothing more than wishful thinking?

An hour passes—maybe more. The phone finally buzzes, and I lunge for it, my hands trembling as Jack's name lights up the screen.

"Hello?" My voice breaks.

"Ella," he says, his voice warm and steady. "What's going on? Are you okay?"

The relief hits so hard that it almost knocks me out of my chair. "No," I whisper. "I'm not okay. I can't do this, Jack. I can't be with him. I tried, but it's not right. It's not what I want."

"Where are you?" he asks his words like an anchor.

"At my dad's. I couldn't stay there anymore." My voice shakes, but I don't care. Not with him.

"Ella…" I cut him off. "I want you, Jack. I need you."

The words hover in my throat, terrifying and impossible to hold back. My heart races so hard I wonder if it might give out.

"I love you," I whisper. The truth burns as it leaves my lips. "I've loved you for so long. And I don't care what it costs me anymore. I can't live without you."

Silence stretches, taut and heavy. When he speaks again, his voice is soft but sure. "I never stopped loving you," he says. "And I never will. If this is what you want, I'll be here. Always." The tears return, but they feel different this time. They're lighter and softer, not tears of sadness but of joy.

"Thank you," I whisper.

"Don't thank me," he says. "Just come back to me."

"I will," I say, my heart steady for the first time in weeks. "I promise."

That night, lying in bed at my dad's house, I let hope take root. I don't know exactly how—but I know I need a plan. My future is uncertain, but one thing is clear: I won't live a life built for someone else. Not anymore. I will fight for what I want, for the life I deserve. And this time, I won't let it slip away.

Chapter Thirty-Five

Two days blur past in a haze of emotions as I try to keep it together for the kids. By the third morning, reality presses in like a storm crossing an open field—impossible to outrun, and too close to ignore.

Every bag I pack feels like another weight of guilt. I'm not just loading the trunk—I'm carrying my shame, my fear, my hope for escape. I climb into the driver's seat, the kids settled in the back, wave to my dad, and dial Maya's number before pulling out of the driveway.

She picks up on the first ring. "Hey, girl. Are you okay?"

"I'm better than the last time we talked," I say, forcing my voice to sound steady.

"Are you heading back?" she asks softly.

"Yeah. I have to face things sooner or later."

"What's the plan?"

I clench the wheel, steadying my breath as I speak. "I need to tell Nathan I want to separate. That'll give me time to find a lawyer and file for divorce."

Maya is silent for a beat. "Doesn't he leave for Maryland

soon?"

"In two months."

"If he leaves quietly, maybe you won't have to light the whole place on fire." But her voice betrays her doubt, and we both know the odds of that are slim.

Tears well, and I don't even try to hide them. "I need you, Maya."

"What do you need? Whatever it is, I'm here."

"I need you and the girls to come to Eastwell tomorrow just in case things go sideways." My voice cracks, but desperation pushes through.

"We'll be there first thing in the morning."

Relief washes over me. Maya has always been steady, the one person I can count on, and hearing her confidence gives me just enough strength to keep driving.

The interstate stretches ahead, endless and empty. The hum of the tires is the only sound besides my racing thoughts. Doubt creeps in as I stare straight ahead, knuckles tight on the wheel. Can I do this? Can I look Nathan in the eye and tear our lives apart? Can I chase my heart without burning everything down?

The kids stir softly in the backseat. Their breaths ground me. I have to do this. For them. For myself. For the chance at a life that doesn't feel like drowning.

By the time I reach Eastwell, night has fallen, the shadows stretching long across the driveway from the streetlights as I pull in. I kill the engine and sit there for a moment, the weight of what waits inside pressing down on me. My phone buzzes with a message from Maya.

Maya: *We're leaving early. See you soon. Love you.*

I respond quickly, my fingers trembling.

Me: *I love you too.*

I cling to her words like a lifeline, take a deep breath, and ready myself to face him.

When I look up, Nathan's already outside—staring and waiting. The moment the car stops, the kids jump out, running straight into his arms. He looks up, testing the waters with a fragile smile. I step out, close the door behind me, and brace myself for the moment his arms wrap around me. He presses a light kiss to my head, and my stomach twists.

There's no going back now.

"The girls are coming up tomorrow," I say, making sure my voice doesn't waver.

He steps back, brows knitting. "Why?"

"I just need them here." My tone leaves no room for argument, and for once, he doesn't try. He just nods.

"Okay."

☾☾☾

Later that night, after the kids are in bed and I've showered, my phone buzzes on the bathroom counter. I wipe my hands and pick it up. Jack's name lights up the screen—a Whispyr message.

Jack: *How are you?*

Me: *I'm okay. I'm telling Nathan I want to separate.*

Jack: *When?*

Me: *Tomorrow. After the girls get here.*

Jack: That's a great plan. I hope it goes smoothly. You don't deserve any more stress.

I exhale slowly, letting his words sink in. Even from hundreds of miles away, Jack steadies me—like a lighthouse through fog.

Me: *Don't worry. I'm sure he won't do anything stupid.*

Jack: *Okay. Let me know how it goes.*

I hesitate before typing the next message, my fingers

trembling.

Me: *Jack?*

Jack: *Yes?*

Me: *I have a question.*

Jack: *Go ahead.*

Me: *Did you see anyone after we broke up?*

Jack: *No. I didn't.*

The tightness in my chest loosens, but my heart still aches.

Me: *Okay. Thanks.*

Jack: *Good luck. I love you.*

Me: *I love you too.*

The conversation ends, but the words linger. I stare at the screen, my heart torn down the middle. Tension settles over the house like fog—thick, unspoken, unavoidable. Even as he moves through the motions—brushing his teeth, turning down the bed—I can feel it. He knows something is coming.

After I finally climb into bed, my phone buzzes again. My pulse jumps, and I reach for it, careful not to wake Nathan. I check the screen.

It's Jack.

Jack: *In the stillness between now and forever,*
I will think of you—
the scent of your hair lingering like a memory,
the curve of your smile breaking through my guard,
the way your eyes unravel me with a glance.
I will remember the shape of you,
how your body molds into mine,
as if we were carved from the same breath.
The taste of your skin.
The warmth of your embrace.
The quiet shelter of your touch—
they will echo in me always.
Your words, steady as stone,

have braced me against the storm,
made me bold enough to face this world.
And your love—
your love feels otherworldly,
as if it fell from the stars...
just to find me.

Me: *Oh my God, it's beautiful.*

His words reach inside me, grabbing the strength buried deep within and pulling it to the surface. I let out a breath I hadn't realized I'd been holding. The weight that's crushed me all day lifts just a little.

I slide out of bed, grab a pillow and blanket, and pad into the living room. I won't share a bed with Nathan again. That version of me is gone. Tomorrow, I'll be ready to fight—for myself, for what I want and deserve.

I sink into the couch, clutching my phone as if it can hold me together. Before I drift off, I save the poem—a soft light I can carry into the dark.

For the first time in a long time, I don't just believe I matter. I know it, deep in my bones.

Chapter Thirty-Six

As the sun peeks through the blinds in the living room, its rays nudge me awake. I sit up, my heart racing as I reach for my phone. I remember falling asleep clutching my phone. Now it's gone—and I know instantly, something's wrong.

I throw back the blanket, searching the cushions and the floor—nothing. The creak of footsteps upstairs makes my stomach lurch. I follow the sound, rounding the corner to the staircase, and freeze.

Nathan is descending the stairs, my phone held high in his hand. His face is unreadable, but his eyes burn with something I've never seen before. My shoulders tense, hands curling at my sides.

"Why do you have my phone, Nathan?" My voice sharpens.

"Looks like I should've been checking it more often," he snaps.

"What are you talking about?" A sick heat rises in my throat.

"Why is Jack sending you love poems?" His words hit like

a slap, sharp and stinging.

The poem. The one I saved on Whispyr. My stomach churns.

"You had no right to go through my phone!" My voice comes out stronger than I expect.

"I have every right! I'm the one paying for this, Ella. What else are you hiding?" His words are forceful, but I can only hear the desperation beneath them.

I straighten my spine, forcing myself to hold his gaze. "No, Nathan. It's not yours. And neither am I." Just then, there's a knock at the door. I glance at my watch—8:05 a.m. It must be the girls. This is it. My rescue party is here.

I walk to the door, my body trembling but my resolve solid. When they see my face, Maya, Tara, and Claire stand there with coffee, donuts, and faded smiles, trying to gauge the room.

"Everything okay?" Tara asks, her voice light but her eyes scanning me.

"Yeah, everything's fine," I lie, forcing a smile.

They hug me, their warmth wrapping around me like armor. The kids barrel down the stairs, their laughter slicing through the tension.

"Aunt Maya!" Emmett's voice rings out as he throws himself into her arms.

Maya turns to Nathan, her smile friendly but her tone dipped in warning. "Hey, Nathan. Long time no see."

"Hey, you three," he says, stiff but polite. He gives them quick side hugs before disappearing into the kitchen.

Maya leans in, her voice low. "What's going on?"

My eyes meet hers, and I whisper, "I'll tell you later." We speak in some girl-coded language, and she doesn't press.

"Let's take the kids to the park," Claire suggests, her excitement sparking a frenzy of activity. It's the distraction I need. Once we get there, Nathan hovers, his eyes heavy with suspicion. I send Emmett to play tag with his dad, using the moment to spill everything.

"Jack sent me the most beautiful poem last night, and Nathan went through my phone this morning and saw it," I say, my voice shaking.

Their faces fall. Maya's eyes darken. "What now?"

"I don't know," I admit. But even as I say it, something inside me knows change is coming.

The day unfolds quietly, a rare stillness in the air. We spend a few hours at the park, the kids laughing as we catch up on each other's lives, the sun's warmth softening the edges of everything. But peace is always fragile. It can shatter without warning.

Nathan corners me in the kitchen while I'm fixing lunch, his broad frame blocking the way. I shift, trying to slide past him, but he moves too, mirroring my steps with a low chuckle vibrating in his chest.

"We need to talk," he says, his voice quieter than usual, as if he's holding something back. I push past him, plates trembling slightly in my hands, pretending I haven't heard.

After lunch, I take the kids out onto the back porch to let them play. I stand there, watching them run barefoot across the concrete, and let myself breathe. But the moment doesn't last. When I try to go back inside, Nathan is there again, leaning against the door frame, his hand gripping the knob.

"Nathan, move."

His lips curve, but there's no humor in it. "Oh, you want back in now?"

My heart stumbles. "It's my house too."

"Well, I pay for it, don't I?" he says, voice sharp enough to sting.

He finally lets me inside after he gets some satisfaction

from his actions.

Later, I have to clean Emmett's knee after a scape. There are no supplies downstairs, so I carry him upstairs, balancing him against my hip. The house feels heavier with every step. When I reach the bathroom, I can feel Nathan moving behind me, his presence closing in.

I keep my focus on Emmett, wiping his wound clean with peroxide and putting a band aid on, but when I look up, Nathan is standing in the doorway, blocking it.

"We need to talk about this." His voice snaps, the words cutting the air.

"Not right now," I say, steadying my voice as my pulse kicks against my ribs.

I step toward him, but he doesn't move. He stands in the doorway, his silhouette swallowing the light behind him.

"We need to talk about that poem," he snaps.

"Not now," I say, voice steady though my pulse is a riot.

I step toward him. He doesn't move.

"Nathan, let me out." He stays put.

"Let me out!" I scream.

"No."

"Help!" I scream, my voice splintering as I hear footsteps pounding up the stairs.

"What's wrong?" Maya appears, her eyes wide as she looks over Nathan's shoulder.

"He won't let me out of the bathroom," I say, tears threatening to break free.

"Nathan, let her by!" Maya snaps, anger hardening her words.

"Nathan, I want a separation. I want you to leave this house," I say, my voice pulling strength from the years I've spent shrinking.

"I'm not leaving, and we aren't separating." The look in

his eyes sends a chill down my spine—the kind of fear you feel when you realize someone isn't who you thought they were.

"We're calling the cops," Tara says, her voice steady as she enters the scene.

"Call them!" Nathan barks. "They won't do anything."

Tara grabs her phone, her fingers quick as she dials. Minutes later, the police arrive, crowding the tiny house. They take statements from me, the girls, and Nathan. The officers look at me closely.

"Are you scared of him?" one asks. I swallow, but the truth breaks free. "Yes."

They nod, speaking quietly to each other before making a call. After contacting Nathan's supervisor, they decide he will leave and stay with a friend for a few days to ease the tension.

But the tension doesn't ease. Heavy and sharp, it lingers long after the door shuts behind him. He's gone now, and that gives me not only time to breathe but also time to figure out my next step.

The house feels different now—emptier, but not in a bad way. It's space. Air. A beginning. And for the first time, it belongs to me.

Chapter Thirty-Seven

The past few weeks blur into late nights, heavier thoughts, and quiet survival. After everything falls apart, the girls stay with me for a few days—hovering, fussing, making sure I don't shatter the moment they leave. And maybe I need that. Nathan keeps his distance, though he still calls the kids almost every night, his voice soft and steady like he's trying to convince himself this is temporary.

Jack and I talk every day. His voice tethers me, the only solid thing as the ground keeps shifting. Being away from Nathan clears my head enough to make me face reality: I need a plan.

Step one is finding a job. I manage that many weeks ago—waitressing at a local bar and grill. It's not glamorous, but it works. Nights allow me to be with the kids while Nathan is at work during the day. And with him leaving soon, I'll need the extra cash for a security deposit and the first month's rent once I'm on my own. So, I spend my mornings scrolling through listings, imagining lives in tiny apartments with chipped paint and secondhand furniture and my nights dodging leers and fake smiles.

The money's decent, but the customers—God, the customers. Half of them don't even bother hiding their intentions, scribbling numbers on receipts like I might call. Some even leave room keys—like I'm for sale. It'd be laughable if it didn't make my skin crawl.

I tell Jack about it, of course. He plays it cool and says he understands it's just part of the job, but I hear it—the tightness in his voice, the edge that slips through no matter how hard he tries to hide it. And I hate that it bothers him, but his jealousy makes me feel warm inside, essential and cherished in a way I haven't felt before. I have to do what I need to, and I just hope he'll keep showing up.

Tonight, the house is quiet. The kids are asleep, and I collapse onto the couch, my feet aching from a double shift. The TV murmurs in the background, just noise to drown the silence., but it isn't enough to drown out the weight in my chest. I grab my phone without thinking, dialing Jack before I can talk myself out of it.

He picks up on the second ring. "Hey." His voice is soft like he's been waiting.

"Hey," I breathe, settling deeper into the couch. "You busy?"

"Never too busy for you."

The words tug at something fragile inside me, and I close my eyes. "It's one of those days where I feel like I could vanish," I say, my voice barely more than a breath..

"Tell me."

So I do. I tell Jack about the shifts and the customers and how one guy follows me to my car tonight until the manager steps in. I don't tell him how my hands shake unlocking the door or how I double-check the locks when I get home. But I don't have to. Jack hears it anyway.

"Ella, that's not good," he says, his voice tightening. "You shouldn't have to go through that alone."

"It's fine," I lie.

"No, it's not." The silence stretches between us, heavy and loaded. "You need to be careful."

"I will be."

"Promise me."

"I promise." I used to say things to keep the peace. Now, I say them because I mean them.

The words feel too small to fill the distance between us, but they ease something in him. His voice softens again. "How are the kids?"

I smile despite everything. "Good. They miss you."

"I miss them too." There's a pause, and when he speaks again, his voice is quieter. "And you?"

The question steals the air from my lungs. I should brush it off, make a joke, and keep it light. But I can't. Not with him.

"I miss you, Jack."

He exhales like he's been holding his breath. "Good. Because I can't stop thinking about you." And just like that, the ache eases, if only for a moment. Because even though everything around me feels uncertain, Jack is still there, steady and sure, pulling me back when I feel like I might drift too far.

After we hang up, I sit there for a long time, letting the quiet settle over me. The steps I'm taking force me to confront the fact that I'm not as fragile as I once thought. I've been figuring things out, one hard decision at a time, and I'm stronger than I've ever given myself credit for. It's not perfect. I'm not perfect. But I'm still standing. And that has to count for something.

☾☾☾

I wake up early the following day, and the air is still cool and damp from the night. I sip coffee at the kitchen table while the kids sleep, their soft breathing carrying through the thin walls. I think about what Jack says—how I need to be careful—and I know he's right. But I also know I can't let fear shape me anymore. I've already spent too much time shrinking myself to fit into spaces that didn't deserve me.

This morning, I decide to scroll through some rental listings. I take down addresses, check locations on local crime maps, and even make a call or two. My voice is steady when I ask about prices, deposits, and move-in dates. It's not a huge thing, but when I hang up the phone, my fingers don't shake.

☾☾☾

Later, I take the kids out for ice cream. We sit on a bench under the shade of an old oak tree, and for the first time in weeks, I laugh at something silly Emmett says. His face lights up, and I see how he's watching me. Maybe he's worried too. I reach out, brushing his hair back, and promise to keep showing up for them. For me.

That night at work, I carry myself differently. My shoulders stay back, my chin lifts, and even when another guy leaves his number, I don't flinch. I toss the receipt in the trash without a second glance. I think about Jack and how his voice steadies me, but I also think about the fire starting to burn in my chest. I'm done feeling small. Done being afraid.

I don't look over my shoulder when I lock up and head to my car. Not because I'm careless but because I'm claiming something back—my confidence, my control. It's been a long time since I've felt like this—like I'm strong.

And this time, I know it counts.

Chapter Thirty-Eight

The following week feels like a test I'm not sure I'm ready for. After getting Nora off to school, I find my familiar spot at the dining room table. Each morning begins the same—coffee, classifieds, and hopeful scribbles in my notebook that feel more like lifelines than plans. Afternoons blur into tours of places too small to hold my hopes—each one faintly scented with mildew and resignation. And the evenings—those are the hardest. Work keeps me on my feet, but my mind wanders, drifting between exhaustion and determination.

I haven't told Jack yet, but there's one apartment I can't stop thinking about. It isn't perfect—the carpet is old, and the kitchen cabinets stick when I pull them open—but there's something about the way the light pours through the living room windows that makes me feel awake and grounded. I toured it two days ago. Afterward, I submitted the application and told myself not to get too attached.

Still, I imagine us there. The kids' laughter bouncing off the walls. All of us curled up on the couch, watching movies, eating popcorn out of mismatched bowls. For the first time in weeks, it actually felt possible to picture a future not completely weighed down by everything falling apart.

But later that same day, the listing agent called. They'd gone with someone else.

I remember just sitting in the car afterward, staring at the dash. Not moving. Holding back tears. But they came anyway. It wasn't just disappointment—it was a full-body exhaustion, like hope itself had caved in. I have finally worked up the courage to tell Jack.

I wait until the kids are asleep and the house is quiet. When I call, he picks up on the first ring.

"You ok?" he says, like he already knows something is wrong.

I don't trust my voice, so I just exhale.

"Ella, what happened?"

I tell him everything: the tours, the applications, the rejections. By the time I finish, my voice is shaking, and I hate that I can't hold it together.

"I'm tired, Jack. Not just in my body—but in my bones. Every step forward feels like a fight, and I'm losing ground."

"You're making great progress," his voice is so warm, so sure, it almost makes me believe him. "You're figuring it out—one breath, one day at a time."

I close my eyes and let his words sink in. "What if it's not enough?"

"It is," he says. "You are."

I don't know how to respond, so I don't. I let the silence stretch between us until I finally feel like I can breathe again.

Our conversation continues late into the night. His laughter and voice relax me, and his words give me renewed energy.

☾☾☾

The following day, I wake up early. The house is still, and the light filtering through the blinds feels softer than usual, almost forgiving. I make coffee and sit at the table with my notebook, flipping to a blank page. And then I start over.

By noon, I have three more tours scheduled. I load up Emmett and head to the appointments. None of them are perfect, but I don't need perfect. I just need somewhere we can feel safe and start over.

The first two apartments are a bust—one smells like smoke, and the other has a broken lock on the front door that the landlord promises to fix but never seems to get around to. By the time I reach the third place, I'm ready to give up.

But then I step inside. It's a small two-bedroom house, but the floors are clean, and the windows overlook a public golf course. The kitchen has just been updated, and the cabinets don't stick when I open them. It feels right. And for the first time, I let myself hope.

I submit an application. This time, I don't get attached—just keep moving forward. When I tell Jack about it later that night, he doesn't try to reassure me. He just listens, and somehow, that's enough.

I take my mind off everything and take the kids to the park. We bring sandwiches, place a blanket on the ground, and sit under a tree with branches stretching wide and low, engulfing us in the shade. I watch them play, their laughter ringing out, and I feel something shift inside me. I'm not where I want to be, but I'm closer. And for now, that's enough.

☾☾☾

The next day, my phone rings while I'm folding laundry. It's the landlord. My heart pounds as I answer. "Ella?" he asks. "Good news. The place is yours if you want it."

I almost drop the phone. It feels like I've crossed a finish line I didn't even know I was racing toward. "Are you serious?"

He laughs. "Completely. When can you sign the paperwork?"

I schedule a time for the following morning and hang up. All I can do is sit on the couch for a moment, the laundry half-folded, my hands trembling. Then, I lay back on the sofa and let out a deep breath. I did it. I found a place for the kids and me.

Later, I call Jack to tell him the news. His voice lights up the way it always does when he's happy. "I knew you'd find something," he says. "I watched you lose everything and build it all back with kids on your hip and pain in your chest. That's strength, Ella. I'm proud of you." And I realize I'm proud of myself, too.

"Now, when I visit, I have a place to stay," he says enthusiastically. The thought of him here and with me in my place sends a bolt of electricity through me. After letting him go, I just lay there in awe of myself. I'm succeeding now and standing on my own.

☾☾☾

Over the next week, I pack boxes while the kids bounce between excitement and nervousness. Every night, I fall into bed exhausted, but it's the good kind of tired—the kind that comes from knowing I'm building something better.

Jack calls every night. He can't help physically, but his voice carries me through. When I finally get the keys and step inside our new place, I feel something I haven't felt in a long time.

Peace.

☾☾☾

When moving day finally comes a few days later, the kids are buzzing with excitement, their laughter filling the empty spaces of the house. Nathan helps me load up the moving truck with his friend. We have to be out of the house before the deadline, and the lease is under his name—so I guess he doesn't have much of a choice. When the kids and I arrive at the house and wait for the moving truck, Nora's eyes light up as she turns to me, her voice brimming with curiosity.

"Which room is mine?" she asks, scanning the layout like she's mapping out her future.

I point to the formal dining room, its bare walls and echoing floors still waiting for a purpose. "That's going to be your room," I say, hoping she won't see how shaky I feel inside.

She doesn't question it or even pause to consider that it isn't meant to be a bedroom. Instead, she walks with me into the space, her steps light and full of possibility.

"Where will you put your TV and your bed?" I ask, trying to keep up with her energy.

She launches into her plans, waving her hands as she describes where everything will go. Her bed is in one corner, the TV is against the wall, and there are lots of posters to make it hers. It isn't just a room to her. To her, it's more than a room—it's the beginning of something safe. Watching her claim it so quickly makes my chest ache in the best way.

Emmett's room is right across from mine, since he is the youngest. I need him close. The bunk bed from Nora's old room will work perfectly—Emmett can take the bottom bunk, steps away if he needs me. It isn't a big house, built back in 1923, and it shows its years in the creaks and quirks. But it sits on a corner lot, tucked into an old neighborhood with low crime, and the trees feel protective.

As I move through the rooms, it strikes me—I have never truly lived alone. In college, I had a roommate. Then I met Nathan, and we folded into each other's lives too quickly to notice what we were giving up. The thought hangs heavy and surreal. This is my space now, and that truth's echo feels thrilling and fragile.

As I walk through the house, beaming with possibilities, I start to see my new reality: I'm doing this. On my own. And I'm not failing. I am here alone, and it is terrifying.

But in the middle of the fear, something inside me feels anchored and strong. Courage. I haven't even realized it's been growing inside me, one tiny seed at a time. Jack has planted and watered it with his unwavering attention and belief in me when I couldn't see my strength.

I breathe in the moment. And for the first time in a long time, I don't want to run—I want to keep going. One step at a time.

Chapter Thirty-Nine

Moving into the new house feels like the start of something good—something I'm not quite ready for. The kids run through the half-empty rooms, boxes everywhere, their laughter echoing off bare walls, and for the first time in what feels like forever, I let myself breathe. It's not perfect, but it's ours. That has to count for something.

I should feel relief—maybe even pride—but all I feel is pressure. Boxes need unpacking, furniture has to be assembled, and work doesn't slow down just because my life is in transition. I throw myself into it all, determined to keep moving forward. Still, the weight of everything settles deeper into my chest each day.

I manage to find a lawyer to help with the divorce. It's a local one with great reviews. Filing feels like the logical next step. I sit in the tiny home office I've carved out of a corner in the living room, staring at the papers in front of me. My pen hovers over the lines, my hands shaking as I sign my name. I tell myself it's just paperwork—one more task checked off the list—but it feels heavier than that.

When Jack calls that night like he always does, I see his name light up the screen—and I freeze.

I could answer. I want to.

But instead, I let it go to voicemail.

☾☾☾

Days blur together. Mornings are a rush of cereal bowls and backpacks, afternoons filled with work and errands, and evenings spent sorting through legal forms or wiping down counters.

I fall into bed each night, too exhausted to think, too drained to feel.

I'm stretched thin—between the house, the job, the kids, the paperwork. Every day feels like triage. One night at work, I lean against the back wall of the restaurant, blinking back tears as I wipe down a sticky table. My knees ache, and my hands are raw from scrubbing dishes between customers. I can't remember the last time I ate a full meal sitting down.

It's all too exhausting for me. I've started to pull back from Jack; he hasn't done anything wrong, but I just don't have time. I often wonder if it can even work between us. The way we met. The affair. How could we ever trust each other? I feel like I'm suffocating with everything that is happening, and some things just end up falling off my plate, and right now, that thing is Jack.

Jack keeps calling and texting and checking in. And I keep letting the messages pile up. I know it's not fair, but I can't reach out. It feels like one more thing—one more person pulling on me.

When I finally call him, his voice is quieter than usual.

"Hey," I say, curling up on the couch.

"Hey," he echoes, and something about how he says it

makes my stomach twist. "I was starting to think you forgot about me."

I force a laugh. "No, I've just been busy. Work, the kids, the move—"

"I get it," he says, cutting me off. "You've got a lot going on."

"Jack—"

"Can I just ask you something?"

I swallow hard. "Of course."

"Am I just a backup to you?"

The words hit me like a slap, and I freeze. "What? No." I pause, ashamed. "I've never seen you that way, Jack. I'm just… barely holding myself together."

"Because that's what it feels like," he says, his voice tight. "Like I'm just here, waiting around until you need me. And I get it, Ella. I do. But it's hard not to feel like I'm the last thing on your mind."

I press my hand to my forehead and slide my fingers through my hair, searching for the words to make this better. "I'm sorry," I whisper. "I didn't mean to make you feel that way."

"But you did," he says softly. "And I don't know how much more of this I can do."

Tears burn behind my eyes, but I blink them back. "I'm trying, Jack. I'm just—drowning right now."

"I know," he says, his voice softening. "I know you are. But so am I."

The silence that follows feels heavier than the conversation itself. I want to reach through the phone and pull him closer, let him know how much I need him, but I don't know how—not without asking him to wait even longer.

"I don't want to lose you," I finally say, my voice breaking.

"Then don't," he says. "But you have to let me in, Ella. Or

this won't work."

I nod, even though he can't see me. "I'll try."

"Okay." His voice softens again. "I love you, you know."

"I love you too."

When the call ends, I sit in the dark, the phone still pressed to my ear. And for the first time in weeks, I let myself cry—not because I feel weak, but because I finally understand just how strong I have to be to keep all of this together.

A few days later, Jack calls again. His voice is lighter this time, almost hopeful.

"I've been thinking," he says. "Maybe I should come visit this weekend."

The suggestion catches me off guard, but for a moment, I let myself picture it: the kids playing in the yard while Jack helps me hang pictures or build shelves. It feels easy and comforting.

"I'd like that," I say softly. "I think the kids would too."

"Really?" His voice lights up, and I feel a pang of guilt for how happy it makes him.

"Yeah," I say. "It would be nice to have you here."

But before we hang up, something pulls at me. A quiet knot in my chest I've been trying to ignore.

"Jack?" I ask, my voice softer now.

"Yeah?"

"I need to ask you something, and I just… I need the truth."

He hesitates. "Okay."

"When we broke up. Did you sleep with anyone else?"

There's a silence. Not long—but enough to change something inside me.

"No," he says. "I didn't."

I close my eyes, wanting to believe him. Needing to.

"Okay," I whisper. "Thank you."

He doesn't say anything else, but his breath lingers in my ear like a promise I didn't realize was already broken.

As the week drags on, reality starts to set in. Now that Nathan's gone, the kids are quieter than usual, their sadness filling the spaces he used to occupy. I try to push through it, to convince myself that Jack coming won't make things worse—but doubt creeps in anyway.

☾☾☾

By Friday, I can't do it.

I call Jack that afternoon, and my stomach sinks when he answers. "Hey," I say quietly. "I need to talk to you."

"What's wrong?"

I swallow hard. "I think we need to hold off on the visit."

The silence stretches, heavy and sharp. "Why?" he finally asks.

"The kids," I say. "They're still adjusting to Nathan being gone, and I just—I don't want to complicate things by having you here right now."

"Complicate things?" His voice is tight, hurt. "Is that what I'd be? A complication?"

"No, Jack, that's not what I mean." I close my eyes and try to steady my breathing. "I just need more time."

He doesn't say anything at first, and when he finally speaks, his voice is quieter. "Okay. I get it."

"Do you?"

"I don't know," he admits. "But I'll try."

After we hang up, I sit at the kitchen table, staring at the phone and wondering if I've made the right decision or pushed him further away. My life is finally going to plan—my plan—so why am I pushing him away? Maybe it's the aftermath, or maybe it's something simpler—maybe I'm just starting to enjoy being alone. Waking up in a quiet house. Picking the music. Drinking my coffee while the sun rises without answering to anyone. I've spent so long tangled in someone else's needs—I'm finally remembering how to listen to my own.

Chapter Forty

Just when I think I can exhale, life twists again. Before I call Jack, I park the car and sit still—just me and the weight of everything. Ten minutes. No noise. No questions. Just me, staring out at the trees swaying in the breeze, wondering if being alone would hurt more or less than this kind of love.

I used to crave silence like this. Now it feels heavier—like it's asking me to choose. Work has been grueling, the late nights wearing me thin, but then my manager pulls me aside and offers me a promotion to bartender. The pay is a lot better, and with the kids and the new place, the extra money isn't just helpful. It's necessary.

I should feel excited. I am excited—for about two minutes. Then I call Jack.

At first, his congratulations sound genuine, but the warmth in his voice fades too quickly.

"More attention?" he asks after I explain the new role.

"It's not like that," I say, brushing it off. "It's about tips and flexibility. I can make enough in fewer hours to still be home for the kids."

"Ella," his voice tightens. "You know what bartenders deal with."

"I deal with them already," I say, my voice sharper than I mean. "This doesn't change anything."

"It does for me," he shoots back. "It means less time to talk. Less time for us."

I exhale, already tired of the argument. "Jack, I need this job. I can't keep scraping by. I thought you'd be happy for me."

"I am happy for you," he says, but his words feel stiff and hollow. "I'm just scared I'm going to lose you."

"You're not going to lose me," I tell him, but even as the words leave my lips, I feel them unravel. A crack I can't seal.

"I hope that's true," he says.

"I have to get ready for work. Tonight's my first bartender shift."

"Well, I hope you have a great night," he says, low and distant.

After dropping the kids off at the babysitter's house, I start my shift. I'm nervous—I don't know how to make all the drinks yet, and the thought of a busy bar makes it hard to think clearly. But the night is uneventful, and the bar never gets so crazy that I can't manage. The tips roll in, and the witty banter from the customers is fun. Of course, some of them ask me out and buy me shots, but I never entertain it. I just say I'm seeing someone and give the shots to other girls.

During some downtime, I grab my phone and text Jack.

Me: *I'm thinking about you right now.*

He responds almost immediately.

Jack: *I'm thinking of you, too. We can talk after your shift.*

Me: *Just talk or something else?*

My heart flutters at the thought of us doing a video call and having phone sex. We haven't done that in a while, and

it's one thing we can still do to break up the distance.
Jack: *I wish I were there to run my fingers through your hair and squeeze your butt through those jeans.*

His words send a jolt through me, my pulse quickening. I settle myself and shoot him a quick reply.
Me: *I'll get out of here as fast as I can.*
Jack: *Good. I'll be waiting.*

When the bar closes, I rush through my closing work—wiping down the bar, restocking the beer, cleaning the bathrooms in the back. I work fast, knowing Jack is waiting at the end of it. We've been tracking each other's phones lately, trying to stay close even with the distance between us.

When I finish and close out my register, I shoot Jack a quick text.
Me: *Almost done. Please don't be asleep.*

His response is faster than I expect.
Jack: *I'm awake.*

I walk out to my car, accompanied by one of the kitchen staff, and climb in. I sit there for a second and realize, in my haste, I've forgotten to put up the mop bucket and mop. I leave my stuff in the car, including my phone, and head back inside to finish the job.

About twenty minutes later, I get back in my car, grab my phone, and see two missed video calls from Jack. I quickly dial him.

"Hey, I'm headed home now," I say, my voice bright with anticipation.

"Hey. Why were you in your car in the parking lot for twenty minutes and not answering my calls?" His voice is tight, irritated.

"Oh, I left the mop bucket and mop, so I had to go back inside to put them away. I left my phone in the car," I tell him.

"Oh. Okay, that makes sense," he says, but his questioning

tone lingers.

"Are you accusing me of something?" I ask, my disbelief sharp.

"Not really, but it just seems weird. Your phone showed you in your car for twenty minutes. Wouldn't you take your phone if you had to go back in?"

"I should have. Yes. But I was in a hurry to get home and speak with you, and I didn't take it inside with me," My frustration rising.

Our conversation continues on my short ride home, and things settle between us—mostly. Before I pull into the driveway, I tell him I'll video call him right back. He agrees, and once I get settled, I call him. Seeing his face brings both joy and discomfort.

"Ella, are you talking to someone else?" he asks.

"I'm not," I tell him, but the words do little to settle him. His tone gives him away—he's been drinking.

"Share your screen. Show me your Whispyr," he demands, sharper now, no room for grace.

My stomach drops. I hear it in his voice—not curiosity, not even jealousy. Distrust.

He doesn't hear my no—he only sees suspicion.

"I'm not showing you my Whispyr," I say firmly.

"Why not?" he snaps. "What else are you hiding?"

"I'm not hiding anything. I just don't want to set a precedent," I tell him, holding my ground.

"If you asked me to show you my Whispyr, I would. Because I have nothing to hide, Ella."

"I'm not showing you my Whispyr. If you don't believe me, that's your problem, not mine," I say with a strength I barely recognize.

Our conversation doesn't get better or worse. We're at a stalemate, and we both know it. I'm in disbelief that he doesn't trust me. I've been loyal to him, even from afar. I've always told him everything, even when I got hit on, and how I handled it. I'm barely surviving the divorce, the move, the constant need to see him—how can he treat me this way?

After letting him go, I sit there in the dark, the soft glow of my phone screen the only light. I can't make decisions based on what he wants, and I can't constantly reassure him. He has to trust me. I have to make the best decision for me. And until the divorce is finalized, I have to make as much money as possible.

☾☾☾

The following week stretches me thin. Between the kids, the new job, and the divorce paperwork, there's not a moment to breathe. I don't feel like a person anymore—just a list of tasks waiting to be completed. Jack's texts stack up unread until late at night when my eyes can barely stay open. He calls, but I let it ring more often than I answer. I tell myself he'll understand. But he doesn't. I feel it in his clipped replies, in the way his words linger, heavy with things left unsaid.

Then comes the lunch date with my manager, Cheryl. We've grown close, and she's been mentoring me at work, even watching my kids when I need her to.

"Emmett and I are meeting Cheryl for lunch," I mention casually to Jack over the phone.

"Oh," he says, hesitating. "How's she doing?"

"Good," I reply quickly. "We haven't had much time to catch up lately, so it'll be nice."

"Send me a picture of you two," he says, laughing. "I want proof she still exists."

I laugh too, but it catches in my throat. It's a joke, I tell myself. Just a joke.

But as I hang up, the moment sticks to me. At the restaurant, my phone buzzes.

Jack: *Has Cheryl made it there yet?*

I bite my lip.

Me: *Not yet. She's running late.*

I hand my phone to Emmett because he's starting to get cranky. Right before I order, Cheryl texts me that she can't make it. Since I'm already here, I just go with it.

☾☾☾

After lunch, I check my phone and see I've missed two video calls from Jack. Once we're in the car, I call him back.

"Hey," I say when he answers. "Did you call me?"

"Yes. I tried to video call you. Why didn't you answer?" His tone is tight, frustration threading through every word.

"Emmett had my phone, so I didn't know you called," I tell him.

"Didn't your watch buzz?"

"I'm not wearing it. It's at home on the charger," I reply.

"Okay," he says, but I can tell he still doubts me.

Our conversation continues, mostly smooth, but the gnawing doesn't leave me. Why doesn't he trust me? What's happening between us? Maybe the distance and my newfound independence are scaring him. But something deeper stirs in me. His questions, his tracking, the way he doubts me even when I give him no reason—it all feels too familiar. That tightening in my chest. That need to explain every move.

I don't want to admit it, but part of me is starting to wonder if Jack's protectiveness is slipping into control. Not like Nathan. Not yet. But enough to make me pause. Enough to make me feel like the girl I've fought so hard to outgrow.

That night, I lay awake, staring at the ceiling. Guilt gnaws at me, sharp and unforgiving. Maybe it's the exhaustion. The pressure. The constant spinning plates.

Jack's slipping through my fingers—and maybe I'm the one letting go.

Not out of fear. Not even out of anger.

But because I finally know what it means to stand alone.

And I'm not sure I can unlearn that.

Chapter Forty-One

The tension between Jack and me only grows worse in the days after the lunch issue. I feel it in every unanswered text, every missed call, every awkward excuse I send to avoid talking to him. The space between us stretches into a chasm I no longer know how to cross.

Jack has always been patient, but I can tell that patience is wearing thin. His regular calls during his lunch break go ignored, and his texts sit unanswered for hours. I know it's not fair, but I tell myself it isn't intentional. I'm just too busy trying to keep my life from falling apart to explain myself to him. Shouldn't he understand what my life looks like right now? He went through this same thing a few years ago, struggling to keep his head above water. Now it's my turn, and he can't be here to steady me.

But Jack doesn't see it that way.

When he tries to call me today, I'm taking the kids to the movies. Maybe a movie will break the monotony of boxes and chaos. I let the call go to voicemail and send him a quick text.

Me: *I'm at the movies with the kids. Can I call you later?*

Jack: *I'm at work, and we need to talk.*
Me: *Ok.*

His words sit heavy in my chest. We need to talk. I hate seeing that through text, and my mind spins in a thousand directions, even as the animated movie plays out on the screen. I try to stay present for the kids, but my heart pounds so loud I can barely focus.

Near the end of the movie, my phone buzzes in my pocket. I slide it out, my stomach twisting.

Jack: *I can't do this anymore.*

My heart lurches. I stare at the screen, willing it to be a joke. But then, another message flashes across:

Jack: *I won't be someone's backup plan. Obviously, I'm not your priority, and maybe I never was. I deserve better than this. Goodbye, Ella.*

Panic slams into my chest, stealing my breath. I fumble to call him immediately—then stop.

What if he doesn't answer? What if he does?

I press the button anyway, my hands trembling as the phone rings.

"What do you want, Ella?"

"What do I want? Are you serious right now?" My voice rises, sharp and defensive. "You're just going to end things like this? Over text?"

"What else am I supposed to do?" he fires back. "You don't have time for me anymore. You barely talk to me. And when you do, it's all excuses. I'm tired of feeling like I'm chasing after you."

"You're not chasing after me!" I snap. "I'm drowning, Jack. I'm doing everything I can just to stay above water."

"It doesn't feel that way," he says, sharper now. "It feels like I'm already losing you."

"Then why aren't you helping me float?" I shoot back.

"Why does it feel like I'm still doing this alone?"

"Because you keep shutting me out," he fires. "And I can't fix what I can't reach."

"I never asked you to fix anything!" I cry. "I just needed you to stay."

Jack goes quiet. For a breathless moment, I think he's hung up. But then his voice comes back, quieter now, rough.

"I never walked away, Ella. I've been here, waiting, trying to make this work. You rejected me when I asked you to move in. I offered to come visit, but you told me no. I asked you to come see me, and you said you couldn't because you had to work. But I can't keep waiting forever. I need more than this. I need to feel like I matter to you."

Tears burn at the corners of my eyes, but I refuse to let them fall. I take a shaky breath. "I have valid reasons for all of that. You do matter to me, Jack. But I don't have anything left to give right now. I'm making tough choices—doing things I don't want to do but have to. I need your support."

"I've supported you," he says, his voice breaking. "I've supported you through everything. But I can't be the only one trying anymore."

I swallow the lump rising in my throat. "So that's it? You're done?"

"I don't know," he admits. "But maybe we're already gone."

When did the man who once made me feel free start feeling like just another name on my list to disappoint?

Maybe it's not him who changed—maybe it's me.

Maybe I'm just too tired to carry another heart besides my own. His words echo in my head like a door slamming shut, one I'm not ready to face.

After we end the call, I just sit there, staring at the screen, my heart pounding painfully in my chest. I want to scream, to cry, to throw the phone across the room—but instead, I curl into myself, my shoulders shaking, then breaking.

The first sob punches out of my chest like a fist. Then another. And another.

I bury my face in my hands and let it all pour out: the frustration, the loneliness, the grief over what I've lost—and what I'm still terrified to lose.

My cries are ugly, choked, and gasping, but I don't care. I can't hold it in anymore. I cry for everything. For Jack. For Nathan. For the life I thought I wanted… and the one I'm still trying to build from the wreckage.

And when it's over, I'm still here. Still alone in this quiet room, surrounded by nothing but my own silence—and maybe, just maybe, a little more truth.

I thought I could handle it all—work, the kids, the divorce, and Jack.

Right now, I feel like I'm losing everything. And the worst part? I'm not sure I even want to chase after what's slipping away.

Chapter Forty-Two

The next few days drag on like so many before. I'm buried in household chores—laundry piling up, kids' homework scattered across the table, grocery lists half-finished—while working some nights and trying to manage everything else.

This afternoon, I sit on the living room sofa with a laundry basket of clean clothes in front of me, the kids chasing each other around the house like it's a racetrack. A headache presses at my temples, and I rub them lightly with my fingers, staring at the dim light spilling through the curtains. My phone buzzes on the coffee table—a low, insistent hum that sets my nerves alight. I flinch, heart kicking up, already knowing who it is.

Jack. Again.

It's been three days since he ended things. Three long, aching days. And despite everything, he keeps calling. I've ignored the first few calls, let them drift to voicemail, but this time something inside me wavers. I pick up the phone and read the latest text.

Jack: *I'm sorry. I need to talk to you. Please, Ella. I miss you. I want* *to fix this.*

My heart clenches, but I tell myself not to respond. He hurt me. I need time to figure out what to do next. How could I have been so stupid? I trusted him. I changed everything. Left my marriage, uprooted my life… all for a relationship I thought was solid. And the second I falter, even for a moment, he accuses me of cheating and ends things.

Instead of answering, I call Maya for advice. She picks up on the first ring, as always.

"Hey!" she says, bright and warm.

"Hey, girl," I reply, my voice tight.

"What's going on? Everything okay?" she asks, concern slipping into her tone.

"It's Jack," I admit, my words tumbling out in a rush. "He broke up with me a few days ago. Accused me of cheating, of being distant. Now he's trying to get me back."

"Do you want to take him back?" she asks without missing a beat.

"Yes," My throat tight. "I do. I love him, Maya. I hate that I was distant. I know he doesn't like me bartending and getting hit on constantly."

"Well, you can't help it if guys hit on you," she points out. "You're doing what you have to do to survive until you can move and be with him."

"You're right," I agree, though my voice feels small. "I know he's trying to see it that way."

"Maybe just take some time to think, okay?" she says gently. "Make sure you make the right decision for you."

We only talk a little longer. I ask about her boyfriend and what's going on in her life. She tells me they are moving in together, and she's getting ready to tell her parents. She's making big strides, and everything seems to be falling into place for her. I wish I could say the same.

The calls from Jack kept coming over the next few days, but I kept ignoring them. I have to. It's all I can think to do. A relationship is built on trust, and I don't know how we can work if he doesn't trust me. I didn't fight my way out of my marriage just to fall into another relationship full of suspicion.

My focus stays on work, the kids, and trying to untangle the mess of my life. But that night, another text flashes across my screen, and my heart skips a beat.

Jack: *I haven't been honest with you. I need to come clean. Please call me.*

My stomach drops. My thumb hovers over the screen.

I shouldn't call. I know that.

But I do.

He answers instantly. "Ella."

"What's going on?" I demand. "What do you mean you haven't been honest?"

He hesitates, and my pulse pounds in my ears. "Jack, tell me."

"I lied," he says quietly. "About when we broke up before. When I told you, I didn't sleep with anyone else."

My breath catches in my throat. "What?"

"I didn't want to hurt you," he says. "It meant nothing, Ella. It was a mistake. When you went back to Nathan, I thought it was over between us. I didn't know how to tell you when you came back. I didn't want to lose you."

The air leaves my lungs like I've been punched. I shoot to my feet, pacing the room as tears fill my eyes.

"You lied to me..." The words barely leave my mouth. "After everything we've been through?"

"I'm sorry," he says, his voice cracking. "I swear, it didn't mean anything."

My fingers fumble with the necklace he gave me, the one I've worn every day since he fastened it around my neck.

"We were supposed to be different," I whisper. "You promised me we were above everyone else. And you threw it away."

"Ella—"

"No!" My anger rises like a wave. I yank the necklace off and drop it onto the table. "You lied to me, Jack. I can't just forget that. I've been over here being loyal to you."

"I was looking at jobs closer to you…hoping I could build a life with you. You weren't the only one trying to close the distance. I can't believe you would do this to me!" My knees buckle, and I collapse onto the cold tile. I press my palms to the floor like I can stop the world from spinning out from under me.

"And you couldn't communicate any of this to me?" he says, finally getting a word in.

"I wanted it to be a surprise!" I shot back, the chaos inside me threatening to consume me whole.

He tries to speak, but I hang up before he can. Tears pour down my face, my body wracked with sobs.

☾☾☾

The next few days pass in a blur. He keeps calling, but I let them all go to voicemail. I can't bear to hear his voice. I feel hollow like the part of me that believed in love has been shattered.

Finally, I call Maya. She picks up on the second ring, her voice warm and familiar.

"What's wrong?" she asks immediately.

I break down, telling her everything—how Jack lied, how betrayed I feel, how I don't know what to do.

"Ella," she says gently. "You can't be mad about something that happened after you broke up."

"That doesn't make it okay," I snap. "He lied about it. For months."

"I get that," Maya says. "And you have every right to be upset. But maybe this isn't about Jack. Maybe this is about you."

"What do you mean?"

"You've been so focused on holding everything together—your job, the kids, and Jack—that you haven't figured out what you need," she says softly. "Maybe this breakup isn't the worst thing. Maybe it's a chance for you to focus on yourself for once."

I sniffle. "I don't even know where to start."

"You start by taking care of yourself," Maya says. "You're stronger than you think, Ella. You don't need Jack or anyone else to hold you up. You can do this."

I stare at the necklace sitting on the table. For the first time, I feel like maybe Maya is right. I've spent so long trying to make everyone else happy that I've forgotten how to care for myself.

"I just don't know if I'm ready to let go," I whisper.

"Then don't," Maya replies. "Not yet. But don't hold on too tight, either. Give yourself space to figure it out."

I nod, wiping my eyes. "Thanks, Maya."

"Anytime," she says. "You've got this."

That night, I sit on the edge of my bed, the necklace still sitting on the table. I reach for it, my fingers brushing the crescent moon pendant—cool, familiar. But tonight, it feels like a weight I'm not ready to carry.

I don't need it. Not as a reminder. Not as proof. I drop it in the drawer and close it softly. I'm not ready to let go.

But I am ready to stand.

Chapter Forty-Three

The days blur together, stitched with the hum of the bar and the clink of glasses—just enough noise to keep the ache quiet. Work becomes my hiding place. I fill every shift I can, staying long after closing to clean tables and stock shelves. Anything to keep my hands busy and my thoughts quiet.

But silence always finds me. It lingers between conversations, settles over me at night when the kids are asleep, and the house feels too big and empty. I tell myself that staying busy is the same as moving on. Some days, I almost believe it.

This afternoon, while I'm wiping down the counter before opening the bar, my phone vibrates. His name lights up the screen.

Jack.

I should let it go to voicemail, but my hand moves faster than my resolve.

"Ella," he says, breathless like he's been holding it in for days. "Thank God. I thought you'd never answer."

"What do you want, Jack?" My voice comes out sharp,

edged with exhaustion. I don't bother to soften it.

"I need to see you," he says. "We need to talk. In person."

I shake my head even though he can't see it. "I'm working, Jack. I don't have time for this—especially not another guilt trip." "You never have time anymore." His voice darkens. "It just feels like I'm the only one trying lately. Are you seeing someone else?"

My stomach twists. "No, Jack. This is about me trying to get my life together and you refusing to let me."

"That's not fair," he says, his voice tight. "I've been trying to be there for you, and you keep pushing me away. If you don't want me, just say it."

I swallow hard, the words catching in my throat. Silence presses in on both ends of the call until he finally speaks again, softer this time.

"I can't keep doing this, Ella. It feels like I'm chasing after someone who doesn't even want to be caught."

"Maybe you shouldn't be chasing me," I whisper. "Maybe I need to figure out who I am before I can figure out what we are."

"Ella—"

"I'm sorry." My voice cracks. "I just can't do this right now." For a second, I picture him here, sitting at the table, waiting for me to stop running. But it's not enough. Not anymore.

I hang up before he can respond, my hands trembling as I set the phone down. But for the first time in weeks, my heart feels steady.

☾☾☾

The next few days are quiet—too quiet. I tell myself it's for the best, but the silence carves something raw inside me.

Maya's words echo in my head. You need to focus on yourself.

So I try. I clean the house from top to bottom, take the kids to the park by the river, and run until my lungs burn. The sun hangs high when we reach the park, spilling golden light over the water. It's calm—glass-like. No waves, just steady movement, flowing wherever it wants. It reminds me of myself, drifting but still moving forward.

At work, I throw myself into learning new cocktails and perfecting my routines. When coworkers ask about the necklace I've stopped wearing, I pretend not to notice. No one knows I've already interviewed for a new job—at a bank. It doesn't pay as much, but it means stability. Routine. More nights at home with the kids. A life that feels manageable again. I haven't told anyone yet. I want to make sure it's real before I let it slip.

But the doubts creep in when the nights stretch too long and the house is dark and quiet. What's best for me? Do I still love him? Could I uproot the kids again? Was it really a mistake or a lie? The questions circle endlessly, leaving me restless.

A week later, my phone buzzes again.

A text from Jack.

Jack: *I miss you. I can't stop thinking about you.*

I stare at the screen, my thumb hovering. But this time, I don't reply.

Instead, I call Maya.

"I can't stop thinking about him," I admit as soon as she answers. "But I don't think I can trust him anymore."

"You're not supposed to figure it all out right now," she says. "Take the time you need. If he cares, he'll wait. Don't let him make you feel guilty for needing space."

Her words hit me hard. "I don't know how to be without

him."

"You already are," Maya says, her voice strong and sure. "And you're doing better than you think."

"Really?" My voice wavers, hungry for reassurance.

"Yes. Look at everything you've done—new house, new job, the kids settled in school. You're filing for divorce, Ella. You're doing an amazing job."

Her words settle over me, soft but solid, and I blink back tears.

"Thank you," I whisper.

We talk a little longer, catching up. Maya tells me she finally came out to her parents. They met her boyfriend, and surprisingly, it went well. Hearing her happiness feels like sunlight breaking through the clouds.

By the time we hang up, something inside me shifts. For the first time in weeks, I smile—a real one—and feel the weight on my chest lift just a little.

I walk past the dresser, my eyes grazing the drawer where the necklace now lives. I don't reach for it. Not because I've forgotten, but because I'm starting to remember who I am without it.

Maybe I'm not lost after all.

Maybe, finally, I'm finding my way back to myself.

Chapter Forty-Four

The weeks collapse into each other—work, kids, and the tug of single-mom life. Days vanish too quickly. Some nights, though, stretch forever. I stop answering Jack's calls and texts. Not because I don't care—but because I don't know how to trust him anymore.

Trust.

That word circles in my mind like a vulture. Can we build something real without it? Without trust, wouldn't everything eventually collapse again? I don't want to go down that road. Not again. I've learned too much about him—and myself—to settle for less than I deserve.

I'm not seeing anyone, even though offers have come my way. I'm not ready. My heart isn't ready. I need time—to untangle the mess of emotions Jack left in his wake, to find steady ground after the collapse of my marriage. Healing can't be rushed. And I have a sinking feeling that letting go of Jack will take longer than letting go of Nathan.

But I have to try. For my kids. For me.

I'm learning to make my own decisions, not ones clouded

by someone else's expectations. Jack was a critical part of my journey, but that doesn't mean he's meant to stay. He helped me see my worth, but it's up to me to claim it. To believe it. To live it.

I decide to stay in Eastwell. My dad keeps nudging me to move back home, but I can't do it. I need to stand on my own two feet. I want to make my mark here, even if it means starting small and rebuilding from the ground up. I owe myself that much.

And I'm doing okay. Maybe even better than okay, considering everything I've endured and everything still ahead of me. I've started to trust myself again—my instincts, my ability to make choices that put me and my kids first. That feels big. That feels like growth.

There are still hard days when loneliness hits like a wave I can't outswim. But I hold on. I breathe through it. I remind myself the emptiness won't last forever.

Jack once felt like home—safe, familiar, comforting—but now, he feels like a storm I can't weather. A storm that might sweep me off my feet but could also leave me shattered. And I'm tired of rebuilding myself after him.

I want more. Stability. Peace. Something real. Something I can trust.

And maybe—just maybe—I have to let him go to find it.

I'm finally finding my life, even though it feels more complex with each passing day. The divorce isn't finalized yet. My lawyer says his representation reached out, and once I finish my paperwork, it shouldn't take much longer to be done with it all.

Nathan still calls to talk to the kids and makes vague plans to see them someday. But he seems to have given up on trying to win me back. And for the first time, I feel like myself again—not Nathan's wife, not Jack's secret, just me.

The days are long and exhausting, but I'm getting through them. I'm doing it—on my own. And for now, that's enough.

Later that afternoon, I drop the kids off at the babysitter's house and head to work. My shift starts with a flurry of silverware wrapping and bar stocking. I have to waitress tonight, but I still help the bartender, knowing how hard it can be.

Later in the night, as I round the corner toward the bar to place a drink order, I look up—and there he is.

Jack.

My breath catches. The bar hum fades behind me, the only sound now is the thud of my heartbeat in my ears. My legs move before I've made a decision. I'm across the room, falling into his arms. The hug between us is desperate and fierce, my arms locked tight around his neck as if letting go might make him disappear. The tension that's been coiled in me for days, and weeks unspools in an instant. For the first time, I feel at ease. The thoughts that swirled in my mind dissolve, and for once, I'm grounded in the moment. Tears burn at the corners of my eyes, but I swallow them back.

"I can't believe you're here," I whisper, pulling away just enough to meet his eyes. Eyes I haven't stopped thinking about, even through all the anger and pain.

"I had to see you," Jack says, his voice a little too fast and thin. He looks thinner, more tired than I remember. His hands twitch on the bar top, like he's holding something in or barely holding it together.

Our conversation is fragmented. I'm defensive; he's anxious. There's still familiarity between us, but tension hums in the air. I catch the restless bounce of his leg, the nervous way his fingers trace idle patterns around the rim of his glass. And still, I stay. I sit across from him, arms folded tight, my expression guarded even as my pulse betrays me. Because no matter how much his leaving gutted me, no matter how the sting of resentment lingers, being near him feels like surfacing after drowning.

Twice, I slip away to the back of the restaurant, pressing my palms hard against the cool porcelain sink in the bathroom, willing the tears to stop before they start. I can't let him see me like this—can't let him know how easily he still undoes me.

Work drags. The minutes stretch as I try to keep busy. The tables are few, the night slower than most, and my restless energy coils tighter with each pass around the room. Jack lingers at the bar, his presence magnetic, pulling at me no matter how much I try to resist. Finally, I give in.

"Let me show you that spooky section upstairs I told you about," I say, letting a small smile break through the tension. My voice feels steadier than I expect. Maybe it's the dim light or the weight of his gaze, but I want to be alone with him. I want to feel him again.

We slip through the back, where no customers or staff are around. The air grows heavier as we pass stacked boxes and shelves lined with kitchen supplies. The quiet buzzes around us, amplifying every footstep and breath. In the hush of the supply closet—brooms, mops, and cleaning products stacked on metal shelves just out of view—he kisses me like he's been holding it in forever.

"See how messy this is?" I say, my voice softer now, words stretched thin between us.

He barely glances at the room. His eyes find mine, dark and searching. And then he moves—one step, then another, closing the distance until his face is inches from mine. I don't breathe. I can't. I hesitate. My pulse thrums. I'm not sure this is a good idea—but I'm too tired to keep pretending I don't want it. And then his lips are on mine.

I gasp, the shock of it fusing with the warmth spreading through me. My hands find his shoulders, his chest, anything to anchor myself as the kiss deepens. It's heat and desperation, all the words we haven't said pouring into this moment. I never thought I'd feel this again.

When the bar closes, he lingers near the door, waiting. I walk out with him, my heart warring between wanting him to stay and needing him to leave. The air outside is sharp, but it does nothing to clear the haze in my head.

"I'm happy I got to see you," he says, his voice quieter now, softer.

"I'm glad you surprised me," I reply, though my chest feels too tight, the words barely making it out.

His eyes don't leave mine. "Even though you wouldn't ask me to come, I knew you needed me here."

Before I can answer, he steps closer. He pulls me close, wrapping his arms around my waist, and then his lips find mine again. This time, it isn't soft. It's fire and need, his hands sliding lower, gripping me as if I might slip away. A slight sound escapes me, half moan, half surrender, and I let myself fall into it. Into him.

But reality presses back too quickly. I break away, breathless.

"I have to get back inside before my manager gets upset," I say, though my body screams to stay.

"Come see me tonight?" His voice holds something fragile beneath the heat.

"I'll try," I whisper, already unsure.

When my shift ends, and I've restocked silverware and cleaned the bathrooms, it's nearly 2 a.m. The drive home feels too long; my thoughts are tangled with everything that's happened. I can't keep running in circles with him, but I can't let go either.

I call him.

"Hey!" he answers on the first ring like he's been waiting. "Hey," I say, matching the warmth in his voice, even as my nerves twist.

"Are you coming?" he asks, his words filled with hope and something heavier.

I hesitate, staring out at the empty road. "I can't. I have to get home. The babysitter's waiting."

I hear the breath he lets out, sharp and short. "Tomorrow then? Coffee?"

"Coffee," I agree, but doubt coils tight in my stomach even as I say it.

My phone buzzes on the nightstand before I can even get dressed the next morning. Jack's name lights up the screen. "I want to come over," he says. No question. Just need.

I open my mouth to say no, but the word doesn't come. Instead, I hear myself say, "Okay."

He shows up with coffee and donuts, nothing elaborate, just familiar comforts in grease-stained paper. I don't need flashy gestures, but this feels honest. It feels like he's just trying to reconnect. Still, his actions tug at something inside me. Maybe it's the effort, or the memory of quieter mornings when things didn't feel so complicated. We talk and laugh, but the air between us feels charged, every glance lingering too long, every touch burning too hot.

When he leans in and kisses me, the ache unravels me. I give him a look full of need and turn, leading him down the hall and into my bedroom. The world outside falls away as we make love, his touch grounding me even as it sets me on fire. But even in the closeness, doubt coils in my stomach. Is this reconnection or relapse? But he doesn't stay. He leaves soon after, mentioning plans to go out with some old friends. I watch him go, feeling the weight of distance settle over me again.

☾☾☾

Later that night, I'm wiping down the bar when I see him walk in. My stomach tightens—not with excitement this time, but with unease. He lingers; we barely speak. Then there's the moment. The new guy, the one stocking beer leans close to ask me a question. I feel Jack's eyes lock onto me, heat rising behind them. When I look up, the jealousy on his face is unmistakable.

My heart sinks. This isn't what I want. Not the tension, not the games. And yet, here we are. He waits outside after my shift, leaning against his car.

"Who was that?" he asks, his voice tight.

"Who?" I feign innocence.

"The guy at the bar. The one all over you."

"He wasn't all over me," I snap. "He was asking about inventory."

Jack's jaw tightens. "I don't like it."

"Well, you don't have to," I say, stepping past him. "You don't get to come back and act like you own me."

His hand catches my arm—gently but firmly. "Ella, wait." I freeze, my heart pounding. His eyes soften, fear replacing anger. "I just don't want to lose you again." He says he doesn't want to lose me, but the truth is—I don't think he ever really found me. Not who I am now. Not who I'm becoming.

I shake my head and pull away. "Maybe you already have."

I walk to my car, my steps heavier than they should be. My heart aches, but I know. If I can let him go, maybe I'll finally see who I was meant to become.

Chapter Forty-Five

I haven't spoken to Jack in weeks. After many unanswered calls and unread texts, I finally blocked his number. It's not out of anger—at least, that's what I tell myself. I just need space—to breathe, to think, to figure out what I want.

And it's working. Slowly but surely, I feel myself coming back to life.

I'm finally getting a handle on everything that's required of me. Late one afternoon, the kids' laughter echoes through the house. I sit at the dining room table, pour myself an iced coffee, and open my laptop. Pulling up my budget spreadsheet, I see my bills are paid, my savings account is growing each month, and for the first time in a long time, I don't feel like I'm treading water.

My phone rings, breaking my concentration. It's my dad.

"Hey, Dad," I answer, leaning back in my chair.

"Hey, sweetheart. How are you doing?"

"I'm good," I say, and for once, I mean it. "Busy, but good."

We talk briefly, and I open up more than I expect. I tell

him about the kids and what they've been up to. I tell him about getting them into private school all by myself, how I navigated the application process, figured out the finances without anyone's help. Of course, he asks when we're coming to visit and when we're moving down. It's become a running joke at this point.

My dad is quiet for a moment before he says, "I'm proud of you, Ella. You've come a long way."

I smile, feeling the weight of his words settle over me. "Thanks, Dad. I'm finally starting to get my feet under me."

I go on to tell him about the divorce with Nathan. He has hired a lawyer, which means it could get messy. I hope there will be no long legal battles, no messy fights, just an ending—clean and final.

"It's weird," I admit. "I thought it would feel more dramatic, but it doesn't. It just feels... done."

"That's probably a good thing," my dad says. "Not everything has to end with fireworks. Sometimes it's better when it's quiet."

"Yeah," I say, nodding to myself. "I think you're right."

The conversation shifts to my job. I tell him about getting hired at the bank as a teller—a steady job with regular hours and benefits. It's not glamorous, but it feels stable, and I need that right now. I keep my bartender shift, just one night a week, mostly because I like the people. And the tips don't hurt. He agrees with that decision, as I knew he would. He never liked me working around a bunch of drunk guys.

My dad teases me about being a workaholic, but I just laugh. I like the work. It keeps me grounded, keeps me busy, and lets my mind rest on the tasks.

After we hang up, I sit there for a while, letting the conversation replay in my head. I still miss Jack sometimes, but not the way I used to. The ache isn't sharp anymore—it's dull, distant, and manageable.

What hurts more is the lie, the betrayal—the realization that I let myself believe in something that may not have been real.

Maybe Maya's right. I don't need Jack. Or Nathan. Or anyone. I look around my house—the clean counters, the organized shelves, the walls I painted myself—and I feel something shift inside me. I did this. I did this. Piece by piece. And I'm not finished yet.

☾☾☾

Later that night, after the kids go to bed, I pour myself a glass of wine and sit on the back porch. The full moon hangs low and orange on the horizon like it's trying to stay a little longer—for me, maybe. I remember the nights Jack used to point it out, saying it felt like a sign like it belonged to us. It used to feel like ours. Maybe it still does. But now, it's just mine.

I pull the blanket tighter around my shoulders and let the silence settle over me. I used to hate nights like this—too quiet, too still. Back in the old house, I'd sit on the edge of the couch, phone in hand, waiting for someone to fix me. Now, I don't need fixing.

For the first time in a long time, I'm not afraid of being alone. I feel strong. Capable. Enough. I glance at my reflection in the glass door—faint, softened by the glow of the porch light—and let myself smile. It's not flashy. Just a quiet, knowing smile. I see myself. Really see myself. And I like the woman looking back.

I pick up my phone and scroll through my contacts, pausing for just a second when I see Jack's name. I don't need a goodbye. I just need to choose myself. But instead of unblocking him, I delete it. Then I set the phone down and look back at the moon, letting the night stretch before me like an open road.

I'm not sure where this path will lead, but for the first time, I'm not afraid to walk it alone.

☾☾☾

The next day, I wake before my alarm and slip out of bed without waking the kids. I put on my new running shoes and step outside, breathing in the crisp morning air. Running has become more than just exercise—it's my quiet time, my escape. Each step forward lets the tension drain from my body, replaced by the steady rhythm of my breathing and the pounding of my feet against the pavement.

When I return home, the sun has risen, and the house is stirring. The kids are already dressed, sitting at the table, eating cereal, and chattering about their day. A big smile breaks out across my face as I pour myself a cup of iced coffee and join them.

During my lunch break, I fill out paperwork for savings accounts I've started for the kids. It's a small step, but it feels significant—a reminder that I'm planning for the future, not just surviving the present.

As I walk out, my phone buzzes. I check it out of habit, even though Jack's number is long gone. It's Maya.

Maya: Thinking of you today. Proud of how far you've come. Don't forget to celebrate yourself now and then.

I smile and text back.

Me: Thanks. I will.

☾☾☾

Later that night, I curl up on the couch with a blanket and a book. The house is quiet, and for the first time in what feels like forever, I don't feel the need to fill the silence. I let myself enjoy it.

I go to bed lighter. Stronger. Not just ready—willing.

Chapter Forty-Six

This afternoon, I find myself back where I once stood many months ago. It's the spot we've returned to again and again—a quiet bend in the river where the water stretches vast and endless, the current always steady. I can still see the gazebo close by, this is where I came with Jack, where I've found myself when searching for peace and where I've come to pour out tears of sadness and joy. It's unhurried. Like me. I stand at the river's edge, the sun warm on my skin as the kids' laughter echoes across the water. I watch them skip rocks, their faces lit with joy, and I feel a peace I haven't known in years.

In these past few months, my life has changed in ways I couldn't have imagined when this all began. I've unraveled and rebuilt, layer by layer, until the woman standing here feels solid. Rooted. Strong.

Heartbreak, single motherhood, the long nights of questioning—it's all shaped me. But it doesn't define me.

Around this time next week, I'll be standing in a courtroom, finalizing my divorce. One more step, and that chapter will finally close. I expected to feel more anxious, but instead, I feel steady—like the river. I've already let go of the past. I'm ready to step into what comes next.

I glance back at the kids, their voices carried on the breeze. They're happy. Thriving. And that matters more than anything. I've made a home for them—a life filled with laughter and stability. I've done it on my own. No Nathan. No Jack. Just me.

Turning back to the water, I let my gaze follow its smooth, glass-like surface. It reflects the sky, serene and unbroken, but I know the current runs strong and powerful beneath. I see myself in it—calm on the surface, always moving forward. I've learned to trust that strength, to rely on it when everything else feels uncertain.

I pick up a smooth stone and weigh it in my palm before sending it skimming across the water. Ripples fan out—momentary disturbances that fade almost as quickly as they appear. The corners of my mouth slide upward. Life will always bring ripples, but I know now how to stand firm and let them pass without losing myself.

The sun dips lower, casting golden streaks across the river. I call the kids, and they come running, breathless and smiling, their pockets full of rocks and treasures they've collected along the shore.

"You're really strong, Momma," Nora says, placing her tiny hand in mine. "Like the river."

I swallow hard, her words lodging somewhere between my heart and my throat. I squeeze her hand gently and whisper, "You have no idea."

As we walk, I think about the road ahead. It isn't perfect. It won't always be easy. But it's mine. I've built something solid—a foundation no one can shake. And just like the river, I'll keep flowing, steady and strong.

When we reach the car, the sky softens with evening light. I take one last look at the water, then turn the key in the ignition, feeling the hum of possibility in my chest. I'm ready.

But as I drive, memories tug at me—faint shadows of who I used to be. Jack's cologne, faint, bourbon-sweet, lingers in the passenger seat, clinging to a hoodie he left behind. A small thing, but it holds weight. A reminder of the man who helped me find myself again. I let it stay for a moment. Then I roll the windows down and let it go.

The kids chatter in the back seat about their day—who skipped the most rocks, who found the smoothest stone—and I let their voices fill the car. It grounds me, reminds me why I've fought so hard to create this life.

☾☾☾

At home, after bathing the kids and tucking them into bed, I sit in the quiet of my living room. The walls no longer feel empty. Photos of the kids line the shelves, little pieces of our story woven into every corner.

I pour myself a cup of tea and step outside to the porch, letting the night air wrap around me. As I pass the glass door, I catch my reflection—barefoot, tired, my hair in a messy knot—and I smile. Not because I look perfect but because I look like me. Finally.

I look up at the stars, each burning steady, unshaken by the darkness. That's what I want to be—constant, steady, unshaken. Not too long ago, I clung to Jack like he was the only thing keeping me from drowning. But now I see—I was learning to swim the whole time. I don't need Nathan. I don't need Jack. I need me.

I sink into the porch chair, letting my body settle, letting the quiet hold me. And as I sit there, breathing in the night, my mind drifts back to the riverbank earlier today—the kids laughing, water sparkling around their feet. The river teaches me something—it's always carving something new out of what has been, just like me.

And then it hits me: I am the river—steady and strong—and the kids are my current, carrying me forward.

Tomorrow is coming, and I'm ready to meet it—not as the woman I once was, but as the woman I've become.

Life has a way of rerouting us.
The road toward your true path is rarely gentle—
it's rough and often breaks you open

before it builds you back up.

But even the hardest moments can shape who you become.
A difficult chapter in my past pushed me inward,
forced me to grow,
and ultimately led me to discover writing.

This dedication isn't for a person—
it's for the turning point
that helped me become the man I am now.

And I'm grateful for where that journey has led me.

—Joseph

Many Thanks
To KB—

my editor, my friend, and my unexpected guiding light. What began as a simple conversation between two parents became something far more meaningful.

You believed in me long before this version of the story existed—before I even believed could write it.

Your insight, patience, and tough love not only shaped the first book, but gave me the confidence to embark on this one. Thank you for pushing me to begin this year-long journey and for reminding me that purpose often grows from persistence.

To **CB**, *for your incredible editing eye and beta reading—your clarity, honesty, and attention to detail brought out the best version of this story. You helped me find its rhythm when I was too close to hear it.*

To **CM**, *for your thoughtful feedback and willingness to dive in, helping refine the story in ways I hadn't seen.*

And to **DS**—

you were the final leg of this journey,
the final bit of motivation I needed to see it through,
finish this book and close that last chapter.
Thank you for reminding me that sometimes the finish line isn't the end—
it's the beginning of something new.

Author's Note

If you're still here—reading this after the last page—thank you.

This story began as a way to make sense of something that shattered me. It wasn't just a novel. It was a mirror. A confession.

A love letter to someone I once knew, and a goodbye to the man I used to be.

Ella's journey is fictional, but the ache behind it was real.

So was the spark that made her feel alive again.

Writing her story meant revisiting wounds I thought had closed.

And slowly, through the words, came healing.

If you've ever found yourself in a life that looked good on the outside but felt empty inside—if you've ever stayed too long because leaving felt impossible—then I wrote this for you. Maybe you've been Ella. Maybe you've been Jack. Maybe, like me, you've been both. We are complex. We are flawed.

And we are worthy of second chances.

This book isn't about infidelity.

It's about awakening. It's about realizing that sometimes the bravest thing you can do is choose yourself—even when it's messy.

Even when it costs you everything.

To the readers who saw themselves in these pages:

You are not broken. You are not alone. You are not beyond repair.

Thank you for giving Ella your time, your tears, and your hope.

Thank you for walking this road with me.

May you keep growing.

Keep healing. Keep becoming.

And may you always remember:

You are the river.

With love,

Joseph Bailey

From Two Doors Away (Book Two in the Two Doors Series)

It's been months since she disappeared from my life.

Day after day of silence. My messages, my calls, my words—green bubbles confirming what I already knew. She blocked me. I start to wonder if she ever thinks about me at all.

Time passes, and I finally do what I should've done long before. I get help. I sit with a therapist every week and face the parts of myself I used to avoid—the jealousy, the fear, the story I kept telling myself that I wasn't enough. Slowly, I pull myself out of the wreckage. I rebuild. I heal. I learn to let her go—not from bitterness, but from strength.

For a while, it works. I stop waiting on her shadow to show up in my life. I let the silence just be silence.

But then, she keeps showing up anyway.

Not her, not in person—but everywhere. Her name at the coffee shop, called out by the barista. Her car on random streets. Our songs on the radio, as if the universe still has something left to say. It feels like the world keeps nudging me: It's not over.

When Thanksgiving comes, the thought of her traveling with the kids gnaws at me. I pick up my phone, search for a florist in Eastwell, and make the call. My voice is steady when I place the order—no overthinking, no second-guessing, just what I feel. When the man asks what I want the card to say, the words come easy:

Ella,

In your eyes, I find my place,
A quiet love, a warm embrace.
Two souls, one beat, forever true,
Home is wherever I'm with you.

I love you, Jack.

After I hang up, I think about canceling it. But I don't—not out of hope or desperation, but peace. I send it because it's true. Whatever happens after that isn't in my hands.

The flowers are delivered, and for days, there's nothing. No message. No call.

I don't fall apart this time. I let her go again—quietly.

And then, a week later, something unexpected happens. My son rushes into the kitchen, holding my old phone—the one I passed down to him a month ago. The screen lights up with her name.

"Dad," he says, wide-eyed, "someone's calling you."

For a second, I think I'm seeing things.

But it's her.

I answer, my voice even. "Ella?"

"Hi, Jack," she says softly.

We talk for hours—about life, about nothing, about everything. She tells me she misses me. And when we switch to video, I see it—the necklace. The one I gave her. Resting at the base of her throat, catching the light.

I breathe deep, steady.

Right then, I know: whatever this is between us, it isn't finished. Not even close. She still feels it, too.

Two Doors Down Book Club Discussion Questions

1. Ella's journey is filled with moments of breaking and rebuilding. What do you think was her true turning point in the story?
2. How did your feelings about Jack evolve throughout the novel? Were there moments you rooted for him? Moments you didn't?
3. The book explores the theme of independence versus partnership. Do you feel Ella needed to lose her relationship with Jack to fully find herself? Why or why not?
4. Discuss the symbolism of the river in the final chapter. How does it reflect Ella's personal growth?
5. What role do Ella's children play in shaping her decisions? Do you think she ever put herself first? Should she have?
6. How does Ella's relationship with Nathan contrast with her relationship with Jack? What lessons did she take from each?
7. Was there a moment in the book where you wanted Ella to make a different choice? If so, when and why?
8. The novel highlights the exhaustion of single motherhood and starting over. How did that aspect of Ella's life impact her emotional journey?
9. Trust is a recurring theme. Do you believe trust can be rebuilt once it's broken? Why or why not, especially in the context of Ella and Jack?
10. Ella often balances survival with desire — what she has to do versus what she wants to do. How did you feel about her choices in work, love, and family?
11. Let's talk about Maya. What did you think of her role as Ella's friend and sounding board?
12. What does "home" come to mean for Ella by the end of the story? How does this definition evolve?
13. Were you satisfied with the ending? Do you see Ella's story as one of empowerment, loss, or both?
14. If you could ask Ella one question at the end of her journey, what would it be?
15. What message or feeling are you taking away from Two

Doors Down? Did it change your perspective on relationships, resilience, or starting over?

Bonus Book Club Fun Questions for Two Doors Down

1. If Two Doors Down were turned into a movie or series, who would you cast as Ella and Jack?
2. What's the perfect drink or snack to enjoy while reading this story?
3. If you could give Ella one piece of advice at the start of the book, what would it be?
4. Which moment in the book felt the most cinematic to you? Why?
5. If you could read a sequel, what would you hope to see in Ella's and Jack's future?
6. Did you see the ending coming, or were you surprised? How did it make you feel?
7. What song(s) would you add to a Two Doors Down playlist

Enjoyed the story?

If this book moved you, inspired you, or simply kept you turning pages, I'd love to hear about it. Your review helps other readers discover the story—and helps me keep writing more.

Scan the QR code below to leave a review, connect with me, or explore what's next.

JosephBaileyAuthor.com

Why This Book Is 292 Pages

The last numbered page says 286,
but this story is 292 by intention.
Those six unnumbered pages at the beginning
are the quiet threshold—
the breath before the becoming,
the settling of the heart
before it steps into something new.

286 + 6 = 292

In numerology, 292 reduces to 4,
the number of foundation, stability,
and the steady strength that rises
when you finally learn to stand on your own ground.

2 is connection—
the delicate space between endings and beginnings,
between who you were
and who you're learning to be.
9 is completion—
the soft closing of the door behind you,
the moment you finally release
what no longer carries you forward.
The last 2 is balance—
the quiet return to yourself,
the alignment of heart and truth.

Together they form 4—
the vibration of rebuilding, grounding,
and the calm certainty
that you can root yourself anywhere
as long as you choose you.

292 is the anchoring—
the moment everything inside you settles,
not because life is perfect,
but because you are finally steady
in who you've become.

For the ones rebuilding.
For the ones finding their footing again.
For the ones growing roots in their own truth—

it was never two doors down.
It was always here,
inside you.

— Joseph Bailey
☾☾☾

www.ingramcontent.com/pod-product-compliance
Lightning Source LLC
Chambersburg PA
CBHW020912310726
48980CB00011B/846/J

* 9 7 9 8 9 9 8 7 2 1 3 1 1 *